Forbidden Forest

THE LEGENDS OF REGIA

BOOK ONE

ALSO BY TENAYA JAYNE

Blue Aspen

The Slayer's Wife

Forbidden Forest

A NOVEL

Tenaya Jayne

COLD FIRE PUBLISHING LLC

ISBN-13: 978-0-9882757-0-6

ISBN-10: 0988275708

Edited by Valerie Hatfield

Cover art by Wicked Cover Designs

Dedicated in loving memory of

Robert and Opal.

I miss you.

Prologue

Austin, Texas

Where shall you go, daughter of Austin? It's Friday night and you're ready to hit the clubs in your new mile high shoes and push up bra. You walk down the sidewalk as though it were the runway, with your girlfriends in tow behind you. Where shall it be? Will you stick with the familiar on 6th St.? Or will you saunter over to Red River? You feel your power over the opposite sex as they ogle you as you pass. Maybe you'll meet Mr. Right tonight or a suitable Mr. Right now. You set your sights on some familiar stomping ground, thinking it's as good as any, but wait. . . What's this? You and your girls feel the pull of the doors to your left. You look up at the sign hanging low over your head: *The Portal*. You can feel the beat of the music in the sidewalk. The vibrations going up the heels of your stilettos are pleasantly buzzing your feet.

The cool air welcomes you in out of the humid summer night. You feel it instantly, some sense of otherworldliness. The place is packed, and the energy of the people dancing is palpable and intoxicating. The spinner, positioned royally above the crowd, breaks your heart with his unnatural amount of masculine beauty. Why have you never heard of this place? Your girlfriends flow onto the dance floor, but you hesitate. Wanting to get the full picture, you back up slowly until your back hits the wall.

There is nothing out of place, nothing to cause you alarm, but you have an unspoken innate knowledge of the strangeness of this place. This club has secrets. You think you are alone in the shadows, pressed up against the wall, when you turn your head to the side. A woman is standing very close to you, looking at you, silently. Your eyes widen, and your mouth gapes as you stare rudely back at her.

Never in your life, not in a movie, or a doctored picture have you seen eyes like hers. Layer upon layer of shades of green, laced with minute veins of gold, and fanned with lashes of deepest ebony. Her eyes seem too big to be real. You'd deal with the devil for a pair of your own. You can't even register anything else about her appearance except you know that she is exquisitely beautiful. Now the power you felt earlier drains away. You feel plain next to her.

"Go on," her voice is both gentle and seductive.

You look back at the dance floor and feel an overwhelming pull to join the crowd, but not before you look once again into those eyes. Turning back to the woman, you find she has gone, as quickly and silently as though she vanished into thin air . . . maybe she did.

1

Forest pressed her back against the cool concrete wall, wanting to remain aloof from the entity of the crowd. She chose her position in the shadows, out of the paths of the roving, multi-colored spotlights. She closed her eyes and enjoyed the feeling of the undulating human pheromones flying around on the air. At the beginning of every shift, she allowed herself a few minutes of this alien/human experience, though she didn't fully comprehend the combination of dancing, drinking, and ear-breaking sound waves. They loved it, however, and never seemed to deviate from the recipe.

These were the people she was sworn to protect. She had developed a light affection for the human race and considered them a benign, if not slightly silly, bunch of creatures. Her religious passion for her job was rooted in hatred of that which harmed the humans, not a superhero tendency to protect the weak.

Forest opened her eyes and focused all her senses to sniff out the illegal suckers that tried to sneak through the portal. She was in the zone tonight, and not for the first time did she feel that hers was the best job in existence. It was a shame she couldn't *legally* kill suckers in her native world.

Over the next two hours, Forest didn't move from the wall. She monitored the light traffic through the portal: two shifters and one elf, each of which nodded to her respectfully as they passed. *Yawn.* The shifters left the club to enjoy the delights of Austin's nightlife elsewhere.

The elf would have been breaking Regia's law had he left the club, but he dutifully seated himself at the bar and ordered a fuzzy navel. He wore a plaid, porkpie hat, pulled down over the tops of his pointed ears. Forest didn't know him personally, but she had seen him in here before. The bartender surveyed him with narrowed eyes as the elf nervously tugged his hat down further and ordered a few more girly cocktails.

Intent on making sure that not one sucker was able to sneak past her, Forest was blindsided by the drunk bubba who had been trying to catch her eye for the last twenty minutes. He had finally decided to stagger over to hit on her.

"Hey babe, you're too beautiful to look so lonely. How's 'bout I buy you a drink?"

"How's 'bout I call you a cab instead?" Forest mimicked his drawl.

"Only if you share it with me, *Darlin*." He leaned in closer, and Forest's throat began to sting from the noxious fume of booze mixed with his natural musk.

"While I appreciate the offer, Jethro, It seems only right to inform you that I'm not actually attractive at all. If you leaned in a little closer, you'd see that you've fallen victim to the effect of beer goggles. A hag like me can't take advantage of a stud like you."

As he leaned in, Forest instantly enlarged her nose, pockmarked her skin, evaporated her front teeth, and added a large black mole with a long hair sprouting from it for good measure.

"You're no hag, baby! You're the sexiest little thing in…I…uh-" He stumbled backward. "*Good grief*! Sorry, sorry…" he stammered, retreating. "I've gotta quit drinking," he mumbled as he turned away.

Forest chuckled to herself once he absorbed back into the crowd. Being a shape shifter sometimes had unusual perks. Once her nose was clear of his funk, she refocused her senses on her job and reconstructed her face.

The club's activity peaked at 1:30 AM. People filtered in and out. The music grew a little louder, the humans a little drunker, the smell a little fouler, and Forest grew a little bored. The night seemed to be shaping up into a frustrating nothingness. She sighed, feeling the weight of her favorite .45 Magnum against her back. She was itching to get her gun off. She hadn't killed a sucker all month; it was messing up her average.

The worst blackguard on both sides of the portal, sauntered into the compass of Forest's senses. Her nostrils flared and her spine stiffened.

Leith.

The fight or flight instinct kicked in. Pulse, adrenaline, breathing, and sweat all accelerated through her body. Her mind banished all reason as she began to quiver with the possibility of taking him down. *Leith.* Reason might have been useful to Forest at this moment, but this was *the* fight she was constitutionally incapable of backing down from.

Her hands began to tingle at the thought of pointing her weapon at him, pulling the trigger, and blasting a hole through his black heart. Her lips curved into a full-on Cheshire cat smile as she envisioned standing victorious over his dead body.

It had to be a coincidence. Leith wouldn't come through her portal unless he was looking for her specifically. That thought made her grind her teeth together. He hadn't sought her out in a long time. No, it *had* to be coincidence. He didn't know her schedule, and the last time she had seen him, he didn't even know the location of her post. Not that he couldn't find that out if he wanted to go digging.

She stood motionless in the shadows, watching him move through the dancing crowd toward the exit. She admired that he didn't slink or attempt to conceal himself. Leith merely walked through the crowd as though he owned the world.

She checked herself. *Bastard.* She hated his arrogance, always had.

Oh, if only this could be the night she triumphed over him. If only she could confront him with her sword and not a gun.

Leith had the sense to go out the back door, which led into the ally. The second the door shut behind him, Forest bolted from the wall, swiftly snaking through the crowd. The ally was long and extremely dark. As soon as she stepped outside and the door closed at her back, she used her elfish power and disappeared. Leith turned around abruptly. His ice-colored eyes looked right through her. He pulled in a deep breath through his nose, but the dumpster next to her masked her scent. His pale eyes darted back and forth, and he sniffed the air a second time before turning back to the looming street ahead. Forest followed a few paces behind. Leith's attire suggested that he was trying to look like a 1960's greaser. Maybe his only reference to a human male was James Dean.

People and cars passed on the street ahead, under the weak protection of the street lamps. Protocol dictated that she make her presence known, state the law he was breaking, give him a chance to return through the portal with a mark on his record, or kill him if he resisted or ran. But this was Leith. If it was anyone but him, she would do what she was supposed to do.

Ten more yards, and he would reach the street. Although invisible, she was right on his heels and the stinky dumpster was now far behind.

Leith stopped and turned, an expression caught between a smile and a sneer on his face. He breathed deeply once more. A feral sound resonated from his chest. She didn't move.

"Show yourself!" he commanded.

Forest's solid form flashed against her will for a split second before disappearing again. Their eyes had locked. Leith lunged. Forest ducked too late. He scooped her off her feet and pinned her between his chest and the alley's brick wall. She sighed and dropped the now pointless invisibility.

"Forest," he growled. "I thought that was your scent. I don't know if this is good or bad luck."

She gave him a malevolent glare. "Bad."

"Ha! I'm sure you think so, given the position of disadvantage you're in." Hungry heat flashed into his eyes, and he looked at her neck.

"Don't even think about it!"

"Oh, but I do." His voice turned to silk. "I think about it all the time. That's how I know this must be good luck. I was thinking about it just today."

Forest shivered with repulsion.

Leith noticed. "See now," he whispered intimately. "See how you respond to me? You've missed me."

He pressed his lips into the curve of her neck where the worst of her scars were. She felt bile rise in her throat. "Let go of me!" she growled.

He laughed, his breath falling across her skin. "In this relationship, I'm the one who commands. You're the one who obeys."

Forest squirmed, trying to reach her .45. He was so much taller than she was; her feet were hanging a good six inches off the ground. Leith pulled his face back from her neck to look in her eyes, and a mixture of emotions crossed his face. She had seen him look at her like that many times. Desire and hatred, envy and fear. She understood it.

"You're packing, aren't you?"

"I'm on duty," she said. "Of course I'm packing."

Leith tightened his grip on her. "Why don't you just give in to me? Why do you insist on trying to kill me when you know you can't?"

"I like to test my boundaries. I know I don't need to remind you how close I came to killing you, not all that long ago." When he grimaced, she smiled. "It must have left one hell of a scar. Can I see it?"

Leith bared his teeth. His glassy eyes were murderous. He pushed his forehead against hers until the back of her head pressed roughly to the wall. She knew he wanted to see her fear. Instead, Forest closed her eyes and let her body go limp.

After a second, Leith relaxed a fraction and pulled back from her face, only to move his mouth to her ear. "I'll let you see it, Forest," he breathed. "I know you really want to. I'll forget about the Vampire RPG I was going to crash, and you can call your boss and head home early with me."

Forest opened her eyes and smiled thinly at him. "Sure. Why not?"

Heat flashed in his eyes again, and he backed up and dropped her to her feet. Throughout all these years, she was still amazed at his stupidity. As soon as her arms were loose, she pulled her gun on him.

"Stop!" he yelled.

All the muscles in her arm clamped down, and her finger, already half-squeezing the trigger, began to shake as she fought against his command. She'd been *so* close.

Leith reached out and grabbed the gun from her hand, only to swear loudly in pain and throw it from him. He looked down at his hand that was now red and smoking.

"That's my favorite gun. I had it plated with silver. You know how I love silver."

"Well," he sneered at her. "I suppose I have to congratulate you on a clever little move."

His raw hand whipped out, backhanding her across the face, splitting both her lips. She staggered momentarily, but held her ground. Hatred was boiling over inside her. His eyes went wild at the sight of blood on her lips, and he took a step toward her again.

This was where Forest drew the line. She spit the blood in her mouth across his face, savoring his shocked expression for a split second, before disappearing again and taking off back down the alley to the club. He wouldn't follow.

****

Horrified, Leith wiped his hand across his face. He couldn't believe Forest had been capable of showing him such disrespect. He had forbidden her, years ago, of ever showing him disrespect. He didn't consider her attempts to kill him anything other than amusing foreplay. But this? His control over her was weaker than it had ever been. She was learning to fight it. The fact the she could exercise any measure of free will around him caused him disquiet. If she could fight back even half of the persuasion he once held over her, his life really would be in danger.

Leith thought of the scar that ran down the length of his back, from shoulder to waist. That had been excruciating.

He tucked his thumbs in the pockets of his jeans and leaned against the wall. He didn't want to lose his favorite toy. Why had she never been able to see that he loved her? *Lowlife Halfling,* he thought bitterly. If he couldn't keep her, he'd have to kill her.

Licking the blood remaining around his mouth, he stomped off down the street.

****

Forest waited until she was certain that Leith was gone before venturing back into the alley to retrieve her gun. It had landed next to the smelly dumpster. She looked at the overflowing trash receptacle, so very metaphoric to her mood. Every memory and emotion connected to Leith was like that putrid garbage.

She kicked the dumpster as hard as she could, sending the rats living behind it scampering. She shouldn't have to put up with this, dammit. She was a warrior, a formidable one at that.

With her .45 tucked back in the waistband of her pants, Forest retreated back to the shadows of the club. She closed her eyes and leaned her head back against the concrete wall, concentrating on her breathing. She was seething and torn about reporting Leith. *Focus. Focus. Focus.* Reporting him would bring attention to her failure to control the traffic through her post. Nuts to that.

She had two hours and thirty-seven minutes left to work. It was no good—she couldn't do her job when she wanted to kill everyone in sight. She pulled out her phone and sent a text to her boss, Kendel, telling him she was cutting out early. Forest went out the front door and headed straight for her car. Traffic was light, and she zipped through the streets of downtown, jumped onto the Mopac expressway, and arrived back at her luxury, north-Austin condo in no time.

Her mind was in a terrible snarl. She dropped her bag and her keys on the floor and stomped into the dining room. Bracing both her hands on the table, she closed her eyes and tried breathing deeply. But calm would not come. Emotions swelled like a tsunami and came gushing out violently. She grabbed the glass fruit bowl on the table that was full of peaches and threw it against the wall as hard as she could. Shattered glass, splattered peaches, and tears fell. Would her life ever be her own?

Destroying her fruit bowl felt good, but it wasn't enough violence to assuage the storm within. Not nearly enough. Her body felt flattened where Leith had touched her. She wiped at the tears on her face, vomit rising in the back of her throat. Growling, Forest grabbed a shard of broken glass from the floor and went into the bathroom. The lights stung her already burning eyes. She let loose a scream of rage at her reflection. Crying! Crying was weakness.

Forest pulled her shirt over her head and dropped it on the floor. She turned to the side and looked at the pattern of her scars Leith had marked her with so many years ago. Biting down on her bottom lip, she took the shard and stabbed it a quarter inch deep into her shoulder. Wincing, she dragged it in a jagged line down to her elbow, then dropped the bloody glass into the sink and splashed water on the self-inflicted wound. She watched it for a few minutes. A searing rushed through her flesh, causing her to yell obscenities at random and kick the vanity.

She splashed water on her arm again and looked at it closely. It was no good. She healed too quickly to build scars on top of scars. The pattern remained unaltered. Sighing, she left the bathroom.

In her living room, she surveyed the mess. She would clean it up tomorrow.

Dawn began to color the sky as Forest dropped on her bed and fell asleep.

Piles of files were stacked to eyelevel atop Kindel's desk. Every miniscule tidbit of information on all Fortress operatives was heaped before him like a haystack. He must find the elusive needle. The clock ticked loudly, incessantly drawing his attention. He had a weeks' worth of work and only a handful of hours to complete it. They weren't paying him enough for this crap.

He closed his bloodshot eyes and took a few deep breaths. He couldn't pull this off. The weight of his thoughts pulled down on his shoulders like an over-stuffed backpack. What would they do to him if he failed? Fortress couldn't fire him—he was privy to too many government secrets. However, they *could* demote him. Kindel shuddered.

He focused on the piles in front him. He had been through every single page. He knew every operative personally; he managed three quarters of them. And not one stood out as the obvious choice for the black ops mission.

Kindel pushed his chair out and began pacing the floor of his office, too agitated to care that pacing was very un-elfish. The King had clearly lost his head, and the high council stood behind him, cheering on this folderol. They had formed a plan and dropped it right in his lap. He would do all the work, and the council would take all the credit. Like always.

Kindel ground his teeth. He needed an operative who specialized in combat and stealth. He had plenty of those. Not a spy. Kindel hated spies. He needed someone he could trust, someone loyal to *him*. But more than anything, he needed someone versatile and also, unfortunately, expendable. He needed…He needed…

His phone vibrated in his pocket. A text from Forest. He read it, half-smirking, half-scowling. Why did she always call him The Suit?

Suit, leaving work two hours early. Dock my pay if you want. Oh wait, forgot I'm salaried.

—blows raspberry— Forest

Forest! It hit him like a sucker punch from an ogre. He needed Forest. Forest was the solution to his problem. An imperfect, knotty solution, but selecting her made sense.

He ought to reprimand her for her insolence and work habits, but Earth was low on his list of priorities. Personally, he didn't really care if the whole human race was annihilated, but it was part of his job to oversee the portals from Regia.

Kendel dug into the mound of paper and fished out Forest's file. He scanned through it, wishing he could edit out a few little unsavory things. His logic for selecting Forest for this mission was undeniable, as were the strong objections he knew the council would raise. He sat back down, dipped his quill in ink, and began to write the proposal.

Forest's eyes loomed in Kendel's mind. He couldn't conjure her face, as he had no idea what it really looked like. He wished she had been born a pure blood elf, like him, and not some cast off, illegitimate Halfling. As it was, she was considered the lowest of beings in all the world of Regia. His respect for her was second to none because no one else gave her any. She was undeniably shady, and bad tempered, and had a love affair with weapons that Kendel didn't understand. Through the years he had watched her battle harder than anyone else, only to achieve less. She was the only Halfling Fortress Operative in all of Regia's history.

Kendel rolled his thin shoulders and cracked his neck. He knew Forest didn't fantasize about him the way he did about her, and that was best, he told himself. Nevertheless, he longed to see her true face, if only for a moment. But she couldn't have shown Kendel her real face even if she wanted to. When she finally met her destined life mate, she would never be able to hide her true form from him.

Kendel agonized over the mission proposal for the next few hours. He wanted to be realistic and fair to Forest if she succeeded, but not so much that the council would notice his favoritism. Using her was going to be a hard sell. The council met in the morning, and should they approve the mission, Kendel would meet with Forest in the evening before her shift. Kindel smirked. She might be an even harder sell than the council.

****

FORTRESS CASTLE, REGIA

HIGH COUNCIL MEETING

The high council chamber in the heart of the castle was empty except for Kendel. He didn't like being in this room alone. It made him feel like a child, sneaking somewhere he wasn't allowed. A copy of his proposal rested on every seat. Personally addressing the high council was something Kendel had only been called to do a few times before. It was a high honor—one that turned his stomach. He was sure his career would suffer if the council rejected his proposal, but in all of Fortress' operatives, no one made more sense for this mission than Forest. Unfortunately, he wasn't the only one who knew about her prejudice against vampires. Her file documented it. Aside from that, the members of the council might act too high and mighty to care about a Halfling, but they indulged in gossip just like everyone else. They all knew about her.

The chamber doors opened. Security ogres came through first and positioned themselves strategically around the circular room. The six council members lazily filled in. First came Devonte, the Wizard. He was ancient and hunched and could give Oscar the Grouch cranky lessons. Kendel avoided him whenever he could. Wizards considered themselves above the law, and Devonte more than most. The fact that they were a dying race gave them an imaginary license for lawlessness. If Devonte desired more power, he could have declared himself the emperor of Regia, and no one would have stood against him. One wizard could destroy an entire army.

Next into the chamber was Nahcaan, the Ogre. Eight-foot-two, five hundred pounds of exaggerated muscle and a perpetually cheerful mood. One of the most educated and talented ogres in all of Regia, he spoke slowly and evenly. Kendel didn't have the slightest idea which way he would vote on the mission. Nahcaan was excessively logical, but the ogres were faithful allies to the vampires. Always had been, always would be. Could logic trump fidelity?

Zefyre, the Elf priestess, followed Nahcaan. She smiled thinly at Kendel, who felt his stomach flip. She was five hundred years older than him, not that she looked a day over twenty, and had been Kendel's first boyhood crush. It was hard for him not to blush around her as the memory came back into his head of how, when he was fourteen, he had proclaimed passionate love for her. He figured that she would be behind his proposal for the mission out of family loyalty; she was Forest's aunt. But Zefyre would never claim Forest publicly since her brother hadn't owned that Forest was his.

Next came Frost, the Werewolf. Kendel always felt unsteady around him. He was broad as most werewolves were, and always looked as though he hadn't shaved in a week. However, for a werewolf, he was positively posh. A superior politician, slick as they came. What you saw was not what you got with Frost. Frost would probably vote against Forest taking the mission, because that would be the politically correct move.

Fifth in line was Gagnee, the Shape shifter. She was Kendel's idea of the dragon lady. She changed her appearance more often than any other shifter in the whole of Regia. Kendel suspected she did so to eavesdrop on her underlings. Her vote would be the easy yes. Shifters were considered to be second-class citizens; they stuck together fiercely. Gagnee might not approve of Halflings, but the fact Forest's mother was a shifter would sway her.

Lastly, there was Lush, the Vampire, whom Kendel despised, mostly because of his rumored liaisons with Zefyre. He was typical vampire nobility scum, condescending with every syllable. Everything from his clothes to his tone of voice was calculated precisely. Arrogant and ambitious. He was nothing more than a successful social climber.

They sat in a semi-circle around Kendel, methodically smoothing their robes under their butts and looking down at the papers in front of them. Silence fell as they read. He watched their expressions change as they thought about his proposal. Lush shook his head in disapproval when he finished reading and leaned back in his chair, crossing his arms over his chest, waiting for his fellows to join him.

One by one, they put the papers down. It was Kendel's job to begin the tug of war. "Shall we vote, or is deliberation needed?" he asked.

"Needed," Lush said immediately, in unison with Devonte.

Kendel gave a little bow to the council and prepared to hold his mouth shut while the arguing began. It was, as he expected, going to be a long day.

3

The late afternoon sun baked Forest's red curtains. The light filtering through washed the walls in pink. She slept as though drugged in the heat of her condo. The ceiling fan over her bed was off balance, the chain pulls clinking cheerfully, as it buffeted her with hot air.

The vibrating sound of her phone as it knocked repeatedly into her bedside lamp, disturbed her sleep. She rolled over and grabbed the offensive little thing, reading the email from Kendel with blurry eyes. Some of the message registered in her sleepy brain, and she forced herself to sit up. She grabbed the tumbler of lukewarm water by her lamp and drank it down. It tasted stale and dead, and she hated it. Earth's water was one of the few things Forest didn't like about the place. It failed to regenerate her the way Regia's water did, didn't taste as good, and wasn't as pretty. She hissed in pain from what she'd done to herself hours before.

Unable to focus on the email, she headed for the shower, turned it on, and stepped in. The water washed off the dried blood on her arm and swirled pink around her feet. She ran her fingers gingerly along the ridges of her scars. The pads of her fingers knew every line. The cuts she had made hadn't changed her scars in the slightest; they still felt exactly the same. Her shifter abilities allowed her to hide them from the eyes of others, but she couldn't hide them from herself. Those scars were the cruelest things in existence, because they ensured that she could never forget the night she received them.

The water worked wonders in waking her up, and she was able to fully comprehend Kendel's email when she read it again. She read it and re-read it, excitement blasting through her. This was important and unexpected, and she needed to hurry. The email was vague, but she knew that whatever this mission was, it was her chance. A big break, as the humans called it. She had to push back her urge to rush about, in order to get to Regia quickly. Arriving in Regia, sweaty and out of breath wouldn't look very professional. So, instead of flying around, she made herself an iced mocha and stepped out onto her terrace to catch a few minutes of the sunset.

Forest loved Austin. It was a beautiful city, with its hills, and trees, and river. She loved Earth's sun too, so warm, so different from Regia's. She had been all over the earth, but she preferred America, and Texans emulated the kick-ass attitude she herself worked to perfect. She breathed deeply and sipped her coffee, letting all the angst of last night slip away. This might be the last time she saw her beloved Austin for a long while, and she would miss it.

Once the sun dipped behind the treetops, Forest felt it was time to hustle. She tossed the glass from the bathroom sink into the trash and rinsed the blood away, then looked at herself in the large mirror for a moment, calculating. She looked a bit like Wonder Woman. Too sexy for an important meeting in Regia, she decided. There were magazine pictures of different models and actresses taped to the wall around the edges of the mirror that Forest used as inspiration. She filed the Wonder Woman look into her memory before shrinking the long, curly black hair into a sleek red bob. The curvy figure shrank as well into an almost boyish shape, and for a finishing touch, she spattered some freckles across her nose. Her eyes remained the same green they always were, no matter what her shape. She did a quick check to make sure that her ears were not pointing at the top. For some odd reason she always had a hard time controlling them. If she didn't pay attention, they would shift back to their natural shape of their own volition.

There was nothing Forest could find in her closet that would be appropriate attire once she crossed the portal. She slipped on Flip-flops, short cutoffs, and a tie-dyed *Keep Austin Weird* T-shirt. It made her smile when she thought of the disapproving look Kendel would give her.

Lastly, she half-emptied her jewelry box, putting a silver ring on each finger, silver hoops and studs in her ears, and half a dozen silver chains around her neck. Oh, if only she'd been so decked out last night.

Forest quickly cleaned up the peaches and glass before grabbing her keys, MP3 player, and tucking her .45 in her waistband. She set the alarm on the security system and stepped out into the heat. The baking-hot concrete almost melted off the bottoms of Forest's flip-flops as she strode to her car. She felt powerful just looking at the black and red 1971 Dodge Demon 340. Not only was it rare, if she'd had the time, Forest would have taken it to car shows. It glistened in the sunset like an oil slick. She slid sinuously behind the wheel; the leather of the seat scorched the backs of her bare legs. The engine roared to life, literally, a feral demon indeed. She plugged her MP3 player in and turned it to something to heighten her mood.

The Demon terrorized the streets of Austin, rattling every window with the engine's growl and some good old fashioned Beasty Boys, Brass Monkey.

Since she would be leaving Earth for a while, she decided to put the car in her storage unit and walk the rest of the way to the club. She would miss the Demon while she was gone.

The metal of her gun against her back was irritating as she walked down the sidewalk, especially once she started sweating. It would be nice to ditch firearms for a while. They made combat so impersonal, and they were strictly banned in Regia. Forest broke Regia's laws from time to time in regard to human paraphernalia, but she never desired to try smuggling in guns. Regia had enough trouble.

It struck her that if she got a big promotion with this new mission she might have to give up smuggling all together. That sucked.

The club was in sight; the businesses along the street were either closing down or opening up. Among the people on the sidewalk, one figure moving away from her caught her utmost attention. Anger didn't begin to cover it. Obscenities, both Regian and human thumped in her skull. Her fists balled, and she picked up her pace. "Lorcan! Stop!"

The vampire halted and turned to face her. His nostrils flared, and a hiss escaped his lips. Most could hardly tell the difference between Lorcan and his brother Leith, but Forest always knew. Lorcan didn't budge as she strode up to him.

Forest showed no trace of fear as she bellied up to the vampire, who towered at least a foot over her. He looked at her confusedly, but his expression cleared once he looked in her eyes. Recognition dawned on his face.

"*Forest.*" He turned her name into a curse, rolling it in his throat like something he wanted to hock up and spit out.

"You are breaking the law. Please return to Regia immediately, or you will be subject to arrest. If you resist or flee, your life is forfeit and it is my duty to take you out." She sated the script through her clenched teeth.

He laughed at her.

"Rather stupid of you to loiter so close to the portal, Lorcan."

"Get bent, Forest," he spat. "If it weren't out of respect for my brother, I'd kill you right here."

Her thin veneer of control peeled away, and Forest's temper snapped like a twig as she seized one of Lorcan's forearms in both of her hands. His face blanched, and she could see he was fighting the urge to scream like a little girl. The silver rings she wore burned his bare skin, and the pain almost crumpled him to his knees.

"Don't you ever mention Leith to me again, Lorcan!" Forest snarled. "Now let's take this inside."

She towed him by his arm, and he followed like a reluctant dog on a leash, swearing continually. Forest kicked the swinging door to the club open and pulled Lorcan through it. In the dark and loud atmosphere, Lorcan pulled his arm free of her grasp and cradled it against his chest. The burning smell of his flesh reeked. She could tell he was fighting a whimper.

"Why don't you just arrest me and get it over with?" he growled.

"I'm not on duty. So I guess this is your lucky night. You get to go back without even an official warning. But I'll give you one off the record. I see you this side of the portal again, and I won't even bother with the arrest crap, I'll just shoot you."

"I'll not forget the disrespect you've showed me." He sneered at her and whispered, "*Halfling.*"

Forest smiled nastily. "I'd watch my language, if I were you." Her hand reared back, and she punched him right in the mouth, the silver rings on her fingers burning his lips. Lorcan hollered in pain as Forest grabbed him by the arm again and pulled him to the back of the club. Luckily, there was next to no one there this early in the night.

The lone woman in the ladies' room screamed as Forest pushed Lorcan through the bathroom door. She quickly grabbed her handbag off the counter and ran out.

"How dare you!" Lorcan snarled.

Forest just pointed at the last stall. It had an "out of order" sign tapped to the door. "Get your ass back where it belongs."

Lorcan stalked to the stall and punched the door open. He turned to face her. "One day, Forest. I swear I'll kill you. "

"Yeah, yeah. I'm sure."

"I'm gonna talk to him," he threatened. "The next time you see Leith, he'll make you pay for what you've done to me."

She didn't care that he was standing on the threshold of the portal. She didn't care who would hear. She was going to kill him right now. Lorcan's eyes widened. He could move fast when he needed to.

The bullet blew a hole through the stall door as Lorcan closed it. One millisecond faster, and she'd have hit her mark, but he was gone.

Forest looked around the bathroom. Gun smoke hung heavy in the air and mingled with the commercial air freshener. Good thing this hadn't happened during peak business hours. She didn't really care about being inconspicuous to humans, however, her present antics would have landed her a bit more than a slap on the wrist if Kendel ever found out. Maybe she needed a break. Maybe this new mission would be just the thing.

She waited a minute before going through the stall door, not wanting to bump into Lorcan on the other side.

Going through the portal was like floating in a river with a strong current. Once you stepped in, you were powerless against the pull. Humans couldn't use it. The new portal regulation stipulated they didn't recognize them as a race and were closed to them. It was just as well. More than a few vampires had tried to bring humans across. Every human died within minutes. Regia couldn't support human life. Yet that didn't stop human blood from being smuggled in.

As soon as Forest's feet landed in Regia, she felt healthier. Living on Earth full time had a physical price. Everything inside her buzzed, and she felt stronger as she breathed the fragrant air of home. The Portal had dumped her in the gardens next to the Fortress castle.

Time kept a different pace in Regia. It was still midday, Forest judged, looking at the sun. Her eyes stung as they readjusted to the change. Regia's sun was larger than Earth's, but it gave less warmth, and a different kind of light, paler and iridescent.

Regardless of how far you traveled and what wonderful sights you encountered, home was home.

She looked up at the castle. It was much the same as castles on Earth. To a human, Regia would have seemed positively medieval, Arthurian, or the landscape of a fairy tale. Most of Earth's fairy tales were a product of Regians passing through the portals.

Forest's eyes swept over the sprawling capital city of Paradigm that fanned out around Fortress Castle. It was exactly the same as the last time she'd seen it. Regians of every race buzzed around in the late afternoon light, preparing for the coming evening. An involuntary sneer curled Forest's lips as she watched. *Paradigm, what a joke.* It was the only place in Regia where your race or status didn't shut you out. All were welcome and equal, supposedly. A place for everyone, and everyone in their place. Excepting her and any other Halflings. Experience taught Forest that a place with vast cultural diversity had more racial trouble than anywhere else. She never voiced such politically incorrect opinions aloud, but she gave herself an unchecked license to be jaded. Being a Halfling made her a minority's minority.

She walked toward the castle at a brisk pace. She was supposed to meet Kendel in the courtyard, and she was overdue. He would be annoyed.

A tall rock wall surrounded the courtyard, and the whole place was protected by enchantment. She wouldn't have been able to enter if she wasn't recognized by the magic. It was a necessary protection in a world full of shape shifters and elves that could become invisible at will.

As soon as she crossed through the stone archway, she spotted Kendel at the far end, pacing back and forth. She could tell he was tired, and agitation pulsed in the air around him. Once he spotted her, he quit pacing and crossed his arms over his chest. "You're late," he scolded. "I told you to hurry."

"Sorry, Kendel, I ran into Lorcan on the other side of the portal. I had to deal with it. And you really need to get the construction crew to move that portal."

"Why? It's in a women's restroom, is it not?" Kendel raised one thin eyebrow. "Are not all the women in there asleep?"

Forest laughed. "No! In the human world a restroom is where they *relieve* themselves."

"Oh? Relieve. . . oh." Kendel's high cheekbones turned slightly pink. "I'll get the ogres to fix that."

"Thanks. Now tell me what is going on."

"Hand it over first."

Forest placed her pistol in Kendel's outstretched hand. It hovered an inch over his skin before disappearing. He would keep it safe, and she was happy to be rid of it for a while.

"Check your phone," he ordered.

Forest pulled her cell phone out of her pocket. "It's working fine."

"Good. Switch to channel three and punch in your security code."

"Why am I doing this?" she asked as she tapped in the numbers.

"Devonte created a new secure line for Fortress. I swear, enchanting the phones is the only useful work that wizard does."

Kindel took her smart phone and scrolled through the menu. "Yours is nicer than mine." He complained.

"Latest model. Came out last week."

Kindel smirked and handed her phone back. "It was originally your idea for Fortress to embrace the technology Earth provided, wasn't it?"

"Yeah, like five years ago. Not that I got any credit for it."

"I'm not sure you'd want credit now. Cell phones have flooded our black market ever since."

"So? They don't work. The unfortunate buyer gets to play Angry Birds until the battery runs out. Now tell me what's going on."

"What the devil are you wearing?" he asked, surveying her multicolored tie-dyed shirt.

She smiled. "I don't keep proper Regian attire in my Austin closet, Kendel. I didn't wear this to piss you off, at least not specifically. I just didn't have what I needed."

He waved her excuse away, haughtily, with his long spindly hand. "It doesn't really matter at the moment. You won't be going before the council anyway."

Her heart sank. Did that mean that she didn't have the job after all?

"They agreed that time is too short and have placed enough trust in me to do the briefing, seeing as my ass is on the line here as well. Let's sit down."

They sat on a stone bench, and for a moment, all Kendel did was look at her. Forest forced herself to hold his gaze and not show the awkwardness she felt. For all intents and purposes, he was her boss, and it was unfortunate that Regia had no sexual harassment laws. He had no idea that she knew how he felt, but it was obvious when he looked in her eyes. He was not the first, nor would he be the last, to be beguiled by her eyes.

Kendel sighed and turned his gaze to the ground in front of him. "Civil war will commence within days."

"Not again," Forest whined.

"The Ogres have sided with the Vampires, naturally. Likewise, the Shape-Shifters will join the Werewolves."

"And the Elves?" Forest asked.

"Neutral…For now."

Forest snorted. The Elves were on no side but their own, and they never made alliances unless they were the ones who benefitted.

"What about the Wizards? Where do they stand?"

"Officially, they don't stand anywhere on the matter. Devonte supports the vampires, but he has about as much care for this war as he does for the lint in his navel. The council has yet to hear an official response from them. I don't know if they will respond at all. As their numbers continue to diminish, so does their taste for involvement in anything outside of their own survival."

"I suppose it's better that way," she said. "Evens the playing field. Just one wizard taking a side can change the outcome of war. How many do you think are left?"

"Maybe nine or ten."

"So, what does the council want with a lowly, level six operative like me?" False modesty rang thick in her voice.

Kendel snorted. "By rights you should be a level eight, at least. Successful completion of this mission would secure your promotion…uh…among other…things."

Forest began to feel uneasy. She didn't like the way Kendel was speaking. He was looking uncomfortable too.

"What does the council want?"

Kendel shifted in his seat and grimaced. "Please don't take offense. I'll tell you now that the council does not want to offer you this mission. It is because of time and desperation that they do so. They have agreed, but they say it is against their better judgment."

Forest was used to this kind of crap. She didn't have the energy to be bothered. "Because of my parentage?"

"Yes, however, more because of your own prejudice. They are unsure if you can be trusted to fulfill your duty when it goes against personal loyalty. I have assured them of you. I vouched."

Forest's eyes narrowed. Kendel vouching for her? Suspicious indeed. "If they don't trust me, why are they offering me the mission? Why can't they find someone else?"

"Because you are the only operative Fortress has who can execute it. Because you have the needed stealth of being a shifter, coupled with your elfin gift of invisibility, and because of your shady connections with the Werewolves. But lastly, because no one knows the Wolf's Wood the way you do, and that is the path you must take while protecting a, ah, most…important person."

Forest just stared at him for a moment. "Oh, no way. How could you do this to me, Kendel?" she demanded.

He said nothing, looking shamefaced.

Forest stood up abruptly, outrage bursting in her head. "You want me to transport a vampire through werewolf territory in a time of war, don't you?"

Kendel sighed. "Yes."

"You've cracked your cabbage. Shifters always side with the Wolves, you know that. This, this *person* and I are enemies in a pending war. This is a suicide mission! I'll lose my temper; I'll make a mess of it. I can't do it! I'll kill them or they'll kill me. Let the suckers take care of their own!"

"This is your job," he said flatly.

"I hate all vampires on principal! The council is right not to trust me. I can't do it!"

"Your success would promote you to level eight, give you the respect of the council, and grant you a royal favor. How can you decline?" he demanded.

Forest paused, rolling his words around in her head until they clicked. "*Royal* favor? Who am I supposed to be protecting anyway?"

Kendel looked apologetic as he handed her a black leather bound file. "This is level ten classified."

Her eyebrows shot up, and she blinked a few times before flipping it open. A slur of obscenities came tumbling out of her mouth. Kindel didn't react to her rage of almost incoherent swearing. She quieted abruptly, eyeing Kendel with a small sneer. "I've never known you to pull pranks, Kendel. Good one. You had me there for a moment."

"Forest, it's not a joke."

"*Really?*" she mocked. "*Prince Syrus?*"

"That's right."

"Heir to the throne?"

"Yep," he said.

"I've been on Earth too long and out of Regia's current events, but I did just happen to remember that *he's dead*!"

Kendel gave her a severe, piercing look and shook his head. "It is not a joke."

Forest paced angrily in front of him. "I *thought* he was dead. All of Regia believes he's dead, since that attack five years ago."

"The fact that most believe him to be dead is in your favor. The attack five years ago crippled him."

"Oh this just keeps getting better and better. What do you mean by crippled?"

"He's blind."

4

Deep in Fortress Castle, prince Syrus was sitting in a dimly lit room, listening to Redge, his personal guard, read aloud from Forest's file. The longer he listened, the more confused he became. The information about her was compiled in a choppy way, and Syrus was having a hard time forming a clear idea about who she was. He was becoming increasingly uncomfortable with the position Fortress had put him in and the solution the council had devised. His father believed it to be the time for him to come out of hiding and take his place as commander of the Vampire army. Syrus couldn't do that until his sight was restored, so this secret little excursion through the Wolf's Wood to the rouge wizard, Maxcarion, became necessary.

"Her regular occupation is as a traffic controller in the human world, and she has the highest arrest and kill record in that department. Her average last year alone was..."

Syrus held up his hand for Redge to stop reading. "What does that mean? Traffic controller?"

"Well, it means that she acts as a custodian to one of the portals. Regulating the going and coming. The new amendment of Regia's law only allows Shape-shifters to cross the portals to Earth. No one else is supposed to go there, especially our kind. Those caught on the other side are subject to arrest. Those who resist are killed on sight. From her file, it looks like your new guardian is quite fond of killing vampires."

"Why is she allowed to keep her job?" Syrus asked.

"Fortress is not overly concerned with those she kills. Vampires who cross over tend to run amuck on the other side, due to the *addictive* nature of human blood. Some lose themselves completely. Some just can't handle... "

"I know." Syrus hissed.

"Forgive me," Redge said, "Of course you do. Shall I continue reading?"

"No. Tell me what you know of Forest—word of mouth, gossip."

"I've yet to see her, but I hear she is a creature of astounding beauty."

Syrus snorted. "She's a shifter. Does anyone know what she really looks like?"

"Is it really true a shifter can only show their true form to their destined life mate and no one else?" Redge asked.

"Yes, that's true. Has she found her life mate yet?"

"No, my lord. They say every form she takes is beautiful and that she cannot help it. Her eyes are the only thing she cannot change about her appearance. I asked around court about her. Apparently, your cousin Leith knows her. He said that looking in her eyes is like getting lost, that you can see an entire forest in her eyes."

"*Leith* said that? *Really*?" Syrus was incredulous.

"Yes, my lord."

"Hm . . . It's too bad I can't see her." Syrus sighed.

"You could."

"Yes, but I doubt it would be worth the price I'd have to pay. Anyway, what else do you know?"

"No one I talked to knows who her elf father is. She carries a katana made of folded silver and wears silver jewelry about her body. It's well known that she hates vampires. I'd watch my step if I were you—they say she fights dirty."

Syrus smirked. "And I thought this trip wasn't going to be any fun."

****

Out in the courtyard, Forest was still sitting next to Kendel, perusing Syrus' file. Her mind was already formulating a plan for the best, and more importantly, fastest route. Travel through the Wolf's Wood would only take three days, maybe four if Syrus was slow. Kendel's voice faded into the background, as he kept up a running commentary about Prince Syrus. She wasn't listening, just nodding and grunting periodically. A blip of information about Syrus' tactical background caught her eye. It took her a few moments to notice Kendel's droning had stopped. She looked into his angry face.

"It's so nice to know how much you value what I have to say." Acid dripped in Kendel's tone. "Or how much you appreciate the sacrifices I've made for you throughout the years, not to mention the one today."

"You're right, Kendel. I'm sorry. I just noticed that the file says he's a master of the Blood Kata."

"Yeah. I've heard he's a great fighter."

"But is he still ranked that high, given the fact he can't see?" she asked.

Kendel huffed, "I don't know how they work their ranking system, and I don't care. Syrus, blind or not, can hold his own, so you don't have to worry about that."

"Okay. Fine. I was just asking. *Sheesh.* Tell me what I need to be worried about then."

"Be on your guard, Forest. Don't start any friendly sparing matches with him."

"Why not?" she asked innocently.

"Because your usual advantage of invisibility won't help you against a blind vampire. And you tend to bring out the worst in people. I would hate for him to kill you in the heat of the moment. "

"Whatever." Forest shrugged, rising to her feet again.

Regardless of what she might say, her interest piqued. She was impressed that the prince was a master of the vampire marshal art. Most vampires were no problem for her, but this one might actually pose a challenge. If possible, Forest would pick a fight with him at the first chance. He wouldn't kill her. She was more likely to be the one who lost control and hacked his head off before she remembered what she was doing.

Kendel continued his tirade. "You've got to be in charge. Syrus is rumored to be quite the ladies' man. Don't let him charm you, and most certainly don't let him bite you."

Forest stopped in her tracks and just blinked at Kendel. Then she burst out laughing.

"I'm not kidding, Forest!"

She continued to laugh, her arms wrapped around her torso.

"Forest!" he said loudly over her mirth. "If you allow a vampire to bite you, they will have the power of persuasion over you."

Forest's laughter died in the air, and her eyes snapped to Kendel's. When she spoke, it was very slowly and through her teeth. "I might be considered one of the lowest life forms in all of Regia, but I know about suckers and their nasty habits. Syrus is charming, you say? I'd like to see how charmed I could be by the thing I find most disgusting. Why do you think I wear all of this?" She held out her hands for him to see all the silver she wore.

Kendel held up his hands in surrender. "I'm sorry. I guess I underestimated your prejudice."

They stared at each other one long moment. Forest sighed, letting her anger fizzle. She wished she hadn't lost her temper. Kendel only said what he had because he didn't know about her and Leith. For that, she was thankful. Leith didn't want anyone to know either, and that was the only thing they had in common. As far as she knew, only his stinking brother, Lorcan, knew about them. She was Leith's dirty little secret. And he was her what? Master? Owner? Lover? No, definitely not lover. She tried not to think about it. It was just too ugly.

"Please sit back down, Forest. I'm sorry for my insensitivity. I know I sprang this on you, and it's not a small thing. But I know you can do this. I might grouse at you from time to time, but I have the utmost faith in you."

It was true. She owed her career to Kendel. Oh, she worked her butt off for it and was over-qualified for her rank, but because of what she was, she wouldn't even have a rank if it weren't for Kendel. She owed him her gratitude and loosely considered him her friend. But she knew how he felt about her, so it was best that she keep him at arm's length. She was not about to be someone else's convenience.

"Thank you for that, Kendel." She sat back down. "And forgive me my temper."

"Because the war has not yet begun, and timing is both short and unscheduled, you will need to depart with Syrus tonight. But you cannot head directly for the Wolf's Wood. You must wait for word from me. I suggest you take him to your cottage and hide him there."

"Why?"

"We cannot afford to have it leaked he's alive. He can't stay in the castle, and you must get him through the wood to Maxcarion, the wizard, before the werewolves get a stronghold. As soon as Maxcarion has healed his eyes, Syrus' existence can be made public. After you return, of course."

Forest *could* hide Syrus at her cottage. Enchantments protected it well, and people stayed away from her anyway. She was not what anyone would consider a social butterfly. She maintained the important friendships and connections that made her life easier, and that was it. Friendship, for friendship's sake, was a waste of time and energy.

"All right, Kendel, I accept the mission, and I agree to hide him in my cottage until I get word from you that it's safe to proceed. How long do you think we will need to hunker in my house?"

"Can't say for sure. I wouldn't think longer than a week."

"*A week?*"

Kendel sighed and looked at the sky. "Enough whining, Forest. Evening is coming. We've burned enough time. Get what you need from your closet, and meet Syrus in the lower council room. The two of you are to set off as soon as you have the cover of darkness. Leave through the tunnel."

They both stood, and Kendel clasped both her shoulders, looking sternly into her eyes. "Forget about the war, Forest. Forget that you hate what he is. Forget who he is and just think of him as cargo. Get in, get out, and claim your reward. That's all." His hands squeezed her shoulders before he released her.

"Thank you, Kendel." She pulled her phone out of her pocket and waved it at him. "You'll be in touch?"

"Yes. When I have news or instructions, I'll send emails."

She took a deep breath and squared her shoulders. "Okay. See ya."

Forest stalked away from Kendel toward the castle's side entrance. She paused, briefly, when Kendel called after her. "By the way, Forest, I like the freckles."

Inside the castle, Forest was met by the usual annoyance of security checkpoints. They were a series of enchanted arches. The first scanned for illegal weapons, and when she walked through, it felt as if invisible hands were patting her down. She sighed in irritation as she passed through and the invisible magic hands gave her a firm slap on the butt.

The next arch was enchanted to detect true identity and that felt like swallowing some hot thick liquid that ran all the way down the inside of her body. It was much more invasive than the perverted invisible hands, and it always seemed to take longer for her to go through than anyone else. Forest assumed the magic had a harder time determining *what* she was. As far as she knew, she was the only Halfling permitted in the castle. As soon as she stepped out of it, her name, race, and rank were emblazoned across her chest in a temporary, glowing, magic nametag.

The final arch was larger and decorated with inlaid stones and carvings, all of which strengthened the magic it held. This one examined emotions and intentions. When Forest walked under it, she immediately felt like she was dreaming or high. Flashes of recent events played in her mind along with splashes of color representing feelings. Everyone hated this security checkpoint because it forced you to look at the ugliness inside you, hate, anger, and weakness. The magic was neutral. It had no inclinations of right or wrong, it simply exposed. Still, every time Forest passed through, she felt like a little child who had been scolded and sent to her room. If the magic had detected something like assassination in her mind, it would have solidified around her like ice, holding her in place until security Ogres came.

Forest went to the main foyer and found it empty. Shocked, she darted her eyes around suspiciously. The foyer was never empty, *never*. She pricked her ears and heard laughter coming from down one of the halls. She took off silently in the direction of the noise. The hall was dimly lit with enchanted torches, as all good castles should be. The doors lining the hall led to offices of the highest muckety-mucks in the whole institution of Fortress. They were all closed, except one.

Forest stood silently outside the door, looking in at Zefyre, the Elf priestess, who sat gracefully, an easy smile on her face, while the vampire, Lush, leaned casually against her desk. He was smiling also, until he turned and saw Forest in the doorway. His smile jerked into a sneer as he read her nametag. Zefyre, however, smiled warmly and stood up.

"Forest." Zefyre's voice was surprisingly welcoming. "Is there something I can do for you?"

Forest just blinked for a second like an idiot. "Uh. . ."

Lush snorted in derision. Zefyre shot him an icy look, and he straightened from his casual stance. "I'll see you later, Zef." Lush walked past her, knocking his arm roughly against Forest's shoulder.

"Racist moron," Zefyre said under her breath as he retreated down the hall. "Sorry about that. Is there something I can do for you?" she asked again.

"No. Sorry. I was just confused by the emptiness of the castle, that's all. I followed the sound of your voice." Forest wanted out of here as quickly as she could without being impolite. She had never spoken directly to Zefyre, or any other member of the high council. Apprehension gripped her belly as she tried to figure how to behave. Should she avert her eyes? Or would that seem weak? If she looked Zefyre in the eye, would that be taken as insolence? She decided to look down at the floor.

"Look at me, please." Zefyre's voice was soft and relaxed as she moved to stand in front of her.

Forest looked up and met Zefyre's gaze. Zefyre brow furrowed as her eyes traveled over Forest's face. Then she took a step back and crossed her willowy arms over her chest. "Hmmm," Zefyre said smiling.

Forest had taken the opportunity to take a good look at Zefyre in return. She was beautiful, but then most elves were. She had a regal and authoritative air about her that was not completely cold. Slightly maternal. Her blond hair hung in straight, glossy perfection down to the middle of her back. Her large eyes were layered in the colors of earth's oceans, and the shape of them reminded Forest of another pair of eyes she could easily recognize—her own.

Zefyre gestured to the door in a way that was unmistakable. *Get out.* Forest backed out, her eyes still locked with Zefyre's.

"Good luck on your mission," she said smiling, and shut the door in Forest's face.

Weirdo. Forest headed off to the winding stairway that led to the bowels of the castle and her locker. It was creepy how empty the castle was. The bowels of the castle were not dark and dank, but comfortable and designed to accommodate all the needs an operative might have. The front half was like a day spa. Multiple rooms dedicated to health and wellbeing. The back end was for training and weapon needs; complete with sparring arena and armory. The place was usually filled with movement and sound, but like the halls above, was quiet and empty.

Forest walked swiftly to her locker. Not made of metal with a little combination lock like the one an American high school student would have. Instead, it was a large closet with ornately carved, wooden, double doors. Her combination lock lay in the carving itself. Every operative's locker was carved differently with the best Ogre craftsmanship. Forest's depicted the trees of the woods. The points of the carving had to be touched in the right order and by the only fingers that fit them perfectly. Tiny places slid behind others omitting small clicks, like a Japanese puzzle box. Opening her locker gave Forest a strong feeling of satisfaction . She was the only one who could.

The doors swung wide, and Forest inhaled the wonderful scent of her weapons, armor, and Regian clothing. She opened her trunk and reached for her Katana. She exhaled, gripping the hilt tightly. Reuniting with her sword was always the best thing about coming home. Forest had made the blade herself in the ancient elf style, similar to that of the human samurai. In fact, everything about the elf culture was similar to the samurai, even the clothes they wore.

She pulled the sword from its scabbard and let the light dance across the blade. It was an extension of her arm; the manifestation of her spirit; her closest and most faithful friend. She swung it in a wide arc, and it sang as it sliced through the air. Forest danced with her sword, letting it center her.

She exchanged her human clothes for plain Regian robes and fitted herself with all of her favorite weapons. Small knives hidden here and there—even the pins she put in her hair could be deadly. Once she was dressed and carrying as much as was advisable, she turned to her full mirror and started at her reflection. The image of her true form bounced back at her. She had not looked at it in a very long time and had not intended to now. Strange. Had anyone else been there to look, they wouldn't have been able to see it. All that anyone else would have seen was the freckled redhead Forest had constructed hours ago.

She looked at her real face for a moment and thought about the future. There was only one other person in all of Regia who could see this face, and when she finally met him there was nothing she could do to hide it from him. Her destined life mate would see her true form no matter how she shifted her appearance. She would never be able to hide her scars from him. She knew he would love her anyway because he would be destined to, but the truth would hurt him. Forest hoped there was no life mate for her. With luck, maybe because of her parentage, he just didn't exist.

The reflection drifted back to the redhead. Forest grew her hair out a good six inches and pulled it into a ponytail. Her ears were visible and obviously elf, but now that she was home, she made no effort to curb their behavior. It was time to go and meet Prince Syrus, but her feet seemed stuck to the floor. He would be spoiled, entitled, well educated in books but no life experience, and he was probably more put out at this arrangement than she was. She fully expected him to be rude, demanding, and generally insufferable. From what she knew of him, the only redeeming feature he would have was his rank in the Blood Kata, but that would probably lend itself to excessive arrogance.

Forest rolled her shoulders and took a deep breath. It was just a few days. She could do this. If she could put up with Leith for the last few years and not kill herself then she could do this. Syrus couldn't be as bad as Leith. She took another deep breath, forcing her feet to move. She could do this.

5

Syrus paced back and forth, a squirmy feeling in his stomach, while Redge sat still in the corner. Bemused by the situation, Syrus tried to think his way through his feelings. He compartmentalized his outrage and rebellious intentions toward his parents and tucked them deep inside so he could deal with them later. Everything had to be channeled into survival. He wanted to live. He wanted his sight back. The hunger for it was strangling him. He wanted to see the faces of the people who thought he was dead, when he came back to life. He would squash his enemies under his foot and show them no mercy.

Focus! Syrus ordered himself. How he would be, and what he would do, were thoughts that distracted from the immediate goal. He must survive. He must reach the wizard. He must keep his guide/guardian from killing him. Syrus told himself to be calm and polite to her even if she was caustic in return. She probably hadn't volunteered for this.

Syrus heard her approaching footsteps outside the council chamber door. He turned toward the source of the noise, and Redge stood beside him. The hinges creaked as the door swung open. A sharp pang hit Syrus square in the chest. It lasted only a second and then vanished. The pain knocked the breath from him. When he inhaled again, his senses spun with Forest's scent. Syrus' teeth began to tingle. He would have to stifle his olfactory sense, or she would instantly be able to see how appealing she smelled to him. Just the idea of one taste was enough to contemplate begging.

Forest walked through the door and spotted Syrus and his personal guard standing at the other end of the room. Her stomach swooped as if the floor had just dropped from under her feet. Her brain screeched to a halt. Every muscle in her body clamped down in defense, turning her to stone. She stared openly at Syrus as though her brain could not process the information her eyes were sending to it. Desire. Admiration of beauty. Objection. Hate. Forest's hatred of vampires snapped through her body. She hated him. No man had the right to be what he was. His existence was injustice.

Snap out of it! You have a job to do, regardless of your errant endocrine system. Anger bordering on rage had her clamping her teeth together. She saw him, but he did not see her.

Forest forced herself forward until she was able to get a good look at his ruined eyes. They were the color of black pearls, and he had no pupils. The second she looked in them, a sharp needling pain filled her own eyes. It was a frustrated, grasping feeling. Determination cemented in Forest's spine. She would succeed in getting him to the wizard. She *would* look into Syrus' eyes and *he* would look into hers.

Syrus was dressed plainly, but she would have picked him out as royalty any day of the week. His clothes were made of a loose, ebony fabric—a tunic and trousers with a cloak casually hanging open on his broad shoulders. The hilts of two butterfly swords, one on each hip, were visible through his open cloak. A small flask hung on his belt as well. He wore no shoes. His black hair was long and glossy, bound back in a single braid. The length of his hair was a mark of his rank in the Blood Kata.

As she moved closer, Forest noticed some diverse scars on his hands, paler in color than the soft cream of his skin. Syrus had a beautifully full mouth with which he offered her a greeting smile, resulting in a wayward thought she had to banish from her mind. When he smiled at her she was glad that *real* vampires didn't look like human saber tooth tigers, the way Hollywood painted them. All of Syrus' bottom teeth were slightly pointed along with his top incisors. You could still call them fangs but they weren't elongated, and they didn't slide in and out. Syrus' were subtle.

Time had stopped moving as Forest looked at Syrus, all protocol forgotten. She was staring at him like a halfwit. Someone cleared their throat, Redge, perhaps? Forest shook herself and straightened. What was going on in her head?

"My lord Prince." Forest gave a little bow even though she knew he couldn't see it. The words tasted like bile in her mouth. *Respect, respect, respect.* She chanted in her head.

"Forest." He reached out for one of her hands in a gesture of greeting. She grasped it without thinking. He inhaled sharply and threw her hand away from him.

She remembered too late the silver rings she wore. "Oh! I'm sorry! I forgot that I was wearing them. I'm so sorry."

Syrus shook his burned hand with an irritated expression on his face. He took a deep breath. "You have my thanks and the thanks of my family for taking this mission. I hope these next few days will pass with little consequence and very little danger. And although we are technically enemies, I'm sure that we can avoid killing each other."

A half strangled giggle escaped Forest's lips before she bit down on her tongue. She inhaled twice, working hard to control herself. "Let us hope so, my lord."

"Please call me Syrus."

Forest inclined her head again. "Syrus."

"I assume you have a plan for our journey?"

"A flexible plan. We'll take the tunnel under the castle, and we will travel through the night until we reach my home, in the fringe. It's remote and secluded. If we are lucky, we will encounter no one. We have to wait for a signal from Kendel when it is safe to proceed into the Wolf's Wood."

"Is it time to start?" he asked.

"As soon as you are ready."

Redge walked behind Syrus like a bulky shadow as they made their way to tunnel's entrance. The tunnel would deposit them outside of Paradigm's borders. It was enchanted for quick passage, and though they walked at a normal pace, they covered miles in minutes. Forest wondered if Redge was planning to come too. But as soon as they stepped outside, Syrus and Redge embraced like brothers, and Redge handed him a bulging pack, which Syrus slung over one shoulder. Redge turned and went back inside the tunnel.

"Lead on," Syrus said.

Forest looked up at the night sky, gaining her bearings. Paradigm glowed in the distance behind them, the wilderness ahead. She furrowed her brow as she looked at Syrus. Excitement emanated from him. He shifted his pack on his shoulder, waiting for her to move so that he could follow. Why would he be excited? Maybe it wasn't excitement, maybe it was anxiety. She could understand anxiety. She turned and began to walk, unsure at what pace she should assume. Given the circumstance, if she were alone, or had a companion that could see; she would be moving as briskly as possible. As it was, Forest was walking with a medium gait.

Syrus matched her pace and stayed on her heels with ease. Forest was relieved he had no problem following her without a guiding hand or having to place his hand on her shoulder. That would have made the trip seem twice as long, and more than twice as irritating. After a while of walking in silence, Forest began to notice that Syrus walked so stealthily he hardly made any sound at all. He glided sinuously behind her. She could easily imagine he was stalking her like prey.

Forest glanced up at the clear night sky, struck by the immense odd turn of events. It was hard for her to wrap her brain around the fact that the Prince of Regia was not only alive but was walking behind her, expecting her to safeguard his life. And to top it off, the royal pain was sexy as hell. *Stop thinking like that!* She told herself. The odds of getting through this trip without making a fool of herself were already looking thin.

"What is it?" Syrus asked in a low voice.

Forest jumped and checked herself. She had been looking at him over her shoulder as she walked. "Nothing." She turned her eyes back to the road.

A moment passed.

"Just because I'm blind doesn't mean I don't know when someone is staring at me. I can feel your eyes on me." Syrus' voice went quiet and breathy. "The questions you're too afraid to ask are running over my skin like someone's fingers."

Forest could feel her cheeks burning. "They are?"

"No." He chuckled. "I could tell you were looking over your shoulder by the way your stride changed."

Forest had a split second of indecision whether or not she was angry. The next second she was laughing quietly, and made a mental note that Syrus was ornery.

"So," he asked, "you must have some questions, don't you?"

Forest slowed her pace slightly and looked around, listening. It seemed safe enough to have a small conversation. She was certain, for the moment, they weren't being followed. She had many questions she wanted to ask, but she took a moment to think about how to proceed. This was the beginning of their trip and the beginning of their acquaintance. Much of how things would be between them would be determined with this first exchange of words. If she was to have any standing with him, she had to demand it with her tone and demeanor. He was the prince and she was nothing. However, she had the knowledge and experience that had landed the job, so she was in charge. Casual friendliness with an unmistakable edge of authority was how she intended to treat him.

"Why are you barefoot?" she asked, remembering to keep her voice down.

"If I can feel the ground under my feet, it's less likely I'll fall on my face or in a hole."

Forest thought it best not to ask too many questions, so he didn't get the idea she was overly interested. Asking too much also opened the door for him to ask questions in return, and she wanted to avoid that.

"It was a wizard who attacked you, five years ago?"

Syrus sighed. "Yes. I never saw his face. I'm sure he meant to kill me. I was in a death-sleep for a long time afterward. When I woke up, the whole investigation was basically over, and I was blind. The wizard on the council, Devonte, tried to cure me." Syrus snorted. "There were times that the things Devonte tried on me were more painful than the spell that blinded me."

"So, we're going to Maxcarion, specifically, because he was the one who attacked you?"

Syrus smiled. "You're sharp, aren't you? Yes. He was the wizard who attacked me. It's not believed that he holds anything against me, personally. During the investigation, it was discovered that throughout the last few years, Maxcarion has been a mercenary. Someone else hired him to attack me. He is the best hope I have for restoration."

Listening to him, Forest discovered she liked the sound of his voice immensely. She tried to think about what the last few years must have been like for him. If he was still considered a master of the Blood Kata, he would have had to have made serious adjustments, if not relearn many things to still be able to fight. But she figured that wasn't the case.

He had probably been allowed to keep his rank because he was the prince. She wanted to ask him about his formal training in the Kata, but those kinds of questions were too personal for a new acquaintance.

"What do you intend to offer him as payment?" she asked.

"That's my business," he snapped.

Forest huffed and picked up the pace. Annoyance tinged with reminder that she hated all vampires. This one might be good looking, but so what? Leith was good looking, and nothing would ever cure her of hatred for him. So that was that—she wouldn't even try to soften the edges of her hatred. Since Syrus was bent on being rude, she would be coldly civil and nothing more

She looked around as she continued to power walk. The night was edging toward its halfway mark. The aquamarine moon was at its zenith, casting dim light on the road that stretched out before them. They were approaching a thickly wooded area. It was unlikely they would pass through unnoticed. She turned to tell Syrus this and found him, surprisingly, a long way behind her, obviously struggling to keep up. He wore traces of panic on his face, and she could tell by the way he was walking that he was in pain.

Forest ran back to him, filled with inexplicable concern. He stopped and exhaled raggedly. The scent of blood had her spine stiffening.

"What's wrong?" she asked.

"You were going so fast. This road is rough."

Forest looked back along the road. The moon illuminated the smears of blood on the ground. Syrus' feet were bleeding. So far, she was proving to be a poor caretaker. Well, it wasn't her fault if the great moron refused to wear shoes.

"Come over here and sit down under this tree," Forest said, reaching out for his hand, and then, remembering her silver jewelry, pulled it back again. He had followed her without assistance before.

Syrus took his pack off and sat down with his feet stretched out in front of him. Forest looked at his wounds. They weren't deep and would probably only take a few minutes to heal.

"I need a drink," Syrus said.

"Well, I don't have one for you."

"Sure you do." He wiggled his eyebrows at her.

Her mouth fell open in shock. Was he suggesting that she let him feed from her? Forest wasn't sure how to best express her violent negative response.

Syrus shrugged and reached for his pack. "Some other time, perhaps."

He dug his hand around inside, before pulling out a corked bottle. He ran his fingers over the neck of the bottle where Forest could see a few etched designs. He put the bottle down, reached into his pack, and withdrew another. Syrus ran his fingers over the neck of this bottle as well. It too was etched. His face held a look of indecision for a second before he shrugged, uncorked the bottle, and took a drink. He closed his eyelids, leaned his head back, and sighed.

Forest crossed her arms over her chest. "The etchings tell you what type of blood is in the bottle?"

"Yes."

"What kind did you just drink?"

"Elf." He smiled vaguely and took another swig. "The fastest healers."

She looked at his knobby pack. "Did you only bring blood?"

"No. I have water as well."

"Do you have any human blood with you?" she asked aggressively.

Syrus straightened. "No. Of course not."

Her eyes probed his face. "Hmm." Once again, her eyes itched with annoyance that her gaze was not returned. "Ogre blood has the strongest scent. Do you have any?"

He reached for the first bottle he had pulled from his pack and held it out to her. She took it from him, and one of her fingers touched his. A pain like someone jamming a needle up her finger jolted her, and she gasped.

Syrus, likewise, retracted his hand, as though it burned and swore elegantly under his breath.

"Please take off that accursed silver," he said angrily.

She ignored his request. "I'm going to cover the blood you left on the road so we aren't tracked by it. Don't go anywhere."

"Sure, no problem," he said sarcastically.

The pain in Forest's finger eased and vanished while she trickled the ogre blood on the ground where Syrus' feet had bled, completely confusing the scent. No one would have been able to figure it for what it was.

As she walked back to where Syrus was waiting for her, she began to bristle with anger. It was very early in the game, but he didn't seem to be such a bad guy. Why did he have to be so damned attractive? Leith's face wandered into her mind, and she compared it to Syrus'. Forest hadn't thought superficially about the way Leith looked since she'd been a schoolgirl. Usually when she thought about him, she only saw red and plotted how best to kill him. But now, she found herself thinking about his face.

Most people thought Leith was extremely good looking. Forest had once thought so too. Now his looks were like that of a mannequin to her. Basically perfect, and perfectly boring. Syrus, on the other hand, was not only extremely good looking but his looks were interesting. If Leith had scars on his hands, as Syrus did, he'd have worn gloves everywhere. Leith was a baby, Syrus a warrior. The second she thought that, she corrected herself. She didn't know that yet, but she sensed it.

Syrus was putting the bottle of elf blood away when she reached him. He held out his hand for the ogre blood. "Hold it from the top please," he said. "I don't want to get burned again."

Nor I.

"We are about to go through a wooded area," Forest told him. "We might come across some company in there. We both need to be on our guard."

"All right," Syrus said nonchalantly.

"Put your hood up."

48

The woods ahead were so dense and sprang up so abruptly that it looked like a small mountain instead of a small forest. The road led right into the heart of it. Entering was like going through a huge doorway into a tunnel. The moonlight barred by the thick branches made very little penetration. It was very, very dark within.

The road became narrow, threading jaggedly through the black trees. Forest had only ever been through this wood in the daytime. Many eyes focused on them. Forest and Syrus pulled closer together instinctively. They moved as swiftly and silently as the wind over the ground. She was surprised at how in this moment of danger, they were able to move together like one entity. If the ground was hurting Syrus' feet again, he made no show of it.

The smell of death burned in Forest's nose. They should have circumvented this place. Too late to turn around now. Something was following.

Syrus grabbed the back of her robe. "Faster," he whispered aggressively.

They moved faster. Syrus kept urging her on by pushing his fist into the small of her back. She listened to the breathing and movements of whatever stalked them. It was a Guardian—she was sure of it. Forest swore inwardly. Dread dug sharp fingers into her belly.

The exit of the woods loomed in the distance ahead. It was possible they were being herded into a trap. If that were the case, their pursuer would have a cohort, or a number of cohorts waiting for them just inside the edge of the trees before the wood opened to the sky.

"Syrus," she whispered, "in a second, we must get off the road. And we have to run. Can you?"

"Yes. Just say when. If I lose my grip on you, I'll be lost. Please don't leave me."

"I won't. I swear it."

They continued forward. The closer they came to the end, the more Forest feared she was right. It was a trap. She could smell those waiting to ambush them, hiding in the trees ahead.

"Ready?" she whispered.

Syrus tightened his grip on the back of her robe. *One more breath. . . three more steps . . .* "Now!" she cried, almost without making a sound.

They stepped off the road into the thick of trees. They ran with the speed of those literally running for their lives. A horrible roar came from behind, as well as some loud crashing off to the side. Forest wove through the trees with Syrus right behind her. They had to emerge from the wood! Once they broke free, they would be safe. At least momentarily.

Their pursuers moved at them from the side, trying to cut across. Forest kept pushing forward as fast as she could go with Syrus hanging onto her robe. But they weren't going fast enough. They were going to be caught. Their only hope was to stand and fight. To stop her own momentum, Forest put her heels down and began to slide to a halt. Dirt and gravel flew up on both sides of her feet like swelling waves.

"NO!" Syrus roared.

They were in sight of the edge, and Forest could hardly account for what happened next. Syrus lifted her off her feet and continued running at a speed that made her equilibrium flip. The black trees turned into blurs, and the next thing she knew, he was setting her down on the ground in the full light of the moon. Both of them were panting, and Forest looked back at the woods. A ghastly roar erupted from the trees. The whole forest shuddered in rage.

Forest took a few moments to catch her breath. "How did you do that?"

"Do what?" he wheezed.

"Run like *the Flash?*" she demanded.

"The what?"

"Never mind. I'll concede that Vampires are fast in general, but that was. . ."

He shrugged as though it was nothing. "Just a basic skill of a master of the Kata."

The sounds of more crashing through the woods came from behind them.

"We need to keep moving." Syrus said.

"Yeah. Let's get back on the road."

They began walking again at a medium pace.

"How could you see where to run, once you picked me up?" she asked.

He snorted. "Listen to yourself."

"What?"

" *'How could you see?' I'm blind.* I can't see! It was a risk, I'll admit, but I could sense we were close. I had a bad feeling about fighting the guardians of that wood. What do you think they were?"

"I didn't get a look, but I think they may have been a merge of ogre and werewolves in beast form."

"That's a nasty combination," Syrus said.

"I agree. I hope I don't die in battle in a forest. I don't fancy becoming a guardian for all eternity, especially if I merged with my fallen adversary. *That* doesn't happen in the Wolf's Wood, in case you were wondering."

"It doesn't?"

"No. It's a good thing too. We'd never make it through. No one would. There have been far too many battles fought in the Wolf's Wood. The whole place would be crawling with deformed, hybrid entities."

She paused, then continued. "I'm sorry for taking us through there. It was a bad call. I've been through that wood back there so many times because it's the most direct route to my house from the castle. But I've never gone through at night. I didn't even think about the guardians giving us trouble. It must be all that blood you're carrying—riled them up."

"Hmm . . . Possibly. I probably brought too much." Syrus shrugged. "I was just trying to be prepared for whatever. I swear I'm not a glutton. I need more when I'm injured, and I know that's a possibility."

Vampires are disgusting. She thought. Then she told herself it wasn't his fault that he was born a sucker, any more than it was her fault she was born a Halfling.

Forest glanced at him over her shoulder again and almost stopped walking. He was smiling broadly at nothing at all. She could feel excitement emanating from him again, the same way she had felt it when they had first left the castle.

"Why are you smiling?"

Syrus' expression changed to a childlike embarrassment. "I'm not."

Forest turned her head back around and rolled her eyes. Then she jumped, startled, as Syrus burst out laughing.

"I can't tell you how great this is!" he said exuberantly. "I'm not bored! Nor am I likely to be for the next two weeks!"

"Are you nuts?" Forest hissed. "Keep your voice down."

"Sorry," he said more quietly. "It's just that I haven't been outside the confines of my own castle for so long! *Years.* Now I'm out. It's great."

Forest found his enthusiasm annoying. "You can't see," she said in a clipped tone. "How can there be any difference between there and anywhere else?"

"You're right. It shouldn't matter…But it does."

"Fine. That's great. I'm so pleased you're having a good time. Now shut up, and keep your happy little thoughts to yourself."

Syrus clicked his teeth together. She looked over her shoulder at him again. His face was blank, but she could feel the anger generating from him. She smiled broadly, enjoying the fact she had angered him, and turned her head back around to face the road.

A sharp sting, like that of a bee hit her in the right butt cheek. "Ouch!" Forest jumped and whirled around. "What the hell was that?!"

"What?" Syrus asked blankly, innocent as doves.

Forest snarled. "I know you did that, Sucker!"

Syrus bared his teeth, taking one calculated step towards her. "You will show me respect, Halfling. I am the prince."

"Not right now, you aren't." Forest stepped up to him, mere inches between them. "Right now you are nothing more than my shadow, and you will stay that way if you want to live through this." She poked him hard in the chest with her finger.

Syrus had never been so enraged in all his life. An overwhelming desire to bite her washed over him, making his teeth throb. He knew she was right, but he was determined to put her in her place anyway. In one easy swoop, Syrus pinned Forest's arms to her sides and lifted her off the ground, crushing her against him. His lips pealed back over his teeth as he dipped his head to her neck when the smell of silver sobered him. What was he doing? He had never done anything like this to anyone. Biting someone in anger was one of the lowest things a vampire could do.

Vitriol coated Forest's insides as she thought how similar a position she had recently been in with Leith.

"If you do this," she whispered. "You had better kill me, because if I live through it, I'll make it my singular goal, to end you in the slowest, most excruciating way I can."

Syrus dropped her to her feet, feeling lower and more worthless than he ever had in his whole life. "Forgive me . . . I was . . . angry."

He wanted to touch her even if it burned him. She would never let him, not after this. He certainly couldn't blame her. Syrus took a slow breath, feeling the great weight of loss.

Forest turned her back and marched on. A sob clenched in her throat, tears running down each cheek. Tears Syrus could easily smell.

6

Regia's sun was less than an hour from dawning over the horizon. After their little altercation, Forest and Syrus walked at a brisk pace, without stopping, and in total silence. They made good time and would arrive at Forest's house before the sun broke. When they came close to the remnant town of Anue, she led them off the road, onto back trails. It took longer, and the ground was rough, but there was too great a chance of being spotted on the road now.

Forest wrestled with her emotions. Syrus hadn't really done anything to her. He'd wanted to, but he stopped himself. If only Leith had ever stopped himself, her life would look very different. Syrus was used to having everything he wanted the moment he wanted it. *She was his guardian not a slave!* He shouldn't have forgotten that. But she had started it. Around and around her thoughts went.

She turned and looked at him. Throughout the last few hours when she had observed him, she could see his self-loathing. Now it was obvious he was pouting. She almost giggled—almost.

The tall stone wall encapsulating her land was visible through the trees ahead. Magic and the overgrown foliage around it protected her property. Forest stopped and turned to face Syrus. Just as it had been when she had first laid eyes on him, her whole body seemed to clamp down defensively.

Syrus stopped in his tracks, his eyebrows lifted quizzically. His shoulders tensed as though he thought she might attack him.

"All right," Forest huffed. "We're almost there."

"So why are we stopping?"

"Because we need to talk about what happened earlier."

His expression looked like he had just bit into a lemon. .

"How would it be . . .if . . .Let's just . . .forget about it."

Syrus' mouth fell open in shock. Then he smiled, as if the sun was shining out of his face. Forest looked away from him angrily. Why did she have to find him so appealing? Why did he look as innocent as a child when he smiled? How could anyone of his age have moments that were totally guileless?

"Thank you, Forest."

She had never been thanked with more feeling or sincerity, and Forest found it disarming. She began walking again, more out of self-preservation than urgency. "It was necessary for us to call some kind of truce." She did her best to sound flippant. "The protections on my property prohibit anyone inside that I consider an enemy."

Syrus was amazed that she would tell such an outrageous lie. That type of magic was not only rare, it would have been impossible for someone of Forest's standing to afford. And personally tailored enchantments, like she described, were almost unheard of. He was about to tell her that he was not even close to being such a fool to believe such a whopper, but just as the words were about to tumble from his mouth, he decide not to start another fight. He would wait and see what other lies she told, and he could make a game of trapping her in her own web. That could prove fun.

"You must have a lot of enemies, Forest," Syrus said jovially. "Just who are you trying to keep out?"

"Mostly those of your ilk."

They reached the outer parameter of Forest's land. Syrus could feel the immensity of the wall and couldn't help but be impressed with its size. The creeping vines that grew over the door, hiding it completely, moved aside when Forest touched them. She passed through without hesitation. Syrus would have moved more slowly had he known that she hadn't been lying a moment ago.

The enchantment held Syrus on the gate's threshold. He couldn't move. The magic passed through his body like a ghost blade, before releasing him. The door shut behind him, and the vines crept back into place. Winded and astonished, Syrus had only ever felt such a personally tailored spell in the vampire castle. It made sense for a spell like that to be there, and in the Fortress castle, but on the private property of an illegitimate Halfling, it was absurd!

"I thought you were lying!" he exclaimed loudly. "How is it possible that *you* could have such an enchantment? Are you a wizard's mistress in your spare time?"

Syrus started as a loud beeping filled the air.

"It's all right. . . Just a moment . . . I have to turn off my security system."

He listened to her walk away, and a moment later the beeping stopped. Syrus stood still, afraid to move, in case there were other security measures waiting to snare him.

Forest laughed as she walked back to him . "It's all right now. You can relax. I don't have any tripwires or landmines."

"What was that noise?" he asked, still tense.

"My security system is a . . .ah . . .human thing." Forest was nervous about how he would respond to all of her illegal human devices and paraphernalia.

"Oh?"

"Yeah, humans put them in their houses and then if someone breaks in to hurt them or steal things, this loud noise sounds, and the police are called. I'm obviously not trying to alert the human authorities—" she gave a nervous little giggle "—but if someone was able to get through my outer barrier, I would know it when the security system began sounding."

"Uh huh," Syrus muttered, his face totally stoic.

Forest waited for him to have some kind of reaction. The moment dragged. He set his pack gently on the ground and crossed his arms over his chest. Then he laughed, catching Forest off-guard.

"You have *a lot* of illegal human relics here, don't you, Forest?" he chortled.

"Yes. I do. In fact, 'a lot' might not cover it. I guess it's better that you know before you come inside the house."

"You're a smuggler!" Syrus laughed enthusiastically. "This is great! I don't know much about Earth and not only can you teach me, you have lots of human stuff I can try."

Forest narrowed her eyes and tucked her tongue in her cheek. He wanted to play with her stuff, did he? Well she had more than enough to keep him occupied over the next few days. It was the perfect way to avoid him while they were stuck here together.

"Pick up your pack and follow me inside," she ordered.

"First tell me how you came to acquire your protective enchantments."

She huffed, feeling her exhaustion, and decided to spit the story out with as little embellishment as possible. "A few years back, a wizard was rumored to be traveling through the town we circumvented on our way here. An associate of mine promised to tell me when, and if, the wizard passed through. Once I received word, I set out on the road to see if I could locate said wizard. I found him easily enough and offered him a drink and a place to rest from his travels for a while. He was tired and conceded to spend an afternoon at my cottage. As soon as I had him comfortable, I presented him with an offer he couldn't refuse. That's all. We made the exchange, so to speak, and he went on his way."

"So you *have* been a wizard's mistress," Syrus said with self-satisfaction.

Before Syrus could bat an eye, she pulled her sword on him. The tip hovered half an inch under his chin, and his flesh began to constrict away from the silver blade.

"I am a warrior, not a whore!" she shouted. Her vision blurred, and her body shook with rage. "I paid him in human goods, not with my body!"

Syrus didn't dare move even a fraction. He'd confronted real danger before, and he recognized her threat was legitimate. He'd spoken without thinking and had meant only to tease her, but she was way over reacting. He didn't trust himself to speak, not even to mutter an apology. So he did the only thing he could think of to show her respect. He took one slow step backward and lowered himself onto his knees.

Forest's mouth fell open, the rage draining away into shock. The shock doused the fire in her head with cold water, and her vision cleared. She looked at her sword, held ready to kill as though it were not her hand holding it but a stranger's. The future king of Regia had humbled himself before her in order to win her pardon for the offense. It was not even a great offense given that he was royalty. He had the right to say anything he wanted to her. But he had recognized that she was on the very edge of killing him. She had to give him credit; he was clever. Nothing he could have said at that moment would have eased her rage, so he shocked her out of her homicidal intentions instead.

Forest pulled her sword away and sheathed it, feeling embarrassed and idiotic. She picked up his pack and slung it over her shoulder. Kendel had said that she brought out the worst in people. Now she was thinking she had possibly met someone who brought out the worst in her.

"The house is this way." Her voice was rather weak.

Syrus stood up and followed her without reply. It was a difficult moment to recover from for both of them. He gave himself a stern mental warning to watch what he said to her from now on, and to remember that he didn't know much about her at all.

Forest's house was a small stone cottage; reminiscent of the one Snow White found full of dwarves. It was set in the back of her property with her garden stretching out around it in all directions. Regardless of the circumstance, Forest was happy to be home. Nothing she owned gave her a stronger feeling of pride than her house. During her absence, entropy had grabbed ahold of her garden. She'd deal with the overgrowth and bracken after cleaning the leaves from the fountain. If Syrus would stay inside playing with her many human toys for the next few days, she could work in her garden in peace.

Syrus' senses piqued as he followed her. He was trying to map his surroundings. He would have to come back to the garden later and walk the perimeter to get a better sense of the space. As it was, he was exhausted, and in a terrific, but tenuous, mood. Forest was proving to be more interesting than he had originally anticipated. He certainly wouldn't ever imply again that she used her sexuality as currency, *ever*. Since that obviously had struck a nerve, he began to speculate why.

As they approached the front door, all Forest wanted was to get inside, go into her room, and shut the door behind her. She didn't want to talk anymore. She wanted him to leave her alone. It wasn't fair that she was the one to have to house, entertain, and protect the most important vampire alive. She didn't want him in her house. It was her place of peaceful solitude. A place with no bad memories. She was sure Syrus would think it was a hovel.

"Watch your head," Forest said.

Syrus had to duck as he came through the door. His head spun with all the unfamiliar scents. Her house was full of human materials: paper, fabrics, plastic, metals, and even food. At first, the sounds of her appliances humming seemed loud and annoying, especially the refrigerator.

"You have human machines!" he said enthusiastically. "How do you get them to work here?"

"That was part of the deal with the wizard. All of my appliances and electronics work and I don't even have to pay the utility company. The batteries in my flashlights and MP3 player never die, either."

Syrus didn't know what flashlights or utility companies were, but he was dying to find out.

"Uh. . .if you don't mind me asking. . ." he began demurely.

"What I paid the wizard?" she said rather aggressively.

"Yes."

Forest sighed. "It was extremely cheap, really. Well, it was cheap for someone who has access to Earth. I gave him a 27-inch high definition TV and a Nintendo Wii. Well, that was the original price of our agreement but I could tell he was feeling a little cheated after the amount of effort he had to put into securing my entire property, so I threw in the special Necronomican edition Army of Darkness Blu-ray. He left, the happiest wizard you've ever seen."

Forest could tell Syrus didn't understand half of what she was talking about and that he was about to launch into a game of twenty questions, or one hundred and twenty questions. She just didn't think she had the energy for it.

"Would you like me to put your bottles in the kitchen?" she asked, still holding his pack. "If you want them cold, I can make room in the fridge."

"Thank you. I appreciate it." Syrus could feel her desire to get away from him. "Follow me."

Forest showed him where the kitchen was, and she couldn't escape without giving him a small explanation of the refrigerator. He found everything around him fascinating, even the feel of the linoleum under his feet. She led him to the spare room where she hoped he would stay throughout the time they had to kill. Syrus looked completely out of place for a number of reasons. He was so tall and broad that Forest hadn't realized how small the room really was, until now. The room was also rather girly, like it might have belonged to a human teenager. Forest was glad he couldn't see it. The *Buffy the Vampire Slayer* posters would have surely offended him.

"Do you need anything else?" Forest tried to remember how to be hospitable, not that she'd ever really known.

"No," he said with a hint of dejection.

Syrus sat down on the edge of the bed, his back stiff and his face blank. Forest could tell something was wrong with his mood. She felt a pang of guilt. What was she supposed to do? Her job was to keep him alive. She was doing that.

Forest turned and left, closing the door behind her. She went to the kitchen and turned on the oven, intending to make a frozen pizza for herself. She mopped the floor while she waited and took account of what was in her pantry. She needed more Oreos.

Later, when she plopped onto her couch, remote in hand, intending to watch a movie, her eyes drifted to the door of the spare room. It had been an hour since she had left Syrus, and there had not been one noise from inside. She knew he probably wasn't sleeping. She only needed about half as much sleep as a human and Syrus only needed roughly a third. She imagined him still sitting on the edge of the bed, immobile as stone. The longer she looked at the door, the stronger her sense grew of what was behind it. In the silence, a storm of emotions raged in her spare room, as if she had bottled a hurricane in there.

Forest shook herself and tried to focus her attention on the movie. Her eyes stuck to the screen but her mind was on Syrus. Why did she feel guilty? She hadn't locked him in there.

No, but she had made it plain that she wanted to be alone. Well, she *did* want to be alone. What was wrong with that? *Wake up stupid!* She told herself. *He's blind in unfamiliar surroundings. You may as well have locked him in that room.*

Forest sighed and turned the TV off. She pulled her phone out of her pocket and began drafting an email to Kendel, telling him that they had arrived safely at her cottage. Then she stood up and walked to the door of the spare room. She hesitated, listening. Maybe she shouldn't bother him. Maybe he *was* asleep. He could be; she didn't know his schedule.

Syrus hadn't moved an inch since she'd left him. He had meditated for a while, but her presence just outside the door was distracting him. He waited, expecting her to either knock or go away, but she didn't. She just stood there.

Forest wrestled with whether or not she should knock. If he was asleep, he wouldn't want to be disturbed. But what if he was awake and bored? She thought about how he had been so happy a few hours ago because he said he wasn't bored. Her heart gave a little lurch as she remembered how he looked when he smiled.

She started in reaction to her own thoughts, and the anger inside her that was always ready to kill came to the surface. The only thing he needed was sustenance, and she had shown him where the kitchen was. It was not her job to entertain him. If he was bored, at least he was used to it.

She stalked away from his room and went out the front door, slamming it behind her.

Forest spent the next hour outside, stewing internally. She weeded and harvested her veggie garden, but at that location, she could easily look through the window and see Syrus sitting on the bed, so she moved away and began working on getting the fountain running again. She got through a few basic tasks but there was so much to do because she'd been gone for so long. Finally, she felt so guilty that she couldn't stop herself from going back inside.

She took her harvested veggies to the kitchen then went straight to the spare room and knocked.

"Come in," Syrus said just loudly enough to be heard through the door.

She opened the door. He had turned his face toward her, and she grimaced as her eyes stung again. "Uh . . . Are you . . . okay?" she asked.

"Yes," he said flatly, standing up.

"Are you bored?" Her voice was apologetic.

He smiled at her, and again she was amazed at how innocent he seemed. Innocent and gorgeous.

"I wouldn't say I was bored. I'm extremely frustrated, though. I have so many questions about Earth and all this stuff you have, but I understand that I'm the intruder and you are used to solitude. I know you don't want me here. I don't particularly want to be here. . ." he paused. "I don't mean your house when I say 'here.' I mean the situation. I actually find your house wonderful and fascinating. The fascination is driving me mad though. Just the smells in here alone—I want to know what they are, but I've been sitting still and meditating so I wouldn't give in to temptation and start poking around. I'm trying to respect your space and your things." He paused again, looking like he was groping for the right words. "I don't know the rules."

Forest laughed. "The *rules*?"

"Yes, the rules of your house."

Forest continued to chuckle. "Okay, Syrus, here are the rules: Don't go in my room. Don't touch my weapons, and don't eat the cookies in the pantry. Aside from that, you can do as you like, except leave the property."

"I should have no problem adhering to your rules," he said formally.

Forest laughed again. "Good. Maybe we can refrain from offending each other anymore for the duration of the mission."

Syrus smiled but this time his smile was seductively impish. "*That* is wishful thinking."

Forest's mouth fell open. "Yes, well. . .umm. . .I was going to watch a movie. Would you like to join me?"

Syrus' impish smile switched back to the excited childlike one. "What is a movie?"

"It's like watching a story rather than listening to one."

Syrus' smile slipped. "What a terrible joke, and unworthy of you, Forest."

It only took her a second to realize what he meant. "No. I didn't mean it as a joke. I swear. If I chose a movie that was just mostly about relationships, I'm sure you could follow it. The characters just talk back and forth." She said all this quickly, hoping he would realize she hadn't meant to be mean. "I'll understand if you don't want to. But I didn't mean it as a joke, really."

"All right," he said quietly. "I'll give it a try if you promise not be put out at me if I need to ask a few questions along the way."

"Oh. Sure. No problem."

He followed her to the living room and sat down on the couch. Forest looked through her DVD collection trying to find a movie that was slow. She settled on a Jane Austen adaptation. Surely, he could follow that; it was almost all conversations, and voice-over narration. She could feel his excitement rising again as the movie started.

After a few minutes, Syrus began enjoying the movie and could imagine how great it would be to watch movies once his sight was restored. He listened to the various characters as their relationships developed and they began to have problems. He was able to follow the storyline but as he became engrossed, he forgot yet again to stifle his nose, and Forest was sitting on the same couch.

She smelled so good to him and it had been a long time since he'd had a drink. The idea of going for one of his cold bottles, while her scent was in his lungs, was repugnant. *I want it! I want it! I want it!* Was all he could think of and better judgment gave way to desire.

Syrus leaned back into the couch and angled his body towards her. Forest was avidly watching the movie and didn't notice.

"Forest?"

"Yeah?" she answered absentmindedly, not taking her eyes off the screen.

"I'm thirsty," he said in a half whisper.

"Oh. Me too." Forest paused the movie and headed to the kitchen. "I'm going to have water. Do you want some or would you like one of your bottles?" she asked loudly from the kitchen.

"Yeah, I want some." His voice was thick with innuendo she didn't catch.

Forest filled two tall glasses with Regian water and came back to the living room, a glass in each hand. She set his on the coffee table in front of him. "Your water is here," she said reaching for his hand to guide it to the glass.

Syrus swiftly took hold of her forearm. Caught off guard, Forest stumbled toward him, almost falling on him. He brought her wrist close to his face and inhaled deeply. "This is what I want," he whispered. "May I?" his breath fell across her wrist as he moved his mouth closer.

Forest's hand tightened around her glass and she reacted without thinking. The freezing cold water splashed over his head and shoulders. Syrus jumped and spluttered in shock. Forest skipped back as Syrus sprang to his feet, snarling at her. The next second he bent over, coughing thickly. He had gasped when she doused him and had aspirated some of the water into his lungs. By the time he was able to stop coughing, Forest was laughing uproariously. Forest's laugh was loud and throaty and Syrus found it infectious. He too began to laugh.

"Well, that'll teach you," Forest chortled.

He snorted, feeling just how wet he really was. "You could have just said no."

"I could have, but I made my point so much more effectively with the water, don't you think?"

"Oh yeah," he said sarcastically. "You made your point clear. My clothes will be wet till tomorrow night." Regian water didn't evaporate as quickly as Earth's. "Where did you put my pack? I need my spare clothes."

Forest looked at him, speculating. She'd seen the clothes he'd brought in his pack when she'd put his bottles in the fridge, and she thought this was a good time to bring up her concerns about his appearance.

"You know, Syrus, you have the obvious look of royalty and at the very least, nobility."

"Thank you."

"That's not a complement."

Syrus' eyebrows furrowed in confusion.

"I think we should consider how to disguise you better, especially once we leave here. Would you consider trying human clothes?" she asked.

"Do you have any that will fit me?"

"Sure. Follow me to the basement."

Forest's basement was so full of various human things that it resembled a consignment shop. She went to her clothing stores and began rummaging for what she thought Syrus should wear. She thought it was rather funny that he was standing behind her waiting to be her dress up doll.

"Here." She thrust a pair of jeans and a grey button-up shirt at him.

He pawed at the garments for a moment, seeing what they were with his hands. Then he pulled his tunic over his head and dropped it on the floor. Forest took in the sight of his bare chest, her brain going a little foggy. She blinked when she realized that he was about to pull off his trousers too. "Whoa!" she hollered.

"What?" his voice was alarmed.

"Don't you have any decency?" she demanded.

"Huh?"

"Just because you're blind doesn't mean I am! Change your clothes in your room."

He just laughed at her when she picked his shirt up off the floor and smacked the wet fabric against his chest. He turned around and carried his new clothes up the stairs while Forest followed him. Her eyebrows pulled in confusion as she looked at his back. It looked like a map in scars. Having been through years and years of training, and many more in real combat, Forest could tell what the cause of many of his scars were. He had obviously been through extensive tactical training and sparring. She wanted to ask him about it but felt it was still too personal. Curiosity would soon begin to make the cat ill.

Syrus found his room without assistance. Forest waited while he changed, wondering how the human clothes would look on him. She needed to talk to him about the possibility of cutting his hair. She figured she should bring it up now and give him time to pout and mull it over. He might flat out refuse. The problem was that the length and style of his hair was a mark of his rank.

Syrus came out a few minutes later. Forest sighed sadly like a beggar looking in the window of a shop at something they could never have. He was so beautiful. The jeans she had given him were a little too long, dragging behind his heels, but not so long as to really cause him trouble. He had replaced his belt but had removed the swords. His button up shirt hung open on his chest. He ran his hand down the buttons.

"Would you help me, Forest?" he asked.

"Sure."

She moved forward and reached to button his shirt for him. Her hands trembled ever so slightly as she pushed the first button through the buttonhole and realized just how intimate an action this was. Her eyes lingered on his chest as she buttoned the next one. His chest was scarred as well but not so much as his back. She buttoned the next one, watching his chest rise and fall as he breathed. She was holding her breath without realizing it. Why did this shirt have so many buttons? She did the next one and the next, averting her eyes from his face.

Syrus leaned his head down towards her and slowly reached up one hand, taking a gentle hold of her forearm. Forest froze, looking up into his face that was closer to hers than she had thought, and felt her eyes go wide.

"Forest," his voice was almost a whisper. "May I ask a favor of you?"

". . . Uhh. . ." her throat had gone dry. "What?"

His fingers tightened gently on her arm and his thumb moved back and forth over her skin, teasing out a shiver in her.

"Would you remove the silver you're wearing?"

"Why?"

"I have a feeling that you are going to save my life in the next few days. It would pain me greatly not to be able to kiss the hand that saved me."

Forest's mouth fell open stupidly. *Snap out of it!* A little voice yelled inside her head. She pulled her arm out of his grip, buttoned the remaining buttons at supper speed, and stepped back from him. "Well, if I do save your life, you can ask again, and if I feel like letting you kiss me at that time, I might remove a few things."

Syrus smiled impishly at her. He had caught the fact the she had said, 'kiss me' and not 'kiss my hand', and he was not about to forget it any time soon. But aside from that, his little ruse of ineptitude let him know that she was not immune to him, even though she was scampering away from him now and would probably turn back into the viper any moment. He didn't mind staying on his toes because whether she being friendly or hurling blunt objects at him, Forest was the very opposite of boring.

"So," Syrus spread his arms out. "Do I look like a human?"

Forest considered his question. He could pass for a human celebrity, maybe. She could take him to Hollywood, put him on the red carpet at some random event, make sure his picture was taken and the next day the internet would be buzzing with desperate questions of 'who is this?! We all must know!'

"Close enough," she said. "Look, I need to talk to you about something."

"What?" he asked defensively.

"Well, I know you aren't going to like my suggestion, but we really need to make sure that you are not easily recognizable once we set out."

"I thought that was what the clothes were for."

"Yes. But it's not enough. I want you to consider letting me cut your hair."

"No!"

Forest sighed. "Look, I understand. I do. But if we are apprehended on our journey, the wolves will either kill you and take me hostage or kill me and take you hostage."

"Everyone thinks I'm dead. They won't know I'm the prince."

"Even if they don't realize that you're the prince, your hair marks you as vampire nobility and a master of the Kata. Your capture would be too great a prize for them to overlook. They would try to ransom you, at which point they would learn your true identity. You would be killed in the worst way possible. They would put your dead body on display. The repercussions of your death would be felt through all of Regia. The wolves might succeed in overthrowing your father."

Syrus shuddered. "And what would happen to you?" he asked.

Forest was surprised by his concern. "If they didn't kill me as well, I'd be forced into slavery. The wolves I know have a love/hate regard for me. Philippe would probably claim me. So, basically if you die and I live, my life will suck. No offense."

Syrus was frowning at her. "Why would Philippe claim you?" The idea shot an angry pain into his gut.

"He's got a major Jones for me," she said flippantly.

"So he would force you to be his mistress?"

"Something like that. But that's best case scenario. If we are caught, they must think you are nobody special. We need to think of a good cover story, just in case."

Syrus looked like he was thinking hard. "But when we get back and everyone sees my hair short... that would be humiliating...People would laugh at me. How could I lead the army? They wouldn't respect me."

"Look," she said aggressively, "I don't care about any of that. My job is to keep you alive not fashionable."

Syrus looked highly offended. "This isn't about fashion. You obviously have no idea what this would mean for me. It would be a symbol of shame. You have no concept of how vampire nobility treat those they feel are beneath them. If you knew, you never would have asked such a thing of me."

Forest's insides writhed with rage. "You insensitive, arrogant, spoiled, selfish oaf of a sucker! You're so right! *I* have *no* idea what shame is! Well, you can keep your hair and be the most beautiful and *respected* corpse there ever was. Go right ahead, you thoughtless baboon, and endanger both of our lives so you won't have to lose face! You stupid, stupid, entitled, narcissist!"

Forest turned her back on him, marched to her room, and slammed the door. The next second she opened it again to shout one more insult at him.

"You...you..." words seemed to fail her as she struggled to use the worst one she could think of, *"you...Male!"*

She slammed her door again and locked it. Syrus just stood there, his mouth hanging open. It was the first time in his recollection that someone had insulted him to his face. And she had done a thorough job of it.

"What the heck is a baboon?" he muttered as he stalked back to his room.

Forest lay on her bed, staring at the ceiling. It had felt damn good to say all those things to Syrus. She was sure no one had ever dared speak to him like that before. That knowledge gave her a warm fuzzy feeling inside. She considered it her special privilege. She thought about the way his face had looked when she had called him all those names, and the next second, she was laughing so loudly, she could have been heard from outside.

Syrus listened to her laughter. The sounds of her mirth made him feel even worse, if that was possible. He wasn't angry, which confused him. Syrus felt like she had run over him and now she was laughing at him. He sat perched on the edge of the bed, trying to sort through his feelings. The house fell silent.

Forest watched the sunset through her bedroom window. The deep hues shimmered in the retreating iridescent sunlight. The sky seemed to move in a slow dance of color that didn't exist on Earth. The only thing Earth had that was close to a Regain sunset was the *aurora borealis.*

How was she going to get them through the Wood alive? She had to make him understand the weight of the danger ahead. Could he really be so vain that he would rather die than cut his hair? Could he really be so heartless to not care if she lived or died? She shook herself. Of course he wouldn't care if she died. Why would he? Well, if one of them was going to die on this trip, it would be him. If he did, she would be wanted by the vampires, and they would hunt her down. But she could escape to Earth. She could live out her life there happily enough.

A sudden emotional intensity seized Forest as she watched the sky, and a rogue tear eased out of one of her emerald eyes. This was her home. As much as she loved Earth, she never wanted to give up all that she had fought for and accomplished. If things went awry on this trip, banishing herself to Earth forever felt like letting Leith and all those like him win. She would rather die fighting than cower and run. She would not acquiesce to failure. Failure might get the better of her, but not with her permission.

Syrus idly twirled the ends of his hair around his fingers. He twirled the words she had flung at him around in his mind the same way he did his hair. She had spoken without restraint, and she had told him succinctly what she thought of him. Instead of responding with temper and haughty indignation, Syrus considered this a rare opportunity for him. Forest's respect had to be earned. She wasn't dazzled by the fact that he was the prince the way most women were. In her eyes, the fact that he was the prince was just another strike against him. If he could earn her respect then she could become something odd and wonderful to him: a *real* friend.

Syrus thought about the possibility of Forest's friendship for a while. Given her temperament, he didn't think she could have many friends. He had no idea how to go about winning a friend, but he had to come up with a plan. At first, he had wanted to guard himself from her, but the more he replayed her voice over in his head, he began to want her to know who he really was.

Syrus smiled to himself as he ran through a mental list of all the things he knew about her, so far. She was far more guarded then he ever had been. The woman, no doubt, had many secrets. In the events of their newborn acquaintance, Forest had unwittingly let Syrus know more about her than she had intended. He discovered that he had a growing respect for her and decided that the best way to possibly begin a friendship was to be more open and just be himself. The smooth charm he regularly used on women would fall flat on her and the usual effect of his charm wasn't what he was going for. Not this time anyway.

The knock on her door made Forest want to shout. Why couldn't he just leave her alone the rest of the night? She sighed, steeling herself for what might happen next with Syrus, and opened the door.

"What is it, Syrus?" she asked wearily.

Syrus took a deep breath and then jumped in with both feet. "If you want to hate me for being born the Prince, that's fine, go right ahead. But I didn't choose it anymore that you chose to be born what you are. I'll apologize for my behavior, and I shall strive to treat you with the respect you deserve from now on. But I won't kiss your feet and I won't ask you to kiss mine, either. Deal?"

Forest just blinked at him for a moment. "Okay. It's a deal."

Syrus astonished her again by flashing another guileless smile. "I'll think about what you said about my hair. Just give me a little time."

"Fine," she said shortly.

"It's evening now."

"Yeah. So?"

"Well, what do you usually do in the evenings?"

Forest considered for a moment. He'd taken her abuse good naturedly—that surprised her. She could easily do something that would make the evening fun and memorable for him. "I usually make a fire outside and enjoy the onset of nightfall in my garden."

"That sounds nice. Could we do that?" he asked.

"I guess. And I think we should make S'mores."

"S'mores?"

"It's a human thing. You'll like it. It's very silly. But you have to promise to eat some."

"Oh. So it's human food?" he asked.

Forest chuckled. "I don't know if it's actually food, but they eat it nonetheless."

"I promise to try at least one bite." The childlike excitement was radiating from him again.

"All right. I'll get the stuff from the kitchen. If you want to go ahead and go outside, I'll be right there."

Forest had a difficult time finding where she had stored her marshmallows. When she surfaced from the house, her arms full of graham crackers, marshmallows, and chocolate, she was surprised to see Syrus standing next to the fire pit, a fire already kindled.

"How did you do that?" she asked.

Syrus didn't answer her, he just smiled blandly.

"You aren't going to tell me how you started the fire?" she pushed.

He just continued to smile.

"Hmm…Tricky, aren't you?"

"From time to time. So how does this work?"

Syrus played with the first marshmallow she gave him until it was mashed into a sticky pulp. She couldn't really blame him for finding the consistency funny. When she tried to hand him a wire poker with a marshmallow on the end, instructing him to light it on fire, he just laughed and crossed his arms. It took her a while to convince him she wasn't joking. He burned the first one down to nothing, lost the second one off the end of the poker, and nearly singed his eyebrows on the third as he tried to blow it out. Finally, she was able to help him complete a S'more.

"Okay. Now you've got to taste it. You promised."

Forest watched amusedly as Syrus took a decent sized bite. His face went from initial shock to bemusement as he chewed. Then he smiled at her, sending her into a fit of laughter.

"What?" he asked, his mouth thick.

"You've got marshmallow stuck to your fangs," she laughed. "Oh, if only a bunch of human girls could see you now! You'd ruin their vampire fantasies."

He chuckled, licking at the goo on his teeth. "Yeah, why is that?"

"Well, I guess I could be wrong, but *I* don't consider sticky fangs very sexy."

"I was under the impression that you don't find fangs sexy at all, sticky or otherwise." He raised one eyebrow quizzically at her.

"I don't," she said quickly, brought up short. "Like I said, I was thinking about a human's fantasy."

"So humans know about vampires?" he asked seriously.

"Oh sure. I don't think many of them believe that vampires are real, just myth. Their myths vary about lots of things too."

"Like what? What do they think about us?"

Forest sighed. "There are so many ideas; I don't know the half of them. There are scary vampires, sexy vampires, classic vampires, cliché vampires, hybrid vampires, vampires in space, take your pick. You can't come out in the sunlight or you'll burn to death. You probably know that *that* is true. Earth's sun will kill you. There are some ideas that vampires are really dead, reanimated corpse stuff."

"Eww. That's gross," Syrus interjected.

"Yeah. Let's see, sleeps in a coffin, allergic to garlic, they know about silver. It goes on and on, and they keep changing their ideas. It really is just the fault of vampires crossing the portal and becoming so addicted to human blood that they basically go insane."

"Sounds like it's all great uncle Dracula's fault."

Forest laughed. "A lot of it is."

"You're the one who caught him the last time he tried to sneak through the portal, aren't you?"

"Yup. Is he still mad about it?"

"Oh yeah he is! I try to avoid him as much as I can. He's *so* annoying. And if he doesn't get his fix of human blood every so often, he goes totally crazy. State events are excruciating with him, he always says the most embarrassing and inappropriate things. And he'll drone on and on about the *good old days* in Transylvania, and when he does, the old accent comes back."

Forest shrieked with laughter as Syrus wiggled his eyebrows theatrically at her and said, "You are a beautiful flower, my dear, come closer," in an apt impersonation of Dracula.

Forest was amazed that she could laugh so hard. She hadn't laughed like that in so long it totally escaped her memory.

"I can't tell you how many movies have been made about him."

"Really? Could you get some for me?" Syrus asked. "I bet they're hilarious."

"I might have a few in the basement. I'll have to check."

The fire crackled happily between them as Forest toasted another marshmallow.

"So, do you like working for Fortress?" he asked.

"Fortress just is. I can't allow myself to have opinions about it, but I love being a traffic controller. It's good to have the ability to have some status, and being on Earth keeps me out of Regian politics."

"Is there anything on Earth like Fortress?"

"Sure. Some of them are secret and they all seem to be named with acronyms like, CIA, KGB, FBI, and MI6."

"Have you spent any time as a spy?"

Forest laughed. "Not a real one. Some of what I've done in the past is similar to being a spy, I suppose. When I was first hired at Fortress, I had to take all kinds of aptitude tests; the results were not very flattering. I was given a very low ranking as a possible spy." She was not sure why she had just told him that and wished she hadn't.

"Hmm...I bet it said something like 'too volatile.' Am I right?"

"Something like that," she replied bitterly. "I don't care. I never wanted to be a spy. Everyone at Fortress slots you as a spy if you are a Shape shifter. It's just racial profiling."

"Ah, well." Syrus shrugged. "We are all victims of stereotypes from time to time, aren't we?"

She narrowed her eyes. Yes, he would know something of that.

They were quiet for a while, and Syrus began twisting his wire poker between his fingers. Forest couldn't bring herself to pick the conversation back up, and Syrus didn't seem to care. She allowed herself to stare at him. His expression was blank like he had simply left his body and gone elsewhere. His lack of expression, coupled with his pupilless eyes, was unnerving. He seemed so far away. It was starting to grow dark and the firelight cast shadows about his angular face. The bone structure of his brow and cheeks was so sharp, so masculine, but his mouth was soft and full.

Syrus had a sense that Forest was staring at him. Over the last few years, he had become accustomed to being stared at by those around him. Now he was having a sensation that he couldn't account for: his eyes hurt. It felt like his shut pupils were straining to open, to see. He had the feeling that a fleeting opportunity was passing before him.

Syrus smiled suddenly, making Forest startle guiltily. "You know, I was just thinking how very much I wish I could stare at you as openly and unabashed as you stare at me."

Forest huffed. "If you could see, you wouldn't look at me any longer than was necessary. I'm really quite hideous."

"Well, that was a large complement. Thank you."

"Huh?" Forest asked bewildered.

"Since you think ugly people are not worth looking at, you must think I'm devastatingly attractive. You've been staring at me for a long time." He laughed when she made no reply. "Fascinating that you make no attempt to deny or contradict me."

Forest was burning with embarrassment. She had to change the subject and fast. "How did you get all those scars?" she asked quickly.

"Training."

"That must be terrible—" she said in a falsely sympathetic tone "—being well trained and never getting to really exercise your skills. I think I'd die of self-pity."

Syrus refused to take the bait, he merely smiled at her. "I almost did once. No one thought I would pull through. But then, as you said earlier, I'm a narcissist. I love myself too much to just let myself die."

There was another momentary silence, more uncomfortable than the previous.

"I'm not everything you accused me of," he said quietly.

Forest had been waiting for him to bring this up. She was surprised that it had taken him this long to complain about her insults. "Oh?" she prompted.

"No. I am, unfortunately, some of those things, it's true."

"And you'll enlighten me, no doubt, about which ones," she said acidly.

"No. I hope in the course of this journey, you'll find out for yourself and unwittingly form a better opinion of me."

"I see. You must have a nasty opinion of me in return."

"Not at all," Syrus said seriously. "I have a very high opinion of you."

"Why?" she demanded aggressively.

Forest felt aggravated when he smiled at her again.

"Now, now, you can't go asking questions like that and expect me to answer them. I'd embarrass the both of us."

Forest was embarrassed anyway. She wished she hadn't asked him why. She realized how stupid she'd made herself sound; like she didn't deserve respect from anyone. She hoped that thought hadn't occurred to him.

"Despite all my faults, would you consider being my friend, Forest?"

Forest couldn't have been more shocked if he'd slapped her in the face. "I ... uh..."

Syrus waited for her reply, one eyebrow raised.

"I don't know how," she finally managed.

Syrus laughed, not in mocking, but a release of his own tension. "Neither do I."

"You really want to be my friend?" she asked seriously.

"I swear on my hair."

"Well, that's an oath I can take seriously," she said emphatically.

"Would you tell me about your childhood, Forest?"

Forest hated to admit to herself that she was touched. No one ever asked her about her childhood, not even Kendel. "What do you want to know?" she asked.

"What are your parents like?"

"Dead," she said shortly.

"*Dead*?"

"My mother died during my adolescence. And my father is alive as far as I know, but he's dead to me. I don't even know who he is, only that he is an Elf of some rank." Her voice was completely devoid of emotion.

"Do you think your father knows about you?"

"Oh, he knows about me all right. The only thing he ever did for me was force my mother to send me to the Academy. He was determined that even his shameful bastard would have the best education." Forest threw a marshmallow violently into the fire. "I guess he meant well, but I wish he never would have taken any notice of me at all."

Syrus was listening, but when she mentioned the Academy, he remembered something Redge had said about her. "So that's how you know my cousin, Leith."

Forest's insides went cold. "What?" she asked deadly quiet.

"You know my cousin, Leith. You must have met at the Academy. He spoke of you to my guard, Redge. I thought it odd that you two should have occasion to know each other. Now it makes sense."

"What did Leith say about me?" Forest asked through clenched teeth.

"Oh, I don't remember now. It was something nice though, a complement. Something about your eyes, I think."

Forest realized that Syrus didn't know anything, but she felt like she was going to erupt regardless. All she could do was run away.

"Forest? Forest?!" Syrus called confusedly at her retreating back. He carefully walked around the fire and followed her back to the house. "I'm sorry. Did I say something wrong?" he asked as he closed the front door behind him.

"No. I'm tired and I want to go to sleep now. You should do the same."

"Okay," Syrus said confusedly. "Thank you for the evening. I enjoyed it."

"Good night, Syrus." Her voice was harsh, and she practically sprinted away from him to her room.

"Good night," he said quietly, sure she hadn't heard him.

She leaned against her door after she shut it, breathing heavily. She'd had to get away from him and his questions. She didn't think they could be friends. Friendship was built on knowledge. Knowledge was too high a price. She couldn't afford it. So Leith was his cousin. Just when she was starting to think Syrus was half way decent.

Forest got ready for bed quickly. She was so tired her muscles were rubbery in some places, knotted like macramé in others. She listened at her door for a few moments to see if she could hear Syrus moving around. Silence. Because she thought it best to still consider him her enemy, Forest opened her door a crack to better hear, before turning out the lights and crawling into bed.

An hour later, Forest's eyes were cinched shut but her brain refused to stop whirring like a computer that had been left on too long. She never had any trouble falling asleep, and it wasn't like Syrus was making too much noise—he wasn't making any. She wasn't even thinking coherent thoughts about him, but his face haunted her. Time lumbered on in a slow agonizing dirge as Forest fought to shoo him from her mind and drift off to sleep.

Syrus sat on the edge of his bed again, half meditating. He was tired, but his irritation would not allow him to relax. He could feel Forest all the way across the house. His door was cracked open just like hers, and because there was no other noise in the house, he was able to hear her breathing faintly. She was not asleep. His muscles constricted every time she sighed or rolled over. He had never been so physically aware of another person as he was at that moment, and it was maddening. He knew he wanted her more than he had ever wanted any woman, and he was incredulous of his own desire. He didn't even have a mental picture of how she looked. He had been trying to make one up but was so far unsuccessful. The tones and nuances of her voice were clear in his head and he had been conjuring it for a while, listening to her speak inside his mind.

He was desperate to know why the mention of Leith had set her off. What kind of history could illicit such a strong and immediate response? Leith had obviously mortally offended her. Syrus needed to distance himself from any association to Leith she might draw. He figured that wouldn't be too hard. He wasn't at all close with his cousin. He didn't have many occasions to meet with him. His opinion of Leith was vague.

The night continued to mature, and Syrus was acutely aware when Forest finally fell asleep. He listened to her breathing as she slipped deeper and deeper. He waited. When he knew she had achieved a level of sleep that she would not wake from easily, he made a decision based purely on instinct and frustration. He'd had a very weak moment earlier in the night when he considered reaching for his flask of human blood and taking a small drink. But he knew that would have been utter folly. He wouldn't have been able to do it without making some cry of pain. It would have woken her. So he did the only other thing he could.

The incantation was uttered almost inaudibly, over and over, until he achieved some results, slight thought they were. The pain was not much this time, more of an ache. He felt the usual amount of disorientation as he stood up, seeing blurry flashes of the room he was in for the first time. Nothing was clear. He was only able to see silhouettes and shadows unless the thing he wanted to see was right in front of his eyes. This was his most guarded secret.

Syrus moved silently through the dark house to Forest's door. He stood just outside her room for a few minutes, just listening to her breathing. He pushed her door a fraction of an inch, seeing if the door would creak. It didn't. He pushed it a bit more and cringed as the hinge moaned quietly. Forest shifted but slept on. He only needed to open it a little bit more to pass through. He hesitated, feeling despicable, like some kind of thief. He would have changed his mind about what he was doing, but he really didn't want to do anything. He just wanted to look at her. Even though what he would see was not her true face, he didn't care. He had to have a mental picture of her. Whatever he saw would suffice.

The door made no more attempt to tattle on him. Syrus moved to stand by the side of her bed, finally getting his first look at her. In spite of the blurriness of his vision, his heart clenched painfully, his lungs seized, and he found himself on his knees, literally. Winded and furious. It wasn't fair! Never had Syrus felt such injustice. It didn't matter to him this wasn't her true face. What mattered was that everyone else could see her and he couldn't. He'd lived his whole life and never seen such fierce beauty. Her features were sharp and delicate at the same time with the most perfectly shaped set of lips he had ever seen. His own began to burn with the desire to kiss her mouth. Her hair was long and curly of what looked like a rich warm brown, but he couldn't trust his eyes enough to know the color. Her hair spread over her pillow like a vast net and hung off the edge of the bed. And he was clutched by a desire so strong he couldn't even stop to consider how great a risk he was taking.

With a greater amount of reverent delicacy than he had ever shown anything before, Syrus lifted a handful of her hair and brought it to his lips. His eyes rolled back in his head involuntarily. His insides churned like an ocean storm, violent, tumultuous, and senseless. He almost woke her on purpose, just to see her eyes. He *had* to see her eyes. *He had to*!

Syrus moved like a flash of shadow from her room and back across the house. He had teetered on the edge of reckless stupidity and had no other choice but to run, or jump off the edge. If she would have woken to see him there, kissing her hair, he had no doubt she would have killed him unceremoniously. He deserved it.

His weak sight was growing weaker by the second and it would soon be gone again completely. He stretched his body out on the bed, feeling tired now, at last. The imprinted memory of her beauty lulled him into a sweet and peaceful sleep. No matter how much longer he lived, or if his sight was ever fully restored, she was with him now, imprisoned inside his mind, where he would never let her go.

7

The eastern Regian mountain range was vast and brutal, twisting through the countryside like a vengeful snake with a spine of broken axe blades stabbing the sky. The first row of mountains to the west served as the werewolves' garden fence. Behind it, at the base of the mountains, lay the suburbs of The Lair. The Lair itself was carved out of the stone face of the largest mountain in all of Regia. It was a city, homes of stone stacked atop homes of stone, with a deadly road winding around and up to the very top where the penthouse of the pack leader perched, protected and defiant.

Under the rule of their current leader, Philippe, the wolves had tripled their territory and greatly multiplied their numbers. Within the mountains, they had unofficially formed their own country. As their power grew, so did their opinion that the Vampire king had no right to rule over them. When the vampire prince had been assassinated, Philippe had doubled his efforts to prepare the wolves for a full takeover of Regia. The time was close at hand.

Philippe stood on his balcony in the cool morning sun, looking out over the country. He had a broad square face with a heavy, prominent jaw that was always peppered with wiry whiskers. The tawny hair on his head was long and unkempt, like a cascading apartment complex of rat nests. His eyes were endless black sinkholes; everything around got sucked in. And although his overall appearance gave the impression of total disregard, this wasn't the truth. Philippe honed his appearance to the goal of unadulterated brute. He rarely bathed but kept his fingernails and teeth meticulously clean. When he did have occasion to smile, his smile caused disquiet in those unfortunate enough to witness it.

The sun had ruthlessly ripped bare everything before it, making the landscape appear smooth and bleached. The tops of the trees of the Wolf's Wood looked like a spiky carpet from where Philippe stood. Possession of the Wood was Philippe's secret joy. It was immense, and the roads were befuddling to anyone unfamiliar to them. The perfect place to get lost, intentionally as well as unintentionally. There were places within that were so beautiful, they were almost impossible to describe to anyone who had not seen them with their own eyes. Many unwary travelers who happened upon the Waterfall of Silverlight had forgotten their quests or themselves completely, convinced that they had fallen into a dream. Philippe used the Wood's natural ability to distract like a web, to catch people. Through the last year, the werewolves had worked tirelessly to confuse the roads through the Wood.

In the distance to the west, he could see the tiny outline of the Vampire castle. Philippe smiled as he imagined the old king squinting as he tried to see The Lair. A view to die for, he thought. And many had died for him to have this view. Others would, if they tried to take it away.

At this altitude, the air was too thin and frigid for even the taste of the toughest wolves, but Philippe loved it. His massive shoulders were warm, covered in the pelts of his dead adversaries. He never went anywhere in public without this macabre cloak on. To a Werewolf, to wear the pelt of another werewolf was just like carrying around a corpse. No other leader had ever done something so disgusting or fear invoking before. After his rise to power, no one had challenged Philippe again in case they ended up displayed on his back, forever desecrated and disgraced. And so, the entire werewolf race had submitted to Philippe's eccentric decrees, the strangest being that they all learn to speak French.

The entire werewolf community was bemused and sometimes indignant that their leader was obsessed with Earth's France and that he was forcing his bizarre ideals on them, but none so much as the army officers, who Philippe had demanded change their names to French ones. It was really the only source of weakness in the wolves' offense, because most could only speak broken French, and the officers were commanded to give orders only in French. As a result, there was a lot of confusion during tactical training and more than a little anger from Philippe for their lack of talent in linguistics.

Despite these difficulties, the army was assembled and waiting. Philippe waited for word from his Fortress informant, who was due any day now. Power took patience, he reminded himself. His stomach growled loudly, demanding breakfast. Patience was difficult to maintain on an empty stomach. He pulled himself away from the view and rang for his serving wench.

****

Across the land, over the forests and marshlands, through the towns and cities, to the far reaches of the northwest lay the vampire lands. The Great Vampire City sprawled lazily like a contented cat in the shadow sand of the Desert of Halussis, or what most Regian's aptly called the Dreaming Desert because the black shadow sand was highly toxic. It varied in color from grey to black, and only the blackest sand surrounded the Onyx Castle like a mote. Inhaling the sand or touching it with the bare skin would cause strong dreamlike hallucinations. The vampires were the least susceptible to it, making their land well protected against attack, and also elite. Aside from the Ogres, who were loyal to a fault to the vampires, very few of any of the other races tried to live anywhere near Halussis. The sand was collected periodically by scoundrels and smugglers who sold it in small doses for high prices, much like human drug dealers.

In the cool and naked morning, the Onyx Castle looked stately and ominous. Everything about the castle, inside and out, was in perfect order, down to the smallest detail. The castle and those who lived within were best described like a piece of exquisite jewelry—chosen, cut, set, and polished. No expense was spared. When Queen Cristiana decided that she wanted new bedding, not even the finest fabric was good enough until it was embroidered with gold thread. That was how the queen liked things. Her cast off socks were worth a small fortune.

On this morning, the queen's tiny feet were quietly ghosting through the halls, searching out her husband like a virus. The swishing of her skirts along the floor was the only sound that preceded her. The ogres throughout the castle loved Christiana and were faithful to her above anyone else, even the king. She had carefully nurtured their love. With their loyalty, she could undermine anything the king set out to do with whispers and winks. The ogres were the only ones who didn't feel the chill behind her smile.

King Zeren was aware he was being hunted and was sitting in the dark of his favorite hiding place, certain the queen would never find him. It wouldn't cross her mind that he would spend any time in such an unimportant room in the castle. That was why he used this room when he needed solitude. The only person who knew this was where he went when he was vexed, was Syrus' guard, Redge.

A small band of sunshine coming through a crack in the drapes fell along the floor like a golden road. Zeren rolled his onyx signet ring between his thumb and forefinger like a worry stone. His fingertips caressed the inlaid hieroglyphs on the band while his mind caressed the subtleties of his troubles, not consciously digging into them but letting them float in his head like leaves in a stream. Zeren didn't come to this seemingly unused guest room in the outskirts of his castle to solve problems. He came here to visit memories, delight in past triumphs, wallow in regrets, and fantasize of what ifs.

In this room, Zeren's mind usually focused on Pipha, and he would make time to think on her today. But at the moment, he worried about his son. He was sorry that Syrus had been angry with him when he'd left the castle the last time. Zeren feared he would never see his son again and was irritated that Cristiana refused to speak about Syrus at all. Cristiana was an unnatural woman. And not for the first time did he have a faint twinge of hatred towards her that he quickly tucked deep down inside. Zeren couldn't allow himself to really experience his honest emotions about the queen.

Please come back, Syrus. His mind whispered fervently. *Know that I love you, Son. Come back alive.* There was nothing he could do for his son now; he had to let it go.

Clenching his hands together, he remembered what it had felt like to hold Pipha's hand, and the memory jostled a pain that was sweet agony. Honest emotion was all he could feel about Pipha and his mind caressed his memories again as they floated through his head. Simple details like the way her hair caught the sunlight, the dimple in her right cheek that only appeared when her smile was genuine, and the lilt of her giggle when she'd laugh at his stupid jokes. These memories made him smile, but it didn't take long for bitterness to taint the memories. It was his fault she was dead. After all these years, his mind still cried out to her spirit to forgive him.

Forest and Syrus found a rhythm that suited both of them over the next two days. They managed to be continuously polite when they interacted but mostly stayed out of each other's way. Forest had shown Syrus how to work her stereo and had hardly seen him since. Syrus developed an instant and passionate love affair with American music. Forest didn't mind the base thumping through the house so long as Syrus didn't repeat the same song too many times in a row. He was quite prone to do that with songs he really loved, and more than once Forest had to threaten him with silver burns if he played *Steal My Sunshine* one more time.

Forest still had pangs of annoyance over his presence, but for the most part, she liked having him there. His cheerfulness was infectious. When she had given him a few audio books to listen to, he was so excited, you would have thought she'd handed him the moon. They made a routine of making S'mores every night, and they found they could talk for long periods of time without offending each other, so long as the topics stuck to battle tactics, weapons, and Earth.

Forest got up before dawn on the fourth day of their stay at her cottage and went out in her garden. She needed to focus, and there was nothing better than the cool, dewy morning air to sharpen her mind. She sat by her bubbling fountain, compiling a list of things she needed to do before they set out on their journey. Kendel hadn't told her exactly how long she had before they had to go, and she had been procrastinating over the last few days. She kept her phone on her at all times, in case the eminent email arrived.

Not having any word about what was happening in the impending war was starting to grate on her. She should go to the Fair and see what gossip she could catch. Tek always had the news, and he would need to be restocked anyhow. He always complained when Forest took too long in bringing him stuff from Earth. He said her competitors were overpriced and never had decent merchandise. So she had two major things on her plate for the day: go see Tek, and finally persuade Syrus to let her cut his hair.

Syrus was up and poking around the kitchen when she came back inside. His head was stuck in the pantry and he muttered curses as his hands shifted things around.

"Syrus?

He started guiltily, and he knocked a box of cheerios to the floor, spilling them all over the kitchen. He huffed in exasperation and threw his hands in the air.

Forest chuckled. "What are you looking for? I told you I put the Lucky Charms right in the front."

"I don't want Lucky Charms, I want Count Chocula," he said petulantly.

"Oh. Well, I'm sure your great uncle Dracula would be so proud," she said as she came forward to dig the cereal out for him. "You'd better be careful how much you eat of that stuff. It'll rot your fangs."

He ignored her warning and plunged his hand into the cereal box with gusto, preferring to eat it dry. He couldn't stand milk.

"So, what are we doing today?" he asked.

"*I* have business to attend to in town. We need to get ready to leave. Kendel could send word any time now. When I get back, you should let me cut your hair."

Syrus grimaced and made a little whining noise in his throat.

Forest ground her teeth together. "You have to get over this."

Syrus acted as if he hadn't heard her, stuffing his mouth with another handful of cereal, and turning his back to her. Forest clenched her fists, wishing she had something to throw at the back his head. She contemplated just grabbing a pair of scissors and charging at him.

"Okay. Go ahead and sulk. I have work to do."

TENAYA JAYNE

Forest grabbed a big tote bag from the closet and went down to the basement, boiling with annoyance. She began to fill the bag with the stuff she knew Tek would want the most. The tote was heavy once it was full and her back would be aching by the time she reached the Fair. Right as she was about to leave she found Syrus blocking the front door with his arms crossed over his chest.

"What?" she half yelled.

"I've decided that I'm not going to let you cut my hair, not ever."

Forest's mouth dropped open. *I'm gonna kill him. I'm gonna kill him right now!*

"There are other things we can do to disguise me. I can wear my hair in another fashion, but I cannot simply let you cut it. It's too important to me. I just can't."

Forest's face and voice were frozen impassive. "Are you finished?" she asked in deadly politeness.

He didn't reply.

"I can't wait till we're done with this and you are out of my life!"

Syrus flinched a little before composing his face in a casual sneer. "The feeling's mutual, baby."

He moved away from the door, and Forest exited through it. She walked through her yard, out onto the road. She was so incensed that she couldn't even feel it, she just walked at a brisk pace like a robot.

Forest was half way to town before she could begin to come up with ways to deal with Syrus. She wasn't even capable of thinking his name before that. She would deal with him. She just hadn't yet figured out how. The problem was that he was the prince. Even though they both didn't want anyone to know that, he did have the authority to tell her what was what, even if he was dead wrong. Even if he was a colossal moron!

By the time she reached the Fair, the heavy tote had worn a ridge in her shoulder. A rambunctious open market, the Fair resembled a massive gypsy camp. Distained and shunned by those who thought it low class and thoroughly enjoyed by everyone else. The Fair busted at the seams with the dregs of society, with plenty of illegal activity to go around. No one seemed to care enough what happened in the Fair to police it. The teenage children of the high and mighty often snuck away from their homes to revel in the base pleasures of the Fair.

She walked the heavily trodden path through the brightly colored tents and open fire pits to the end of the row, where Tek's patchwork tent stood, defiantly taller than anyone else's. Forest kept her eyes on the ground so no one would recognize her. Tek had a small wooden sign hanging at the doorway of his tent that read, *Human Relics*. Forest passed through the flap to find him sitting slumped on a stool, his head lolling on his chest, snoring loudly. She took the opportunity to look at his stock. He was low.

She glanced at Tek and decided to see just how asleep he really was. She stuffed a few outdated celebrity gossip magazines into her cloak, along with three bottles of nail polish and turned to leave.

"Thief!"

She ducked just in time as a dart went flying past her ear. Forest turned, laughing, and looked Tek straight in the eyes. "I knew you weren't really asleep, Old Dog."

"Oh, Forest!" he exclaimed, lowering the blowgun from his mouth. "It's about time, Missy! Look at my shelves!"

"I have. Sorry."

She hefted the tote bag onto the counter. His little brown eyes gleamed as he opened it greedily. Tek looked as downtrodden as his shelves. Was he depressed? He always attempted to keep his rough werewolf appearance to a minimum. Yet now, his clothes were dirty with the exception of his black Stetson and his green snakeskin boots.

"So, Tek…" Forest began casually as he continued to pull out and stack things on the counter. "I've only just come back to Regia. What's been going on?"

"Hmm?...Oh this is good." He said pulling out a stack of romance novels. "I'll make a fortune on these… Oh! Fantastic Forest!" he exclaimed finding a bunch of temporary tattoos.

"Tek?"

"What?"

"What's the gossip?"

He shot her a piercing look for a second. "What have you heard?" he demanded aggressively. "It's not true, I swear! Me and Martia are just friends. That's all. Just friends."

Forest blinked at him for a second before bursting out with laughter. "Really, Tek. I've known about you and Martia for a long time. Everyone at fair knows about you two. What are you all uptight about? Did you ask her to mate or something?"

"I did not!" Tek blushed brilliantly. "She asked me," he mumbled.

"You're a lucky wolf. She's lovely."

Tek's cheek pulled up into a small smile. "She is, isn't she?"

"Congratulations."

"Oh shut up. I hate how everyone acts like it's so great." He dug out the last pair of flip-flops from the tote and threw it angrily down on the ground. "It's not my fault I fell for an ogre. I only agreed because I'm too old to breed."

Forest chuckled. "Yes, you two would have interesting offspring. Just think what the Were-soldiers would do to you for that offense."

Tek shuddered at the thought. "Yeah, like I need that kind of trouble. I still have an outstanding warrant on my head."

Forest's face grew serious. "I'm happy for you and Martia. But I wouldn't be if you planned on having children. It's too hard to be a Halfling. I wouldn't wish it on anyone."

Tek nodded gravely. "So what do I owe you?"

"Forget it. Think of it as a mating present. Just tell me the Regian gossip outside of your own dealings."

"Oh, well. I heard that Philippe has been organizing for war, but that he's been acting odd. Odder than usual, that is. Like maybe he's got some secret weapon. The Lair issued a decree for all wolves to engage in social disobedience. Nothing has really happen yet. Everyone was expecting King Zeren to make a swift and nasty military response, but he's done nothing. He has made no statements or appearances, and neither has the queen. It's like he's waiting for something. No idea what. Everyone I know is feeling the tension, but it's all quiet. We're all just spectators, waiting for the show to start."

"I see. Anything else?" Forest asked.

"Oh! You should have been around a few days ago! The Elves came out and publicly gave their support to the Vampires."

"What?"

"Oh yes. Quite the stir it's causing. Apparently, it all happened because the Elves and the Shifters in power got into a huge argument. Something about dishonorable battle tactics on the Shifters side."

"What battle tactics?"

"No idea." Tek shrugged. He scratched his bearded chin for a moment.

"So what do you think?" Forest asked.

"Well, you know I'm a traitor to the core. I think Zeren is a good king. He's lost his edge since Syrus died, but then who wouldn't? I think Philippe hired the hit on Syrus. It's a shame really. This will probably be the war that will shift the balance of power. Not looking forward to it myself. I like Regia the way it is, but Philippe will try to turn it into France. I don't want to change my name to Pierre or Jean Claude."

"Or Peppy La Pue." Forest laughed, but she was feeling tense. The news he had given her wasn't good.

"I've also had word that there is a storyteller traveling through. I hope they will be persuaded to spend a while at our humble little fair."

Even though this news had nothing to do with Forest's purpose, she was interested nonetheless. "Really? I haven't listened to a storyteller since I was a child. I didn't even know there were any left."

"Yeah. Storytellers have been thin through this region for the last hundred years. Why don't you come into the back and have a drink?" Tek invited.

Forest chewed her lip for a second. "Only one," she said sternly.

****

It had begun to rain by the time Forest left the Fair. Her mind churned with the news Tek had given her. She was so engrossed in her own thoughts that she hardly noticed when she reached the outskirts to her land. The rain had thoroughly saturated her, her hair dripping and clinging to her face. As soon as she entered her garden, all thought snapped off like a light switch. Unconsciously she held her breath and didn't move. Syrus was seemingly unaware of her presence, and she wanted to keep it that way.

She couldn't have looked away if she tried. He was at the far end of the garden near the house, barefooted and stripped to the waist, his body moving in beautiful precision, sliding through the raindrops as though he were dancing with the storm. Forest recognized that he was practicing the Blood Kata's forms. She had seen others doing the same moves, had even learned some of them herself. But now all of her memories of watching students or masters of the Kata seemed robotic and ugly next to Syrus' liquid grace. Admiration and awe tainted with a swirl of jealousy. Discipline as beauty.

Then she noticed her sword lying on the ground close to where he was practicing. Outrage and offense slammed into her like a battering ram. *How dare he?! How dare he use her sword?! And he left it on the ground!* She would have been less offended if she caught him digging in her underwear drawer. A scream of rancor rose in her throat, but before she could let it loose, shock choked her silent.

Syrus stood ten feet away from where her katana lay on the ground. He lifted one arm, pointing it at the sword, all his muscles taut. What looked like ghost ribbons undulated from his fingertips. The ribbons wrapped around the sword and lifted it into the air. The sword hovered at arm height, facing Syrus as though an invisible enemy held it at the ready, beckoning him to fight. Astonishment rendered Forest immobile as she watched her sword swing through the air in a wide arch meant to decapitate Syrus.

He bobbed and danced out of the way. Her sword continued to slash and stab. Then it began to gain momentum, and Syrus drew both of his short swords and began sparing. The clink of metal rang through the air. Forest couldn't take it any longer. She ran towards him as fast as she could and dove through the air, catching the hilt of her sword in mid flip. She landed flat on her feet and thrust the blade beneath Syrus' chin. He lowered both his swords and smiled.

Forest could feel the power that had been wrapped around her sword pulling lightly at her hand. "You're file said you were a master of the Kata. Not one word mentioned you were a mage."

Syrus shrugged, still smiling. "Not many know. Those that do are bound to silence that I'm alive at all."

"No one in Fortress knows?"

"No."

"Not even the high council?" She demanded.

"No. So are you impressed?"

Forest huffed. "Yes…Grudgingly." Reeling from the information that he was a mage, her original outrage returned. "I told you *never* to touch my sword."

Syrus smacked her blade away from his throat with one of his short swords. They stood facing each other, breathing heavily.

"All of my senses are heightened when I fight. I'm thoroughly warmed up, and you've been walking a long ways, if I'm not mistaken. What do you say?"

She was about to ask him what he was talking about when he lifted both his swords and bent his knees into an attack stance. She didn't move, remembering what Kendel had said about fighting with Syrus. Adrenaline was building inside her, as she looked at him, poised and ready. She had fought and triumphed over many vampires, many skilled in the Kata, but this was a chance she had never had before: to fight a mage.

Forest took a step back and sank into her own attack stance. Syrus was right about his heightened senses. Even though he couldn't see, she could feel that his physical awareness was greater than her own.

All the sounds surrounding Forest thundered in Syrus' ears: her breathing, her pulse, the rain falling on her skin. He knew exactly where she was by the heat waves rolling off her body. His senses were turned up so high, it bordered on painful. The only thing that dulled his edge over her was the mental image he had of her. He saw, in his mind's eye, the way she looked when she was asleep and now pictured that standing in front of him armed with a sword, and he was half crazed with desire.

Syrus was still smiling at her. "Don't hold back. Forget I'm blind. Try and kill me."

"Fine, but you have to try and kill me as well."

"Agreed. *En garde!*"

They began circling each other, and instantly Forest was struck with the thought that her sight was actually a disadvantage. She was distracted by her attraction to him and the admiration that his movements were beautiful in their deadly precision. Blades flashed through the raindrops. The instant their weapons slammed into each other, she knew she had never crossed blades with anyone this deadly. She easily deflected an overhead strike, the blades clanging loudly. He was holding back, testing her level.

"Stop messing around!" she snarled at him.

"Glad you could tell," he laughed while slashing at the side of her midriff.

She jumped out of the way.

"You're not bad, Forest."

She shrieked in outrage, making him laugh again. "*Not bad!* I'll show you, *not bad!*"

Forest moved like a blur, bounding over the fountain in one long leap. But Syrus moved too quickly, facing off with her on the other side so that Forest had to sidestep clumsily, almost falling into the fountain and half twisting her ankle. Her wrists were jarred painfully over and over as she put up the most aggressive offense she could. Syrus parried her every strike, seeming totally at ease. She could see he was taunting her, and her rage kicked up another notch.

"You're getting emotional, Forest." Syrus said casually as he deflected her attempt to cut off his arm. "You're losing concentration."

Forest felt like she was back in swordplay class at the Academy. She had never fought anyone with Syrus' skill. She knew he was right, but that made her all the angrier, and her swings became wilder. This in turn began to anger Syrus. He threw one of his swords at her head. The sound of it rang in her ear as it missed by a few centimeters. She knew he missed on purpose. Raindrops smacked against the side of the blade as she swung her sword in a wide arch, bringing it down in what would have been a killing strike. Syrus stopped her arm in the air, grabbing her wrist firmly. She tried to pull it lose. Syrus lifted his sword slowly and set the blade on her shoulder.

"You lose," he stated.

She shrieked again in rage, angering Syrus at her soreness. He twisted the sword from her hand and threw it.

"I've lost some respect for you, Forest. I thought you were much more disciplined."

Forest saw red, and she gave no regard to the fact that he was still armed and she wasn't. She raised her arm and brought her hand down on his face in a stinging slap. Shock was plain on his face along with her handprint.

"*Vampires!* Always think you're better than everyone else when really you're the most disgusting race in all of Regia!"

Forest stood panting with emotion, astonished at what she had just said.

"That does it!" Syrus threw his sword and charged at her.

She scrambled backward as he advanced. His face was taut and his blind eyes were wild. She retreated backwards until she could feel the rock wall looming behind her. He stretched one hand toward her, and his lips moved in an incantation she couldn't hear. She felt a pulling at her hands and around her neck. The next second, all the silver she was wearing went flying off her body and landed with a plunk in the fountain. He reached out and picked her up around the waist. Before her mind could think to protest, she wrapped herself around him. Their mouths fused together in a violent, starving urgency. Her arms clung around his neck, and her legs banded around his hips. There was one agonizingly wonderful moment as they strained against one another trying to pull tighter, both their mouths throbbing as blood hammered through their veins. Then it happened. What felt like a lightning bolt cracked inside both of their chests, jolting their mouths apart. The pain hissed and flashed inside them but strengthened the pull between them.

"Don't do this," she whispered even as she clung tighter.

He buried his face in her neck but he didn't bite her as she feared he would.

"I don't want this," she protested breathlessly, her words contrary to her actions.

He pulled his face back, his mouth a breath from hers. "*What? You felt that didn't you? You must have felt that! I want to find out what this is.*"

He crushed his mouth against hers again. Her whole body was screamingly alive as he kissed her. But even as instinct had her clinging, demanding more, a stabbing pain bit deep into her scars and Leith's face flashed in her mind. All of her muscles stiffened, and she pulled her mouth away, fighting to regain control of her body. "I. . .I don't want this!" *There's nothing I want more.*

Forest's lips trembled as she fought to hold herself immobile. She fought until her whole body quaked with the effort. The pull between their mouths was painfully strong. Syrus stood stone still, allowing her to move or pull away as she chose. If she gave in it would unleash a force within her she couldn't account for. Insanity. Desire. Fear.

"Please let me go, Syrus. Please."

A look of crushed disbelief fell on his face. Now he was the one who was trembling. He fought against his muscles as he forced himself to let go. Forest's feet hit the slick muddy ground, and she ran from him. She ran to the gate and shoved her way through, and she continued to run. She paid no attention to where she was going; her body just demanded that she move. The trees clawed at her but she paid them no mind. Forest didn't hesitate even a second when she reached the edge of the river; she dove right in.

The luminous, silvery water was comfortably cool, and it eased the scraping frustration in her cells as it compressed on her. She took one deep breath and slid beneath the surface. Forest pulled herself to the sandy bottom and lay on her back looking up through the water. The surface undulated lazily, textured by the pelting rain.

Relief washed through her, though her mouth still throbbed, forcing her think about Syrus' mouth. A vampire's mouth was the most sensitive place on their body. Kissing Syrus was nothing like kissing Leith. It had been intense, but her mouth was not at all harmed. Forest's lips and tongue always bled when Leith kissed her. The comparison was stark. She had wanted to kiss Syrus, she chose it. She had never chosen to kiss Leith. Everything he did to her was an assault.

The water was such blessed silence. All she could hear was her heart, thumping in her ears, and she could cry without having to feel the tears. She would drown the part of her that longed for Syrus right there along with the insanity inside her that made her shed tears over the loss of the possibility. They could not be together.

****

Night had fallen when Forest finally returned home. She tried to force her mind to be coolly diplomatic, but she was terrified. As she reached her stone wall, she forced herself to focus on her physical state. She was freezing. It had stopped raining, but her clothes were still wet and clinging. Her heart clinched when she entered her garden. Syrus stood with his back to her, poking a stick into the fire. His shoulders stiffened when she approached, but he gave no other sign that he knew she was there.

Forest stood close to the fire, watching him over the top of the flames. His eyes were shut, and his face looked drawn. Forest could think of nothing to say. She felt embarrassed, stupid, and unprofessional. One of Syrus' cheeks was pulled in, as if he chewed the inside of his mouth. The silence was ridiculously awkward and Forest was completely at a loss as to how to break it.

Syrus sighed, rolled his head, cracking his neck, and threw the stick he was holding into the fire. "I've always had the feeling that my parents hate each other."

Forest's breath came out in a whoosh, and she tried not to laugh in the cracking tension. It was amazing the amount of relief she felt that he had spoken first. "Oh?"

"Yes. It seems on the rare occasion that they do speak to each other, they are fighting, or else talking with such cold civility you would think they were addressing an enemy."

"That must have been difficult for you as a child," Forest said.

"When I was young, they fought about me all the time. Then as I grew up, they used me against each other. No matter what the topic was, I was the hinge on the door that they pushed back and forth."

96

Forest was quiet for a moment. "Why are you telling me this?"

Syrus shrugged, but she knew he wasn't just making idle chit chat. "I became a mage after the attack. It was the most wonderful moment of my life. It was even enough to please my mother. Any vampire that becomes a master has the chance at becoming a mage, though very few have the ability. When the transformation happened to me, well…the experience was nothing short of… spiritual. I thought it would be the only spiritual experience I would ever have. That was until a few hours ago."

Forest panicked. "Syrus, don't!"

"No, Forest. We have to talk about it."

Panic pressed down on her lungs, and she found it hard to breathe. She would not, could not tell him about Leith. And if they talked about what had happened between them, she feared it would come up because Leith was a part of it. If Syrus had felt even a fraction of what she had, he would want to be lovers. She couldn't be his lover. She was someone else's property.

"I…Not yet…not now, okay? I'm not ready. Give me some time, please. We'll talk about anything else."

Syrus raised one eyebrow. "Leith?"

"Damn it, Syrus! *Anything* else! Not what happened earlier and not Leith! Why would you even ask about him?"

"Because of the way you reacted the other night when I mentioned you knowing him."

Violent emotions bubbled inside her, and she turned to retreat to the house again. "Why can't you leave me alone?"

Syrus moved quickly and caught her by both arms. "I just can't."

Whatever it was that had happened earlier had caused a shift in the gravity. She felt the pulsing of his blood through his hands as he gripped her arms, and it seemed the magnetism between them had doubled, tripled even. Why was fate doing this to her? Syrus was shaking slightly again as he eased back from her, and she sighed in relief when he let go and took a step away.

"Just tell me something."

"What?" she asked cautiously.

"Just something I don't know about you. Something true."

"My eyes are green," she said.

"I already know that. Redge told me."

Forest thought for a moment. He had told her something personal, and he wanted something personal in return. "My father named me. As far as I know, he has only seen me once: on the day I was born. My mother said that he held me a long time and that we looked into each other's eyes. When he gave me back, he said that my name should be Forest, because that was what he saw in my eyes."

"When this is all over," Syrus said quietly. "I shall look in them myself." He reached and took her hand. "Get lost in them."

He began to pull her to him, but she put her hand on his chest, stopping him. "Look, we can't do this," she said firmly.

"Why?"

Forest could feel her mind spluttering. "Because we, because…because we have to keep our minds clear for the journey ahead. This, whatever this is, is a distraction neither of us can afford." She pulled her hand out of his. "Don't touch me anymore," she ordered roughly.

"Fine," he said in a clipped tone. Then he smirked, catching her off guard. "Don't touch *me* anymore."

"No problem." Forest could hear the acid in her voice and was relieved that she could still serve it up to him. "I'm going inside. I'm cold and tired."

Syrus didn't follow her immediately inside but took his time putting the fire out. Forest threw her damp clothes on the bathroom floor and put on fleece pajamas and thick socks. When she came back and picked up her pile of wet clothes, intending to put them in the laundry, her heart skipped a beat. Her cell phone! She pulled it out of the pocket of her wet pants. It was dead.

When Syrus came in the house, he could hear Forest cursing a blue streak from her room and the whirring of one of her electronics. He was half way to her door, going to ask her what was wrong, when something loud crashed inside, and he thought better of it.

Forest was in hysterics over her phone and trying to dry it out with her hairdryer. Desperation will sometimes cause people to do things they know are asinine, yet they cannot seem to stop themselves from doing them, hoping for a miracle. Forest put the phone down once it was dry and began pacing around her room. She had to calm down.

An hour later, Forest sat on her bed, the comforter littered with clothes, weapons, and first aid items. She had been considering what were the most important things to pack for their journey. She was throwing clothes around, looking for her favorite hoodie when her phone gurgled up a weak beep letting her know that she had in fact received a message. Forest was cradling her phone in both hands pressing buttons gently, trying to coax it to deliver the message it received while she had been underwater.

"Please. Please. Please," she whispered.

The little screen told her the time in London, the weather in Boston, and a factoid about Mount Rushmore before informing her that she had an email from Kendel. Forest held her breath. Some of the message was lost but the words that mattered most popped up. "Leave before first light."

Forest sighed and then laughed, relieved. Her phone wouldn't be any more use to her on the trip. She tried to call, tried to email Kendel. The phone refused to play along. Well, she had been chosen for the job because she knew the Wood better than any other operative, she reminded herself. She would just have to do without any other help from Kendel. She jumped up to tell Syrus they would be leaving in a matter of hours.

Syrus' door was shut. He was listening to *Cake's* version of *Mahna Mahna* loudly. She laughed to herself as she heard him singing along, before knocking. The music shut off.

"Come in."

Syrus sat cross-legged on the floor, playing with a slinky.

"I just got word from Kendel. We need to leave before dawn. So, that gives us about five hours. You should think about getting some sleep."

FORBIDDEN FOREST

"Okay, Mom."

"Well, *I'm* going to sleep once I finish packing. You need to do that too."

"Hm. Yes. Do you have any more human clothes for me?" he asked.

"I'll go down and find some."

Forest was happy to find a new pullover that would fit Syrus, along with two other pairs of jeans and a few T-shirts. As she walked up the stairs, she remembered that they still had not figured out their cover story if they were captured, or how to change Syrus' hairstyle.

"Here," she said tersely, dumping the clothes on his bed. "Fix your hair. I'm going to finish packing, and then I'm going to sleep. So, leave me alone."

Syrus grunted in response as she shut the door behind her.

9

Kendel sat in the back of the high council chamber, wishing he had a stiff drink. It was a nightmare that had been going on for hours. Kendel kept his opinions to himself and let the rest of them shout. The high council allowed the low council in their beloved chamber, but the real problem, aside from the tantrums, was that the king and queen were there and they had thrown a wooden shoe into the machine. Kendel had considered discreetly recording the whole thing with his phone and sending it on to Forest, but as soon as the queen began speaking, he knew he would never even tell Forest half of what was said that day, as most of it was disparaging towards Forest herself. Kendel forced his mind to hum as things were said against Forest. If he even alluded to what he was thinking, it would cost him his job. And if he lost his job, Forest would lose hers as well.

"I want this mission aborted," Queen Christiana said quietly as she addressed the council. "There is no call for this misconstrued plan to continue any further. An entire platoon will be dispatched as soon as this meeting is adjourned to go and collect Prince Syrus and bring him back to the safety of the Onyx Castle. Scouts can be sent in search of this wizard, although I don't see why he would be any more successful than Devonte has been in restoring my son's sight. Syrus is the future king of Regia. He must be kept safe from Philippe, this backward befuddled organization, and social-climbing, bastard Halflings."

Kendel watched King Zeren while the queen spoke. It was obvious the King did not agree with his wife, but he made no move to speak against her. The whole mission had been the King's idea to begin with. Kendel was taken aback by the king's passive resignation. No, he downright resented it. This was the first time Kendel had thought Zeren weak.

When Christiana finished and re-seated herself, the finger pointing and arguing began again. Finally, when the vehement council members had exhausted their vocal chords, the call for a full council vote was made.

Kendel watched and voted that Forest be allowed to complete the mission with a few others. The majority voted against, and Kendel was forced to send Forest an "abort mission" email.

****

Forest made sure Syrus had everything he needed packed tightly in a Spiderman backpack. He wanted to use the pack he had brought with him, but he became enthusiastic about the backpack Forest gave him when she showed him all the handy little pockets. She transferred all the blood he brought into stainless steel sports bottles, and as an afterthought, made sure he had a flare gun and showed him how to use it. After she had packed, un-packed, and packed all his things, she was satisfied and bid him goodnight.

Forest retreated to her room and was just as conscientious packing her stuff as she had been with his. The looming danger had distracted her marvelously from her thoughts of Syrus' mouth and how she wanted it on her own again. When she had stuffed the last pocket and zipped the last zipper, the lights went out, and Forest climbed into bed. She hovered on the edge of sleep, unable to fall into the abyss.

She ghosted through the darkness of her house to his room. Resting her forehead against the door, her hand caressed the knob. Did she dare turn it? The door eased open. He lay in bed, sitting up on his elbows, facing her. She hesitated.

"Come here," he commanded in a whisper.

She pulled the cover up and slid beneath it into his arms. His lips brushed against hers, and she moved down, resting her head over his heart.

Forest eyes fluttered open in the dark. She'd been dreaming, alone in her bed, but she didn't feel like she was alone at all. Forest sat up, and her breath caught. A silhouette stood in her doorway.

"Am I dreaming?" she whispered.

"Hmmm? Dreaming? Maybe," Syrus answered.

Forest got out of bed and walked over to him. Her eyes adjusted to the darkness, and she could see him now. He reached out for her, but she stopped just beyond his grasp. He sighed and let his arms fall back to his sides.

"Is there something wrong?" she asked.

"Yes and no."

"Why are you standing in my doorway like a psychopath?"

Syrus turned his face away from her. "It's you. You bother me. I can't sleep. I lay in bed, and all I can hear is your breathing, your heartbeat. I can smell you. You're driving me crazy. I've never met anyone who bothers me as much as you do."

"Well. I don't know what you think I can do about it?"

"Would you let me drink from you? You cannot imagine how badly I want to. I wouldn't take much, I promise. And I'll be very gentle. Please?"

Forest's brow pulled down as she considered how to answer him. She wasn't tempted to agree to his request, not in the slightest. However, the humble way he had asked her made her almost regret that she couldn't allow it—almost. In any case, she wasn't keen to suffer from the physical pain it would cause. She was almost certain that the second Syrus' teeth broke through her skin her scars would scream as though they'd been injected with acid. On the other hand, his demure begging made her feel powerful and, though she would never admit it to herself, a little hot.

Forest sucked in a deep breath. "I don't want you to have control over me," she answered honestly.

"That wears off pretty quickly. I wouldn't use it anyway. And it's not actually control, more of a susceptibility to my suggestions and requests."

"I don't need any more scars. I have enough already, thanks." she said in a clipped tone.

"Scars? My bite wouldn't leave any scars. I'm not asking to mark you."

Forest blushed, thankful he couldn't see it. She forced herself to swallow. "I—umm--I don't think—" she said slowly.

Syrus took a step back and held up his hands in defeat. "I'm sorry. Forget I asked."

Forest stood there woodenly. A dull ache spread through her heart. Syrus made her hate Leith more that she already did. She looked out her window at the sky. "Our time here is short now. Maybe we should just finish getting ready and take off."

"Okay. Just one more thing before we leave though," Syrus said.

"What?"

"Will you cut my hair?"

Forest's mouth fell open. "Are you sure?"

"Yes."

Syrus perched on a barstool in the middle of the kitchen, a towel draped around his bare shoulders, while Forest got her hair scissors out of the bathroom cabinet. He was toying with the end of his braid, bemused. Was he really going to do this just for a chance to touch her again? Hell yes, he was.

When Forest came back into the kitchen she felt acutely nervous. She hadn't consciously realized how badly she wanted to touch his hair until then. Not only were they about to engage in something highly taboo in Regia, purposefully touching a vampire's hair was considered an intimate action.

Forest laid her hand gently on his shoulder. "Now you're sure? Totally sure?"

Syrus chuckled. "I'm nervous enough as it is, Forest. You don't have to make it worse."

"Just say it again, please."

"Do it."

Forest put the scissors in the pocket of her jeans and reached to remove the metal clasp at the base of his braid. Her hands shook. She clenched them together and took a deep breath. There was nothing personal in this action, she reminded herself. As soon as the clasp was loose, she began unwinding the intricate lacing of his hair. A shiver rolled through her as the hair ran in between her fingers like silk spun from shadows. She almost couldn't bring herself to cut it. She had been unconsciously running her fingers through it, mesmerized how the light slid along the shaft.

Syrus' whole body covered in goose bumps. His fingers dug into his knees. "Forest," his voice was husky. "*Please.*"

Forest shook herself and pulled out the scissors. "Sorry."

She knew the only way she was going to get through this was to just do it quickly. She grabbed a large handful of hair and wacked it off just under his ear. She didn't let it fall on the floor; she laid it gently on the counter. It didn't take long before it was all short and she was evening it up. Forest shook the towel he'd been draped with while he ran his hands through his hair. Forest figured that he would have some plan for the hair she'd cut off, but when she looked down at it she was seized with possessive desire. "Syrus, may I keep your hair?"

He turned and faced her. He looked fantastic with short hair. "Why would you want it?" he asked.

"I don't really know," she answered honestly. "I just do. I promise to keep it safe."

Syrus crossed his arms over his chest. He looked annoyed. "Tell you what," he said slowly, "I'll sell it to you."

Forest's stomach tightened. "What's your price?"

"I want…"

Forest held her breath unsure what she would, or wouldn't, refuse.

"Let me touch your face," he said quietly.

Forest exhaled. "My face?"

"So I can know what you look like."

"Syrus, have you forgotten I'm a shifter? My appearance changes with my whims."

"I haven't forgotten. I just want a mental image of you, even if it's wrong."

She had no idea that he was lying, that he already had a mental image of her, and that it was artifice so he could get his hands on her again.

"All right."

Syrus moved toward her slowly, but in such a way that had her backing up until her butt hit the edge of the counter. She thought about how she looked at that moment and decided to make a little change before he touched her. She had to stifle the giggle in her throat as she quickly enlarged her forehead and nose so that she looked grotesquely bizarre.

He raised both of his hands and lightly touched both of her cheeks. Forest's eyes widened as she felt her head and nose shrink back down without her consent. His fingertips ran along the length of her eyebrows, down the edge of her ears, the length of her jaw. She should not have allowed this, she realized violently. Forest closed her eyes as his fingers skimmed her eyelashes. She began to shiver. When his thumb ran over her bottom lip Forest had to grab the counter for support.

"You're beautiful, Forest," he whispered.

He cupped her face with both his hands again as though he meant to kiss her, and rested his forehead against hers. His eyes reflected like silver mirrors. All the color drained from Forest's face. A small-strangled gasp escaped her throat. She pushed him roughly away, sprinting to her room.

"Forest?" he called after her.

She locked the door behind her and slid down it to the floor. Now she knew, now she understood. In the reflection of his dead eyes, she saw her true form. Syrus was her destined life mate. Everything that had happened between them made sense now. They had bonded the second they had kissed, but their connection was incomplete and out of order. Had he not been blind, their first and strongest connection would have been made the second they had made their first eye contact.

Syrus knocked lightly on her door. "Forest? Are you all right?"

"Yes. I'm fine," she said, trying to keep her voice steady. "I just need a minute to myself. I'll be right out."

"Okay."

Forest held her head in her hands. What was she going to do?

Well she knew one thing she was *not* going to do. She was not going to tell Syrus. He might suspect it given that they had forged one connection already. Forest could have kicked herself for that, but she couldn't deny that she had wanted to kiss him. She thought about the stories she knew about people who had rejected their life mates and the ramifications of that decision. There were other stories of those who had made eye contact with their life mates, like in a crowd, and because of circumstances, had never been able to meet each other. The stories always talked of the pain that was involved. Well, Forest would just have to deal with it. Pain was her daily companion. She was used to it.

But what about Syrus? What about the pain it would cause him? Forest didn't want to think about it. The thought of his pain added a coating to hers. In one instant, she had transformed from a reluctant and occasionally surly guardian to one that would give her life without thought or hesitation. She made a firm decision right there that she would do her job to the best of her ability and when they reached the wizard, she would abandon him before his sight returned. Yes, that was exactly what she would do.

Forest took a deep breath and stood up. Regardless of the emotional turmoil she was in, they had to leave now. She rested her hand on the doorknob and hesitated. She had to act as if nothing had changed. She had to act exactly the same way she had been. No, that wasn't right. She had to be more defensive than ever. She couldn't let him in any more than she already had. She was really worried about how she would respond to him now that she knew what he was to her. She didn't know how strong that instinct would be, and if she was capable of fighting it for long.

Syrus was waiting for her by the front door, pacing back and forth. He was barefoot, like always, in light stonewashed jeans, and she was pleased to see that he had figured out how to get the pull over on by himself. She watched him from her doorway as he slid his arm through the straps of his backpack, anxiety emanating from him. He turned his head toward her as she came out. "Is everything okay, Forest?" he asked mildly.

"Yes. I'm trying to think it through, make sure we haven't forgotten anything important. You seem to be missing something vital."

Syrus' hand immediately went to the flask he always had on his belt. His face relaxed as his hand closed around it. "What have I forgotten?"

She smiled. "Don't you feel a little off balance?"

His expression told her he had no idea what she was talking about.

"You'll have a hard time killing anything unfriendly without your weapons."

Syrus' cheeks flushed as he turned back into his room to get his two short swords. Forest strapped her own pack on, and when Syrus came back out, he had his swords on his hips.

"All right," he said loudly, pulling his shoulders back and lifting his head up trying to shrug off his embarrassment. "I'm ready to go."

The sunrise was clawing its way to the horizon. Forest locked the front door behind them, armed the perimeter alarm, and gave one last loving glance at her property before they passed through the gate and into the world.

10

Tension hovered in the air of the Onyx Castle. The upper hand was being fought for with whispered orders and skilled manipulation. Queen Christiana was using her influence with the ogres in her service to try to undermine the King as much as possible.

Zeren, unable to veto the vote taken in the council, held a private meeting with the squad set to retrieve Syrus from Forest's care. There he appointed Redge to lead the bogus mission. Giving authority to Redge was Zeren's ace in the hole. Christiana could cause plenty of trouble, but Zeren squeezing Redge into the mix had trumped her best scheming.

Moments before the squad left the castle, Zeren met secretly with Redge.

Redge came quietly into the dark room and inclined his head to the king. Zeren strode up to him and grabbed him by the shirt. "Do what you have to," Zeren said desperately. "Give them a chance. You spoke to Kendel?"

"Yes, my king. He's with us. Forest and Syrus should be on their way now. I will delay as much as I can without invoking recalcitrance within the squad. We will track and protect them."

Zeren eased his grip on Redge and smacked him once on the back. "Good. Good." His eyes seemed to lose focus. "I have a premonition about this, Redge. It's the strangest thing. I feel that Syrus is on a great precipice. He must be allowed to finish this. I feel there is more than his sight on the line. Does that make any sense?"

Redge thought back to the night that Syrus left. There had been something elemental in that room as soon as Forest had come in. "It makes sense, my King. I feel it too."

Zeren backed away from Redge and began pacing back and forth. "You're the best of them, Redge."

"Beg pardon, your highness?"

"Syrus doesn't consider you a servant. He thinks of you as a brother."

"Yes. And I him."

"You have the End of the Bridge, just in case?" Zeren asked.

Redge pulled the chain with the little red transparent ball on the end of it out of the front of his shirt. Zeren nodded and Redge tucked it back in. "I've never used one before."

"It will only work once and you must not open it unless there is no other alternative. Keep it hidden, and if luck is with us, you will bring it back intact." Zeren waved his hand in dismissal. "Go and keep your eyes open and your ears pricked. Remember Syrus is the future of Regia."

Redge bowed and quickly left the room.

****

The hooded messenger trudged into Philippe's apartments. With a small flick of his finger, the servant closed and locked the heavy doors, leaving them alone. The mole never came herself, she always sent sacrificial messengers. Philippe took a deep drink from a large goblet before standing up and approaching the messenger. He pulled the hood back and hissed, his lip curling in disgust at the female vampire. She gave him an equally disrespectful glare. Philippe stepped back from her and reseated himself.

"What crime did you commit, girl, to receive so great a punishment as to be sent to me?"

"Theft," she answered curtly.

"You must have stolen a great treasure, tell me what it was."

"Some of the queen's jewelry."

Philippe barked out a laugh. "Stupid girl."

He narrowed his black eyes at her. Her skin was the color of warm cream, and Philippe thought she looked soft. Her platinum hair was wrapped and braided intricately around her head, her large amber eyes filled with insolence, and her pouty crimson lips twisted in a sneer. She was dressed plainly, but Philippe wasn't fooled. He recognized the evidence of breeding. Maybe he'd keep her for a while after he retrieved the information she had for him. He hoped he wouldn't have to torture her to get it. Not that he minded torturing, but vampires always seemed to fight longer than most.

"Are you prepared to deliver your message?" Philippe asked.

"I am."

"What forms of torture would you prefer me to use to get the whole truth out of you?"

A small smile flashed through her sneer. "None, I'm sure."

Philippe barked another laugh. "I know *that's* the truth."

The young woman lifted her arm, raising her hand towards him. The light glinted off the large gold ring set with a glowing orange stone. The ring was ornately carved and the stone gave off its own light, pulsing and flickering. Philippe gazed at it blankly. After a moment, she realized he didn't know what she was showing him.

"It's a collar," she said emphatically as though he were a halfwit. "I have no choice but to tell you the truth and deliver the entire message."

Philippe rose from his seat and grabbed her hand. His eyes danced with the flickering light of the stone and obvious greed.

"Give me the message."

"The time is close at hand, but do not be hasty," Her voice was flat, the words coming from her mouth like an automated recording. "The alliance between the Elves and the Vampires could undo all you have worked for. Zeren has a sting in store for you of a personal nature. Integrate the shifters; they will bring your killing strike. The Ogre's are creating new weapons. I am working to destabilize from within. Gagnee can be trusted, but Frost is a traitor. Do as you like with the messenger, and keep the collar with my complements."

Philippe paced in front of her as she talked, running his rough fingers through his beard. When he turned his lupine eyes on her, she held out her hand again, and the collar verified that she had finished her mission. The glowing stone turned as colorless as glass and slid easily from her finger. She sighed as Philippe took it from her, relived to be free of the cursed object.

"What's your name?" he asked.

"Netriet."

Before she could blink, he grabbed her, threw her over his shoulder, and carted her upstairs. She wished he'd have killed her. As soon as he dumped her back on her feet and grabbed her roughly by the shoulders, she made the mistake of screaming. His fist efficiently knocked her unconscious.

A wave of nausea rolled through Netriet as she regained consciousness. The room swam before her blurry eyes. The taste of blood was in her mouth and throat. She gingerly touched her face. Her nose was broken, and her lips were split and puffy. A generously sized knot throbbed on the back of her head where she assumed she'd smacked it against the floor after Philippe had punched her. Shock and indignation flared in her gut at the abrupt memory. She might be worth nothing, but she had never been brutalized like that before.

Netriet was sure Philippe had any number of unspeakable plans in mind for her, and she was equally sure that she would rather take her own life. She stood up slowly. The empty room swirled around her. A heavy chain pulled on her wrist. She looked down at it. He'd leashed her to the wall.

The night sky beckoned her through a wide-open doorway. It led out onto a balcony. The length of her chain allowed her to step out into the thin open air, but didn't stretch far enough for her to look down. Still, she knew that she had never been up so high.

****

Kendel spent the second consecutive day ghosting around Fortress' castle. He was extremely stiff from standing in a corner all day. It had been a fair few years since he had spent this long of a time invisible. He was certain there was a mole inside Fortress, and he was going to do his damnedest to find them out. Unfortunately, he couldn't fully dedicate himself to the task because he still had regular duties to perform.

Kendel thought about Forest as his back achingly melded into the stone corner. Was she safe? Was she as uncomfortable as he was at the moment? Had she lost her temper and beheaded the future king? He wished he could contact her. And for the first time, he hoped she knew he was thinking of her, wishing her well. He wished she had been around the castle the last few days, because he knew she would have found playing with the new vampire weapon prototypes entertaining.

11

"Just let it go, Syrus!"

"I don't see what the big deal is."

"Yeah, well, you wouldn't," Forest spat.

"Don't start with that 'cause you're a vampire' crap again."

Forest bit down on her lip. "Fine, why don't we just stop talking altogether?"

Syrus was quiet for a minute. "Why don't you just tell me why you hate vampires so much?"

"Like I told you before, it's because of what they've done to me."

"I like how you're able to generalize so elegantly. It's the mark of a true bigot."

"If you think I'm going to rise because you call me names, you're wrong."

"Racist, prejudiced, blinkered, narrow-minded, intolerant, unfair…"

"Let me know when you run out of synonyms."

Syrus was quiet again for another minute. "Seriously, Forest, why can't you tell me?"

"Just let it go," she said again.

"No."

She huffed out a breath. "The way it started is my business, but after that, I never met a vampire who swayed my bad opinion of the entire race. There."

"So, you're saying that you've never met a vampire you liked?"

"Yes."

"Until you met me," he said triumphantly.

Syrus ducked just in time as whatever she'd thrown at him went whizzing past his head. Forest wanted to stop up her ears as he laughed at her.

"Well, maybe the word 'like' is wrong. Infatuated, obsessed, madly in love with. How do those fit?"

Forest stopped walking and faced him. "What are you doing?" she demanded in a quiet voice.

"Just seeing how susceptible you are to the power of suggestion."

"Stop it."

"Ha! I must be getting to you."

"Please! Please stop it!"

The obnoxious grin on Syrus' face vanished, and he was instantly sober and contrite. "I'm sorry, Forest. I'm just really nervous."

"So you're way of dealing with anxiety is turning into a complete jackass?"

His lips twitched into a small smile. "I guess so. I'll knock it off. I just have a hard time not talking when I'm nervous."

"Here, maybe this will help." Forest pulled her MP3 player out of her pocket and thrust it into his hand. "Can you follow me without your hearing?"

"I'll try. I think I can manage it."

Once Syrus had put in her ear buds, Forest walked at a slower pace for a while. He murmured and hummed along to the music but mercifully ceased talking. Forest was so emotionally distraught she felt like she had ripped in two. One half of her wanted as much distance from Syrus as possible. The other half wanted to burrow under his skin. And she wanted to beat her head against the nearest tree until she blacked out, because both halves of her were equally strong and equally demanding. She was so relieved when he had stopped talking and yet had mourned the loss of his voice, annoying as it was.

The beginning of their journey had passed easily enough. Forest decided to keep off the roads, knowing that decision would cost them time, but it maintained the low profile. The terrain was amiable for the first few hours, but now it was starting to become rocky as they began to ascend the oblique hills that would take them behind Kyhael, the elf city.

Forest's eyes constantly wandered over her shoulder to look at Syrus. Every time she looked at him, she hurt. Her eyes ached for his, and a white-hot sting would snake and snap inside her core, not to mention her scars. Every time her heart would clench for Syrus, she would swear she could feel Leith's teeth sinking deeper and deeper into her scars. She turned her eyes back to the ground, and her two halves started arguing inside her head.

You're pathetic! Stop looking at him!

I'll look at him all I want. He's mine.

He's not yours, and he never will be.

No. He is mine . . . and he never will be.

Looking at Syrus when she should have been paying attention to where she was stepping, Forest stuck her foot right in a hole. Syrus caught her by the hand as she stumbled. Neither one of them said anything. Syrus smiled companionably at her and gave her hand a little squeeze. It was as easy as breathing. He continued to hold her hand, and she allowed it. He continued to hum along to whatever he was listening to, his face casually relaxed as though holding her hand was completely natural. Forest could feel her heart running into her hand, and she would have sooner cut it off than let go. They passed the next hour without saying a word. His thumb ran back and forth over her wrist, and tears slid silently down Forest's cheeks.

****

Redge stalled as his men shuffled along in formation behind him. He could see Forest's wall in the dense trees ahead. How long could he draw it out? Were Syrus and Forest far enough ahead of them that they could follow without interference? Redge held up his hand and the troop stopped. "There," he said, pointing out the wall for the rest of them to see.

The troop moved ahead until they reached the wall. "How do we get through the gate?" one asked.

"We don't need to," Redge said. "They aren't here. Use your nose."

Every vampire in the troop took a communal sniff.

"So what do we do now?"

Redge turned and gave his men a stern look. "We follow them."

****

Forest insisted they take a break in the afternoon. They rested under a large tree and shared a snack. Forest tried not to think about how Syrus had held her hand all that time and then abruptly let go of it as if she had an infectious skin disease. She told herself to stop being stupid about it and it was nothing to feel injured over, but since it had happened, she now skirted around him, careful not to touch him at all. They moved about each other like magnets of the same charge.

Syrus drank from one of his bottles and was now absentmindedly eating fruit loops out of a sandwich bad. Forest ate a granola bar and drank a personal sized carton of coconut water as quickly as she could, wanting to get moving again.

"How much progress have we made?" he asked, talking for the first since she'd given him her MP3 player.

"Not that much, and we aren't making anymore sitting here."

Syrus smiled nastily. "Is that your charming way of saying, 'Syrus, get off your butt.'?"

"As you like it."

Syrus chuckled and put everything back into his backpack. They headed off, continuing up the rocky hills. Forest hoped that he would go back to listening to music but she had no such luck.

"Do you think it will be difficult to locate Maxcarion once we are in the Wood?" he asked.

"I don't know."

"Have you ever met him?" he asked.

"I don't know," she said again flatly.

"Do you think Philippe is aware that a wizard is living the Wood?"

"I don't know. Why don't you listen to music and stop asking me questions?" she said testily.

Syrus was quiet for a while, but when she looked at him, she noticed that he hadn't put her ear buds back in. The terrain was getting worse, and both of them were beginning to feel physically taxed. An hour passed in silence, and Forest was feeling more and more uncomfortable. She thought about trying to begin a conversation just to break the tension but found there were no words in her. She would open her mouth hoping to say something trivial and close it again, at a complete loss. Maybe Syrus wasn't bothered by the silence. His face remained impassive, but she could see the weight of his thoughts under the surface.

Two more silent hours passed, and the evening began to blossom over their heads. The only bonus Forest could see to them giving each other the silent treatment was that they traveled much faster. If they kept a steady pace, they would reach Kyhael before the moon achieved its zenith.

****

That night, Lush knocked lightly on Zefyre's back door the way he used to when they had been more than just colleagues, and the memory made him irritable. She opened the door and gestured silently for him to enter. She quickly shut and locked the door behind him, and without a word, walked into her living room. The house was dark, and he might have felt disoriented if he hadn't been there in the dark so many times before. Zefyre's house was large and simply styled in the old Elfish tradition. She had never been happy living in the capitol city, mixed in with all the other races, so she modeled her home to resemble the one she had left back in Kyhael.

A few candles flickered around the living room, and Zefyre sat down on her flat uncomfortable couch and motioned for him to take the chair opposite. Lush's irritation ratcheted up, and he dropped into the seat with a huff. She was trying to manipulate him, and the fact that she could only made him surlier. He wasn't going to let her dictate this...meeting or whatever it was. He knew she was about to play hostess and offer him refreshment or something; he was in no mood for pleasantries.

"So, what do you want, Zef?" he asked aggressively.

She raised one eyebrow and gave him a look a mother might give to her naughty child. "Would you like something to..." she began.

"No!" he snapped.

She *tisked* at him and gave him a small sneer.

"You asked me to come here, now what do you want?"

"I want in-depth details about the new weapons the Ogre's are designing."

His face wrinkled up into a *what the hell* expression. "You have details on the weapons the Ogre's are making. Or were you daydreaming through the last council meeting?"

"Oh no, I was paying attention. Paying enough attention to know that the information at the meeting was patchy and more a dance of misdirection. I want to know what is really going on in the bowels of the Onyx Castle."

Lush leaned back in his chair and gave her a momentary piercing look before shrugging nonchalantly.

Zefyre's eyes flashed at him, and he felt a little surge of pleasure that he had angered her.

"Don't feign ignorance. I know you are in Queen Christiana's pocket."

Lush smiled. "And why shouldn't I be? It's warm and comfortable in her pocket."

Zefyre merely hissed at him.

His smile broadened. "Jealous?"

Zefyre let her face go blank, turned her head to the side and yawned theatrically.

"You've turned into some sort of traitor, haven't you?" he asked.

She didn't respond.

"I should report you."

Zefyre threw her head back and laughed heartily at him. "Don't waste words with stupidity. You know you can't threaten me. I'll win any blackmail game you want to play, and you know it. Now tell me what I want to know."

Lush crossed his arms over his chest. "Everyone's entitled to have secrets," he said dismissively.

They looked at each other like two hostile opponents over a chessboard. Lush could give her the information she wanted without feeling too guilty. He wanted to know what she was up to and feeding her intelligence made them partners. He smiled suggestively at her. She wouldn't get what she wanted without a little give and take. "All this is just a ruse, isn't it Zef?"

"What are you talking about?" she demanded.

He gave her a very hot stare. "You know what I'm talking about."

She returned his heat with ice. "That's over, Lush."

He ignored her rebuff. "So you want to know about the new weapons. Anything else?"

"I want to know if Forest and Syrus were stopped."

Lush stood up. "I'll tell you anything and everything you want to know, but not in here."

"Huh?"

Lush jerked his head towards her bedroom.

"No. I told you that's over."

He chuckled deep in his throat. "Now who's being stupid? You can't really expect me to tell you secrets in bed without first getting into bed."

****

The night was mature when Forest finally glimpsed the pale glowing light of Kyhael. She had not laid eyes on it for many years and had forgotten just how beautiful the straight Zen-like economical lines of the city made of Belliss stone were. Its golden glow made the weary traveler feel peaceful and welcome.

But the warm welcome feeling was deceptive. Kyhael offered the best of Regian tourism to the supper wealthy and maintained a strictly neutral policy on racial background. If you could pay the price, you were welcome. However, beneath the posh, elite surface, Kyhael harbored a meticulously cold and cruel sect of Elves called the *Rune-dy*. The ideology and practices of *Rune-dy* laid a foundation of fear in the other races and was the reason Elves were essentially the most feared race in Regia. The *Rune-dy* perfected the elements of torture and mastered the twisting of science.

Forest found a good place for them to spend the duration of the night. They made camp on a ridge, sheltered by trees, high above the city. "We'll rest here and continue at first light." It was the first words Forest had spoken to Syrus since midday, and they felt thick in her mouth.

Syrus merely nodded, took off his backpack, and sat down on a fallen tree. Forest was cold but they couldn't have a fire, it was too risky. She unrolled her sleeping bag on the ground, thankful she had access to human camping gear. Syrus drank from one of his bottles before tucking into a rice crispy treat. Forest climbed into her sleeping bag. She wanted to sleep a while, but she didn't want to ask Syrus to take the first watch. She watched him finish his dinner, wishing she could come up with some small talk, extend him a verbal olive branch.

He must have been cold too because he began rummaging through his backpack until he pulled out a zip-up hoodie. Forest hadn't paid much attention to what she packed for him because she would have made anther selection. When he pushed his arms through the sleeves and turned his back to her, she let out a burst of laughter that she had to stifle with her hands over her mouth.

Syrus spun around to face her, startled by her outburst of laughter. "What?" he demanded.

The irony had broken through Forest's tension. "You're wearing a *Team Jacob* sweatshirt."

"I'm wearing a what?"

Forest continued to laugh. "I didn't pack it for you on purpose, I swear."

"Is there a reason I shouldn't be wearing this? What is *Team Jacob*?"

"A fictional werewolf."

"Wait a minute. Are you telling me that I am wearing some kind of support werewolves affiliation symbol?"

"Yeah. It's a human thing though. I wouldn't worry about anyone spotting you in it."

Syrus gave a low growl before unzipping the sweatshirt and tossing it aggressively on the ground.

"Hey!" Forest protested. "I'm just letting you borrow that. It's mine."

"Oh. I'm sorry." His voice dripped with false honey. Syrus picked the sweatshirt back up, wadded it into a ball, and then threw it at her, hitting her in the face. "There you go."

"Jerk," Forest said under her breath. "I guess I'm not the only bigot around here."

"I'm not a bigot." He was insulted. "They are our enemies. I don't care if anyone saw me in it or not."

"You could turn it inside out."

Syrus folded his arms over his chest and sat back down on the fallen tree.

"Fine. If you'd rather be cold."

"I would," he snapped.

Forest stuck her own arms in the sweatshirt and zipped it up.

"Hm. It's nice and warm," she said sleepily. She nestled down in her sleeping bag, her eyes going heavy.

Syrus' angry voice broke through her drowsiness. "Don't tell me you're wearing that?" he demanded.

"I am. It's nice and cozy too. Thank you."

Syrus was instantly on his feet. "Take it off!"

"No."

"I'll not travel with a guardian who displays love for werewolves on her person."

"Syrus…" she said slowly like she was reasoning with an angry four-year-old. "I don't care where your support and sensibilities lie, but in case you have forgotten, I am half Shape shifter. Shape shifter's have a natural camaraderie with werewolves. Not unlike vampires and ogres. If you are going to try and form opinions for me and tell me…"

"You're only trying to provoke me!"

"So what if I am?"

Faster than she could blink, he rushed to her and grabbed her by the front of the sweatshirt.

"Hey!"

"Take it off!"

The next second they were in a full-on wrestling match on the ground. He was unquestionably stronger and heavier, but Forest could slip through his grasp with limberness and a few well-placed cheap shots. Grunts, curses, and dirt flew into the air. Even with Forest's ability to evade Syrus' pins, he had almost managed to remove the sweatshirt.

"Ha!" he said triumphantly as soon as he had it in his grasp.

Forest scrambled to her feet as he jumped away from her, sprinting towards the edge of the ridge, laughing manically. She was right on his heel but she wasn't fast enough.

"Don't you dare!"

"Woops!" he said loudly as he threw the sweatshirt over the edge.

"Oh, you *Turkey!*"

"What did you call me?"

"A Turkey."

"Oh, you've bought it now! I don't know what a turkey is, but I don't like the sound of it."

Forest's eyes widened. "No!" she yelped as he grabbed her and threw her over his shoulder.

Forest clamped her mouth tightly together to keep the squeal of laughter inside as he spun in a circle. Thoroughly dizzy, he set her back on her feet. She swayed and giggled like a drunk and crashed into him. He grasped her tightly. She wrapped her arms around his waist, waiting for the ground to stop moving. Her equilibrium righted itself after a minute, and she no longer needed support, but still she hung on. His grasp eased and changed from a simple offer of support into an intimate embrace. Forest shivered as his hands moved up her arms, over her shoulders, and down her back.

"Forest?" he whispered.

She tipped her head back, and all remaining traces of fun were forgotten. The sensation of the pulsing of blood through the veins in his hands as his palms moved on her back was making her feel dizzy all over again. Logical thought was a drowned-out whisper as instinct screamed, *take what's yours!* Forest's eyes rolled back in her head as his mouth came down on hers. The whole forest around them seemed to go up in flames. Passion, in such intensity it bordered on insanity, burned through their veins.

The whispering of logic fought for a stronger voice, and Forest heard its desperate warning. *Let go now! Let go or you'll lose yourself entirely!*

She had no idea how she mustered the strength to pull away from Syrus. She turned her head to the side and placed her fingertips lightly against his mouth. His hands on her back clenched into trembling fists.

"Please." He whispered, his lips moving against her fingertips.

"I'm sorry."

Syrus sighed, and his tense muscles eased in a kind of agonized defeat. Forest laid her head against his chest. "I'm sorry for being mean to you earlier today," she said.

Syrus didn't say anything but refused to let go of her.

"I do want to be friends, Syrus."

"I don't."

"What?" The pain was clear in her voice.

"That's not what I meant. It's not that I don't want to be friends, I just don't think we ever will be. Why is it so hard with you, Forest? Why do you make me hurt so much?"

With his arms around her, Syrus could feel tension roll up her body as tears began to run from her eyes. He felt frustrated that she was crying. He knew she had feelings for him, but he couldn't understand why she held them back like she did. He assumed it was partly because of the vast difference in their stations. He could tell her all day long that it didn't matter to him, but he knew it mattered greatly to her, so it would always be a barrier between them.

Then there was his other suspicion that there was someone else, but he tried to push that thought away, because when he envisioned another man with his hands on Forest, the urge to kill filled him. He wished he could chuck both of their issues over the edge of that ridge as easily as he had that silly sweatshirt. He wished he wasn't the prince. He wished he could kiss her, and she wouldn't run away or bash him over the head for doing so. Syrus wished a lot of things around Forest.

Forest heaved a great sigh and let go of Syrus. He followed her back to their messed-up campsite. She shook the dirt out of her sleeping bag and climbed back inside. Syrus fumbled around with his bedroll until he had it laid out neatly next to hers. "Are you sleepy?" he asked climbing inside his sleeping bag.

"I was before that little incident we just had." Forest lay on her back looking up into the sky. The aquamarine moon was covered over with thick clouds. The only light that existed now was the dim glow that emanated from Kyhael far below them.

"Can we talk?" Syrus asked tentatively.

"Of course. Why do you feel the need to ask?"

"Well, you weren't so nice about it earlier today. Minus the time I was being a, what did you call me, a jackass?"

Forest snorted. "That's it. I'm sorry I was rude, minus the time you were being a jackass."

"Obviously."

"What do you want to talk about?" she asked.

"Asking questions was what got me into trouble last time. Why don't you start?"

Forest turned her head to the side and looked at him. He was on his back as well, his face turned to the sky, his useless eyes open. Forest's fractured heart pulled inward like a fist. More than anything, she wanted to give him back his sight. Even if she never looked into his black pearl eyes once they were healed. Just to know that he was whole, with his power fully restored, that would be enough. She hoped.

Okay, she thought seriously. He was always asking her questions about herself because she never told him much of anything. Maybe it was time to let something loose. Because they would never really be together, she wanted to share some of herself with him, just little tokens, like pieces of broken shells.

Forest sighed, thinking about where they were and decided what she would start with.

"I have never set foot in Kyhael, even though I have all the rights and privileges of citizenship passed down to me from my father. I have often had the desire to see it because of the way people rave about it, but I can never seem to bring myself to go. My mother never understood why I didn't use my elf background to my advantage. She thought it was because I hated my father for abandoning us, but that wasn't it."

"Was it because you thought it would hurt her feelings?" Syrus asked.

"No. I *didn't* want to hurt her feelings, but my real reason was because I felt it was too big of a risk for me. I don't know who my father is. All I know is that he has some rank and power. It was my greatest fear that he may be a priest of the *Rune-dy*. I mean what if they wanted to study me?

The *Rune-dy* commit unspeakable acts in the name of science. I have always been afraid to go to Kyhael and have my father take notice of me. Through the course of my life, the only thing he has ever done for me caused me more harm and pain than anything else I have had to endure."

"Sending you to Academy," Syrus stated in a low voice.

"Yes...I don't hate the fact that I'm half elf, but I chose to hold more closely to my shifter roots out of love for my mother, and also because I was raised in the shifter community. As I grew up and my social circle widened, I began to realize that the shifters were more accepting of me than the elves ever would have been. The shifters have suffered persecution at the hands of every Regian race with the exception of the Ogres. Ogres don't persecute anyone."

Syrus chuckled lightly. "No they don't," he agreed.

They were both quiet for a few minutes. Forest could feel her weariness falling back onto her. Syrus rolled onto his side, facing her, and propped his head up on his arm. "So what is it like, being a Halfling? I say *Halfling* with no disrespect." He added quickly.

"What do you mean, what is it like?"

"Well, you have gifts from both sides right?"

"Yeah."

"Do your gifts clash or compliment?"

"Well, there are drawbacks to not being a full blood shifter, because I cannot ever shift completely. My eyes are always the same, no matter how hard I try to alter them, so I'm always recognizable to those who look close enough. My ears too. I can shift my ears, but they give me trouble and are constantly changing back to their natural shape without my realizing it. I'm not hindered in regard to my inherited elfish ability to become invisible, but sometimes when I'm in battle, I'll shift when I mean to vanish, or vanish when I mean to shift. If I am afraid or stressed, it takes more effort to control what I'm doing. I never slip up when I'm calm."

Forest yawned deeply.

"Get some sleep, Forest," Syrus said warmly. "I'll stay awake and keep watch over you."

Forest was about to thank him when Syrus reached out and gently stroked the side of her face. She bit down on her quivering bottom lip and rolled onto her side, facing away from him. After a few minutes, she fell into the restless sleep of the aggrieved.

Syrus lay still as a stone listening to the faint beating of Forest's heart. His own heart and mind twisted into various knots as he thought about the things Forest had told him. It was the first time she had been truly open with him and it both thrilled and saddened him. His mind replayed every conversation they had ever had, and that amazing core-jolting kiss they shared after sparring, and lastly, the momentary passion a few minutes ago. She would give him mere seconds of vulnerability and then strike out at him violently or run away. The gravitational pull between them was making him demented. Not only did he want to touch her, knowing it would hurt if he did, it hurt not to.

There was no noise in the forest around them. Syrus didn't have to think about listening for danger; it was as natural as breathing since he'd lost his sight. As the night wore on, he began to feel relaxed and tired. As his mind became hazy, he lost his edge on his own physical self-control. He had given no thought to touching her while she slept, but that awful gravity was relentless. He only realized that his hand was about to grab a hold of her arm when he felt his mage power pulsing from his palm. He couldn't bring himself to pull his arm away. He kept his hand an inch above her, not making any physical contact, but his energy extended out and ran back and forth over the length of her arm. The pleasure and relief this small innocuous act brought him was staggering.

Syrus tottered on the brink of completely losing his head and turning the innocuous act into something entirely different when Forest rolled onto her back and whimpered as though she was in pain. She was still asleep, and Syrus realized that she must be dreaming. As more of an experiment than anything else, he reached across her and lightly ran his fingertip over her lips.

She whimpered again and then she spoke. "Don't..." Her voice came out in a whisper. "Please...don't force me...please..." She moaned and her voice became louder and stronger. "No...no...I won't beg..."

Syrus grabbed her shoulder to wake her up. She moved faster than he knew she could, and he found himself pinned under her, his arms trapped under her knees and a knife under his chin. "Touch me again without my permission and I'll have your head, Sucker!" She snarled in his face.

"I won't! I promise! I'm sorry! I only touched you to wake you up. You were dreaming."

Forest's eyes were glazed. She wasn't coherent. The cold night air and a bad burning smell brought her to her senses. She blinked down at Syrus under her, his face twisted in shock and pain as her silver plated knife touched the skin on his neck, burning him.

She pulled it back and jumped off him, mortified. "Oh! I'm so sorry. I was dreaming."

"I know," he said acidly.

Forest burned with humiliation. "I should have told you not to wake me if I appeared to be dreaming."

"Yes, you should have," he snapped.

"I'm sorry," she said again.

"Well, now that you're awake—" he said, lying back and zipping his sleeping bag up to his chin "—it's your turn to keep watch. I'm going to sleep."

Syrus fell asleep thoroughly pissed off and thinking that he'd never met a woman that was this much trouble.

12

Zefyre knew ending up back in a relationship with Lush was a possibility when she decided to solicit information from him. Knowing didn't ease the irritation she felt. Using herself as collateral was distasteful. On the other hand, she couldn't deny that she'd missed him a little since she'd kicked him to the curb. She'd learned many secrets from him that were to her advantage, but now he was growing nosy. He pushed and pushed until she was ready to garrote him, but eventually she caved and told him her purpose. He was her accomplice after all.

Lush propped his head up on one arm, lying next to her in bed, a look of amusing shock on his face. All remains of arrogance and pleasure were gone as his mouth hung open stupidly. She knew he was about to implode, and it could take a long time for him to calm down, so she jumped out of bed and put on a brocade robe. If he shouted and she felt the need to shout back, at least she wanted to respect herself enough not to get dragged into a naked shouting match.

She waited, but he just continued to lounge there in her bed with his mouth hanging open.

"Can't you think of anything to say?" she demanded.

"Well…well, you've turned my world on its head, and I'm having a hard time adjusting to your vision of the future."

Lush sat up and began looking around for his clothes. Obviously, he also considered this conversation too important to have naked. Zefyre went to the kitchen, poured herself a drink, and sat back down on the living room couch.

A few minutes later, Lush surfaced from the bedroom fully clothed and sat down across from her. He crossed his arms over his chest and gave her a calculating stare. "You're going to try and sell me this scheme aren't you?"

"Of course," she said lightly. "You're already a party to it by feeding me information. You might as well subscribe to the ideology."

"So you've been feeding intelligence mixed with disinformation to Philippe via sacrificial messengers?"

"Yes."

"In an attempt to control the outcome of the war?"

"Yes." Lush was quiet for a moment, piercing her with his eyes and scratching his chin. "To what end?" he asked aggressively.

"To destabilize the Vampires *and* Werewolves; causing enough chaos to shatter all forms of existing power and government, so we can begin anew. A republic, Lush! Can't you imagine it? Initially under the stewardship of the *Rune-dy.*"

"*'Under the stewardship of the Rune-dy,'*" he repeated with a disbelieving tone of voice. "Why the *Rune-dy*? They've never showed any interest in power, and they terrify everyone."

"That's why. You just said it. They aren't interested in power, yet they have more than anyone else in Regia. They have just chosen not to use it to make any changes."

"Until now."

"Yes," she said, "until now."

They sat staring at each other in silence for a minute.

Lush narrowed his eyes at her. "You've been playing both sides a long time, haven't you?"

She gave a deep sigh. "Yes. A very long time."

"You were playing me back when you used to tell me you loved me," he accused.

Her eyes flashed. "No! I might have manipulated you at times, but what woman doesn't? When I expressed feelings for you, I meant them."

"Sure. I'll just take your word for it," he said sarcastically.

"Oh, don't go acting all injured. You used to revel in the fact that we could never make our relationship public."

Lush sulked, but he was mulling-over her vision of the future. Being a vampire, he naturally enjoyed that vampires were in power, but he was a politician. Under the crown, he could only advance as far as his bloodline would allow. He saw how he could emerge as a more powerful leader in a new republic. Nothing made him more drunk than the prospect of power, except Zefyre. He was in. There was just one thing he needed squared away before plunging ahead.

"What if we're caught? Who takes the fall?"

"Well that depends on the timing," she explained. "If we are caught and it looks like we are trying to help the wolves gain power, then Frost and Gagnee will take the fall. If things have progressed further and the Elves come under fire, then Kendel will be framed as the mole."

"Why not throw Forest into the fire with him? Anyone could believe she was a conspirator."

"No!" Zefyre said firmly. "She will have a bigger role to play in the new world."

Lush sneered contemptuously at the thought of Forest having any power. "Says who?" he demanded. Zefyre smiled nastily at him. "Her father."

****

Netriet had been sitting on the stone floor for hours, her knees pulled up to her chest. She was hungry, thirsty, and freezing. The only bright side she could find at the moment was that she was alone. Philippe had not come back to his bedchamber since he'd dumped her here. The doors leading out onto the balcony stood open. Thin icy wind blew continually around the vast room. The altitude made her feel loopy, and she suspected she had been unconscious longer than what would have been natural because of it.

She had no real sense of time, but since it was night again, she assumed she was coming up on her second or third day there. Having nothing else to occupy her, Netriet had set her mind to memorizing every nook and cranny of the room, but she made sure to touch nothing. From what she knew about werewolves, she was astonished that they had allowed Philippe to be their leader. However, seeing as he was the leader, why had no one assassinated him? She'd noticed that he wore a cape made from the dead when she had arrived, and the room she was in had the pelts of the dead on the floor like a rug. Why was this tolerated? Netriet was careful not to walk on any of them.

Philippe burst into the room so suddenly Netriet screamed, startled. He carried a large torch, and he began to light the darkened ones in the torch brackets around the room, laughing loudly at her outburst of fear.

"Honey, I'm home," he bellowed.

Netriet pulled her knees up higher and wished she could slide through the cracks in the floor.

"You might want to think about sewing those pretty lips closed," he said. "I don't like screaming, as I demonstrated to you yesterday." He looked over at her face for a second. "Yes. I broke your nose, from the look of it."

Netriet said nothing and averted her eyes. She almost whimpered in relief when he closed the balcony doors, shutting out the cold. The torches began to heat the room, and the warmth felt heavenly. She watched Philippe with a wary eye. He took off his disgusting cloak and threw it over the back of the chair in the corner before sitting down. He gazed at her intently from across the room. His insistent look made her feel examined and violated.

"So, don't you want to know how my day was, Rita? Or whatever your name is."

"Netriet," she answered flatly.

"Ah yes. I think I'll call you Nettie. Does that suit you?" His politeness frightened her.

"Yes...my lord," she said quietly. "That suits me fine."

He scratched his beard. "I'll tell you plainly, I'm not yet sure what I'm going to do with you."

Netriet shuddered.

He stood up abruptly, his chair scraping against the floor. She cowered into her knees as he came towards her . . . but he didn't touch her. She glanced up quickly to see him pull a rope next to the door, sounding a loud bell. He walked past her and seated himself again.

In the next moment, the door flung open, and a buxomly she-wolf came into the room carrying a tray of food and a large tankard. She set them down, curtsied, and received a hearty slap to her backside for her trouble. As she turned to go, she spotted Netriet in the corner and stopped dead in her tracks, her eyes round with shock. She made a strangled little gasp and turned back to face Philippe.

"What is the matter with you, wench?" he demanded.

She seemed to have lost her voice and merely pointed at Netriet.

"Yes, I know there's a vampire in my room. If you would have looked closer you would have seen that she is chained. Don't worry she's no assassin. She's nothing more than a new pet."

The serving wench's mouth hung open and her eyes continued to bug.

"GET OUT!" Philippe roared so loudly it seemed like a gust of wind blew from him, blasting back the wench's hair and flattening her skirts to her legs. She scampered out and slammed the door behind her.

Philippe sighed and took a deep drink. Netriet watched him as he began to eat. Her stomach rumbled. She was taken aback by his manners; he ate his food meticulously and with poise more refined than any vampire noble she'd ever seen.

"Do you think I was too hard on the wench?" he asked her.

"Not at all, my lord. A serving wench is for serving and nothing else, unless she is told so directly. I'd have thrown the insipid creature over the balcony."

"Would you have?" Philippe asked before barking out a laugh. "I think I might like you. Here." He threw a hunk of bread to her as if she were a puppy waiting for scraps.

Netriet had to stifle feelings of being gravely insulted. She was trapped, at least for the moment, and it was better if she amused him. She knew he was capable of unspeakable acts, and the worst thing for her to do was incur his anger. Not without difficulty did she swallow her pride—it was large and dry and seemed to be lodged in her throat—but she had to swallow her pride before she could swallow that bread.

When Philippe had finished his dinner, his eyes became cloudy, and he stared at the ceiling. Netriet got the impression he was plotting or daydreaming. The last thing she wanted was to disrupt him and bring his attention back onto her. She made a point to sit as still as she could and even to breathe quietly. Then he really startled her by beginning to sing to himself in a low mumble. She thought she couldn't understand the words because he was singing so low, but then she realized that she had no hope of understanding the words because he was singing in a language she had never heard before. After a few minutes, she realized that he must have been singing in French. She'd heard the rumors.

When his song was over, he leveled his eyes on her. She looked at the floor. He stared at her for a long time. Finally, he stood up again and walked to the balcony doors. He leaned on the doorframe and gazed out at the night sky. "It's too bad for you that you weren't smart enough to not get caught," he said.

"I'm sorry?" she asked.

"You told me you were a thief."

"Ah, that. I hate the queen. She looks so petite and innocent, but behind that façade is a cold, calculating monster. She always had it in for me. She'd humiliate me in public. So I thought I'd teach her a lesson and take her favorite thing. I pried the central diamond off the front of her crown and sold it for next to nothing to a merchant."

"You're an interesting creature, Nettie."

"When I was found out, it was my confession of the amount I received for the diamond that did more damage to me than anything. I knew the price would piss her off something terrible, but I stupidly believed I'd get out of it with some light punishment, not a death penalty."

"Yes. I also misjudged the weight of a crime once, a long time ago, before I was Philippe." He turned around to face her, a small smile on his face. "That wasn't always my name. Did you know that?"

"I guessed as much. It's not a werewolf name. It's French, right?"

His smile broadened. "Yes. That's right. I ran away to Earth after being convicted of a crime and sentenced to death. I settled in Paris and thrived for many years."

"Then why didn't you stay there?" she asked.

"Ah, well, pretending to be human all the time was rather wearing, and I'd been spotted too many times in my beast form. The humans began hunting me. They are terrible hunters, for the most part, but occasionally an alpha human would surface and give me some trouble."

Netriet began to feel a cold dread spreading through her stomach. She didn't want to hear his tale, but she was in no position to stick her fingers in her ears and loudly chant *la, la, la, la, la!*

"Philippe was the name I had assumed on Earth. Seeing how I wanted to bring Paris back with me, I decided to keep it. In any case, I had to reinvent myself if I was going to come home. My real name still carries a death sentence. It is a pity, for my father gave me a strong wolf name. Do you want to be the only living creature in Regia to know it?"

"Yes and no, my lord."

He chuckled at her. "My real name is Mach."

"Why would you tell me? Why risk so much?" Netriet asked.

"There is no risk. Dead vampires tell no tales." He gazed out of the window and was silent for a time. "To be honest, which is something I have not been in such a very long time, I'm lonely," he said quietly. "I haven't actually talked to someone openly since before I killed my mate."

Netriet watched the back of his hulking figure as he told her his secrets.

"Her name was Tarrin. She was an awful bitch, but she came from a prominent family, and mating with her gave me status. She was too stupid to realize that I'd targeted her. She actually believed I loved her. Well, that and my French accent used to drive her wild." Philippe turned around abruptly. "What do you think about that?" he demanded.

"Like you said, she was stupid. A woman with a title must never trust a suitor with none."

He narrowed his eyes. "Yes. You would not have made such a mistake."

"I should say not!" she said emphatically.

He threw his head back and laughed again. "Thank you for the conversation," he said sincerely. "Power is a frigid mistress." Philippe strode back to his chair and sat down, dropping the relaxed friendliness and looking at her now in a calculating way. "So, now I'm wondering what other information you might have that would prove useful to me?"

Netriet straightened her sore spine. She had been forced to tell him the message by the collar, but she had no intention of telling him anything else. She didn't know much anyway. She was not a traitor to her own kind. The elf was the mole. If she ever escaped, the information she had would cause quite the stir. However, she had to use her head in dealing with Philippe.

"If I knew anything dangerous or secret I wouldn't have been chosen to be a messenger."

Philippe scratched his beard, again giving her that intense stare. "That may be. But I must find out for sure. And…" He pulled the collar out from his pocket. "I need to learn the knack of this object."

Netriet froze inside. Wearing the collar had been the single most awful experience of her life. She hadn't even considered that he would put it back on her. The elf had known what she was doing; he had no idea how to make it do what he wanted. Well, it looked like after some intense pain, she would be spilling her guts anyway and then dying.

All that night, Netriet's cries of pain reverberated through the mountain.

****

Kendel paced a rut in his sitting room floor. He didn't like how complicated his life had become in the course of the last few days. His house was darkened and the only light in the sitting room came from the flickering fireplace. When Kendel's secret guest opened the door and walked into the room, he had to remind himself that it was an honor. Situations that were supposed to make him feel honored and important always made him feel queasy instead.

King Zeren dressed plainly and discreetly in a black hooded cloak. What amazed Kendel was that he was completely alone. There wasn't even a single guard standing outside. Secrecy was all well and good, but the king was being downright reckless.

"What have you learned?" Zeren asked without preamble.

"Our suspicions have mostly led me to more suspicions, my King. There is a mole within Fortress though I have yet to learn their identity. But they are a large spider and have been threading Fortress with their web for a long time. I catch tail ends of web and then it turns to smoke in my hands."

Zeren sighed. "Is there anything that you can tell me for sure?"

Kendel began to shake ever so slightly. He took a deep steadying breath before plunging ahead. "The hit on Syrus five years ago was not contracted by Philippe."

"What?" In the dim light Kendel could see the king's jaw clench.

"No, my King. The hit was contracted by a member of the *Rune-dy*."

Zeren looked like he'd been slapped in the face. But the shock quickly gave way to rage.

"I don't yet know if the *Rune-dy* as a whole is responsible, it may have been a rogue action."

Zeren's flashing eyes stared deep into the fire. "This gives me much to think on," he whispered, and without another word he turned on his heels and left.

13

Kitch had gone past his patrol boundaries, venturing out until the dim light of Kyhael was only a speck in the distance. His mind wandered in the darkness. Patrol was a terrible, boring nuisance. Nothing ever happened in his area or time block. No one traveled through the area at this time of night. It was protocol that he remained invisible for the duration of his watch. He didn't mind that, it made it easier to imagine he was somewhere else. Kitch knew the area backward and forward; the ground, the sounds, and the scents were familiar. So when an out of place scent flew up his nose, he had to stop and smell carefully before allowing himself to be shocked and confused.

Forest held her head in her hands, her embarrassment refusing to go away. Syrus lay sleeping next to her. She couldn't believe that she had jumped on him and burned his neck. She also had the awful feeling of exposure, knowing that she had been dreaming about Leith and maybe she had mumbled something in her sleep. She hoped desperately if Syrus heard anything it was unintelligible.

Forest groaned. She was suffering from such a backward emotion she felt stupid once she recognized it. She didn't want Syrus to know about Leith for many reasons, but mostly because it felt like she was cheating. The stupid part was that she felt she was cheating on Syrus with Leith instead of cheating on Leith with Syrus. Preoccupied by her thoughts and feelings, Forest didn't sense the presence looming in the distance.

She gasped as Syrus sat upright like someone had stabbed him with a cattle prod.

"What is it?"

"Stay here," he ordered and bolted off into the darkness before she could say another word.

Being invisible didn't hide Kitch from Syrus. Kitch smelled the vampire, but he was more than a little taken aback to see him charging at him through the dark. Syrus skidded to a halt in front of Kitch, both his swords drawn.

"I know exactly where you are, elf," Syrus said in a deadly tone. "If I kill you while you're invisible, do you think anyone will ever find you?"

Kitch took a step back, wanting to put more distance between him and this deranged vamp. "Whoa! Let's calm down! I'm just on patrol. It's my job to intercept any travelers in this area and question them. Please lower your weapons. In case you didn't know, our peoples are allied."

Kitch exhaled as Syrus lowered his swords to his sides. He surveyed him carefully. He was certainly dressed strangely and the crop of his hair would suggest that he was a servant, or even a slave. He emanated a powerful aura that caused Kitch's suspicion to percolate, but he knew that just because someone might have no social standing didn't mean they lacked in strength of spirit. Kitch judged that Syrus was of no importance and should be allowed to go on his way. But he was bored and decided to question him thoroughly. "All right." Kitch tried his best to sound authoritative. "What's your story? Why are you traveling through this area with two companions?"

Syrus crumpled his brow. "I have only one companion."

"I'm in no mood to play. I can smell them. You left an elf and a shifter behind."

Syrus smiled at him. "No. There's nothing wrong with your nose, but what you are smelling is a Halfling. Half elf, half shifter."

"*Really?*" Kitch was angry with himself for sounding so juvenile and eager. He tried to pull his voice back to stern. "Okay. Why are the two of you out here and where are you going?"

"Ahh…" This was the moment that they needed a cover story for, and they didn't have one. Forest had talked about coming up with one, but that was all that had been said on the subject. Syrus decided he would go with whatever popped into his head. "Well, we are running away. Our families will never accept us and starting over in a new place is the only way we can be happy."

"What are you talking about?" Kitch ordered.

"She's my life mate."

"Oh…yes, I see how that would be a problem."

Forest, who was listening to their conversation, felt like she was now the one who was stuck with the cattle prod. Did he know, or was that the only lie he could think of on the spot? Either answer made her stomach twist.

"So were you going to try and settle in Kyhael?" Kitch asked.

"No. We really don't know where we'll end up. We just want to avoid the fighting."

"You ought to take refuge in Kyhael. All elves have citizenship. You said your life mate is half elf?"

"Yes, that's right," Syrus said.

"Call to her. I want to see her… I mean meet her."

Forest was about to move out from her sheltered spot so the invisible elf could eye her when Syrus' voice took on a diamond hard edge, freezing her in her tracks.

"You want to see her, eh? Goggle the freak, is it? Make her feel bad about herself and who she is? You've never seen a Halfling before I bet, and now you just have to get a good look. Well, you and your insensitive ignorance can go climb up a slimy tube."

He was so forceful, Kitch took another step back. "All right, all right. I'm sorry. I'm curious, I admit it. And you're protective of your mate, I get it. My apologies. It must be very hard for you to deal with."

"You have no idea how hard it is to be the mate of the most beautiful creature that ever lived. I constantly have to fight others who want her for themselves. You'd probably be no different than the rest of them."

Kitch was at a loss for words. This vampire was clearly unstable. He didn't like emotionality. He would be within his rights to kill him, but he disliked fighting emotional people and this jealous, angry, lovesick vampire on the run was a knot better left untied. Kitch began moving away. "May you fare well in your travels," Kitch said, not taking his eyes off Syrus.

Syrus waited until the elf had gone a good distance. He sheathed his swords and made his way back to Forest. The elf was still looming in the distance, watching from afar. Syrus knew his performance was not yet over, and he could trust Forest to mess everything up by sniping at him or threatening to hack him to pieces.

He could feel the tension radiating off her body as he approached her. Before she could do or say anything, Syrus grabbed her, hauling her up onto her toes, and planted a thorough kiss on her mouth. She was clearly shocked for a second before she caught on and relaxed against him. Then she seemed to explode.

Forest climbed Syrus like a tree and attempted to eat him alive. He almost toppled under the weight of her passion. All of his thoughts of putting on a little show for the elf were now nonexistent. There were no thoughts in his head, only a desperate feeling that begged to be realized and validated. He clung to her with the full strength of his life force, attempting to absorb her. She pulled him along in the smoldering darkness, consuming him from within. Everything inside him rolled and purred luxuriantly… then she yanked away and jumped down. She may as well have doused him with cold water as she had days before when he'd asked to drink from her.

Syrus stood still, waiting for his senses to stop spinning, while she efficiently packed everything up. She thrust his backpack into his chest, and he shrugged it on grudgingly. No one had ever made him feel the way Forest did. He wanted her so much the desire was turning him into an idiot. He wanted to kick things and pitch a fit like a toddler who was denied what they wanted.

"Let's go," she said and began walking.

Syrus followed a stride behind her with a nagging desire to kick her in the butt. He waited to speak until the elf was too far away to be sensed.

"What was *that*?" he demanded.

"You kissed me for the elf's benefit, right?" she asked flippantly.

"I was only trying to lend a little credibility to the lie."

"And I was trying to help. I don't know, do you think I was convincing?" she asked with mock innocence.

"Oh, I'm sure he bought it."

"Do you really think so?"

"Yes, dammit."

"That was a really bad thing to happen though," Forest said seriously. "I hope that elf doesn't run his mouth when he reports back in."

"You're afraid your father will catch word that a half elf was traveling through the area?"

"Yes. Exactly that."

"Do you plan to live your whole life without ever searching for him?" Syrus asked.

Forest thought about his question for a while. "I really don't know."

All that morning, Forest tried to remind herself to enjoy this time with Syrus. If they were successful, they would reach the boundary of the Wolf's Wood that evening. The Wood was vast, and she had no idea how long it would take them to locate the wizard once they were inside. She also knew that they would have to fight for survival there. If they weren't killed or captured, she had less than a week left with Syrus. She had to make the most of it; it would be over all too soon.

The "pretend" kiss that morning had all but wrecked Forest. She was still able to resist, but the internal battle of instinct vs. intellect was growing desperate. Her intellect drew straight and harsh boundary lines, while instinct crept behind, blurring them.

****

Kitch was relieved when Forest and Syrus were out of his patrolling area and no longer his concern. He was so used to coming across nothing and no one that the event of meeting such a loony vampire was enough excitement to last him for a long time. But as the sun brought the day, Kitch received an even greater shock.

He was just getting ready to head home when an entire platoon of vampires tromped into his jurisdiction. His mind raced through all the reasons he could think of why they would be there. Kitch wisely decided to keep still and invisible and let them pass. They moved silently and in perfect formation. Kitch recognized the seal of the Onyx castle on their armor and realized that he had been suckered. The Vampire and the Halfling were important enough to be pursued by royal troops. He'd screwed up big time. Unless it was a massive coincidence—he doubted that. In the interest of job preservation, Kitch decided that he would report about the vampire and the Halfling and leave out the troops on their heels.

When Kitch entered Kyhael, he went directly to the office to report in. He cringed as he entered because Susa sat at the front desk. It wasn't that Susa was overly bad tempered, but she gave Kitch the creeps. She stayed indoors too much, and her skin was a rather unusual and sickly shade of yellow. Her eyes were overly large and red, and she never blinked. But the thing that bothered Kitch the most about her was that she ground her teeth while she filled out reports. The sound always made him envision her gnawing on his bones.

When he entered, she looked up at him with her unblinking eyes and gave him no expression whatsoever, as though she was nothing more than a lifelike automation. "Reporting in from duty?" she asked in monotone.

"Yes."

She scribbled his name and information quickly with her stylus. "Report?"

"Ah, well uneventful from dusk till the third hour of morning when I came across a pair of travelers."

"Race?"

"The race of the travelers?" he asked stupidly.

"No, footrace. Want to have one later?"

"Huh?"

She sighed. "Racial background of the travelers?"

"Oh, well, one of them was a vampire and the other was a Halfling."

She stopped her scribbling and looked up at him. He shuffled his feet and looked away.

"Why didn't you bring them to the city in custody?" she demanded.

"They didn't seem very important. He was a servant; they were just running away from family members that wouldn't accept them as life mates."

"I see. What was the Halfling?" she asked.

"Uhh... I think if I remember correctly, she was half shifter and half...elf...yeah that was it."

For the first time that he'd ever witnessed, Susa blinked. She stood up abruptly and snatched the paper she'd been writing on. "I'll be right back. Don't move! You hear me? Don't move!"

"All right. All right."

Kitch waited, a cold dread sweeping over him like a fever. Susa wasn't gone long. When she came back, she had Prefect Camber on her heel. Kitch swallowed loudly, swearing elegantly in his head. Camber was a high profile gofer, the *Rune-dy's* go-to-guy. He smiled at Kitch in his official *I'm trying to put you at ease* smile. Kitch wasn't comforted.

Camber walked over and placed his hand on Kitch's shoulder as though they were good friends. "Kitch, so good to see you! How's everything at home?"

Kitch found it hard to un-stick his tongue from the roof of his mouth. "Uhh. Fine. Just fine."

Camber slapped him companionably on the arm. "Good. Good man. So, I'm going to need you to come with me. Nothing to worry about, I assure you, just routine."

Routine, my ass, Kitch thought. He had no option but to do as Camber bid. He followed him past Susa's desk and through a long hallway with many open doorways leading off to offices dedicated to the menial jobs and workers. He had interviewed in one of those rooms, but he had never been deeper than this level. Camber led him through a narrow passage that began to snake downward. The Belliss stone walls and floor gave off enough light to make the passage feel warm and safe, an incongruity, because Kitch knew that just being in this tunnel was the opposite of warm and safe. He began to feel dizzy as the tunnel continued to spiral downwards. They must be very deep under the city, but the light was getting brighter. Yet again, the light did not comfort him. They were drawing close to their destination. Hair standing on end, cold sweats, and dangerously close to losing the contents of his stomach, he followed until the passage birthed him into the antechamber of the *Rune-dy's* council room.

Camber turned and gave him an intense look. "Wait right here. I'll be right back."

Kitch nodded, unable to unclench his teeth.

The wall in front of them curved out like a huge bowl. A small circle of light shone through the stone, and Camber placed his palm directly over it. The circle began to grow, quickly becoming larger than Camber. Kitch's mouth fell open as Camber walked right through the stone in the beam of light. He hoped whomever he had to talk to would come out and that he wouldn't have to walk through the stone. The light shrank back to its original size.

Camber had said he would be right back, but it seemed to take him ages. Kitch worked to keep his breathing steady. He hadn't done anything wrong. No one had told him to apprehend any Halflings he might come across. The failure lay with someone else. He was ignorant. The *Rune-dy* couldn't punish him for ignorance. Why did they care about Halflings anyway? Did they want to begin experimenting on them? Kitch shivered as he imagined what the *Rune-dy* might do in such an experiment.

"Kitch!" Camber had returned, his voice pulling Kitch from his reverie. "You can go in now. For your own sake, I recommend you answer his questions succinctly and say nothing else. Don't babble or elaborate and don't even contemplate lying. Stand at an appropriate distance and don't fidget. And for goodness sake, close your mouth."

Camber placed his hand on the light again and stepped back as it began to grow. Kitch made no move to go through once the light was large enough. Camber got behind him and began pushing.

"Wait! Who am I seeing?"

Camber pushed harder and on a grunt said, "Rahaxeris," as Kitch was forced through.

The domed chamber was awash with warm golden light. Circular skylights dropped pools of sunlight on the floor. Kitch stood directly underneath one and looked up into it. They were so far under the city that the sunlight had to travel down a long straight tunnel to reach them. If he squinted, he could see the sky at the end. He was terrified, but the light of the Belliss stone coupled with the sunlight made him feel peaceful, as if it held him in a loving embrace.

Seven stone chairs curved around the wall in front of Kitch. All were empty, except one. Rahaxeris sat in the tallest chair in the center of the others. Kitch froze like a small animal in the hypnotic gaze of a snake. Rahaxeris looked as though he too was carved of Belliss stone. His skin was the same alabaster color as everything in the room. His eyes were a golden hue, and his blonde hair hung straight down behind his shoulders and looked soft, a stark contrast to the sharpness of his face. Of all the races of Regia, Elves had the most angular features, but none more than Rahaxeris. Everything about him—his face, his hands, his eyes, his voice—were all deadly sharp, as though he had been born for the singular purpose of inflicting pain.

"So…" Rahaxeris' voice was quiet, but Kitch still winced. "Tell me about the travelers you encountered last night."

Kitch tried to clear his throat, but it felt like a jagged rock was wedged in his windpipe. "Uhh. Yes sir." *Be succinct.* "Sometime around the third hour I encountered an unusual scent: Vampire, Elf, and Shape Shifter. I was invisible, but the vampire came charging right at me as though he could see me, brandishing two short swords, and spitting threats at me."

Rahaxeris' remained expressionless. "Did he look like a master of the Blood Kata?"

"No. He was dressed strangely. Clothes like I have never seen, and his hair was so short, I took him for a servant."

Rahaxeris sneered, and Kitch wanted to run away as fast as he could. "A servant who can sense the location of an invisible elf in the dark? Not very observant, are you?"

Kitch looked at his feet. "No sir."

"Tell me the rest."

"I asked him his business. He said that he and his companion were running away from their families to start over because they were destined life mates and would never be accepted. I told him I could smell two others but he told me I smelled a Halfling."

Rahaxeris didn't move, but Kitch could tell he had come to the information that interested him most by the glint in his eyes.

"Are you sure of what you smelled?"

"Yes, sir. Elf and Shifter, I have no doubt."

"What did she look like?"

"Uhh…well I didn't get a good look. I wanted to question her as well, but the vampire made a fuss about it, said I was just wanting to ogle the freak, or something like that."

"Did you believe his story?"

"I did watch them from a distance. They were very… amorous."

Rahaxeris sneered again. "Voyeur?"

"No! No sir. Not at all!" Kitch spluttered.

"Is that all? It was just the two of them?"

Camber had warned him not to lie, but what would happen if he told the truth? He could feel that his life hinged on the decision he was about to make. Truth or lie? Or was it too late and he was damned regardless?

"Yes, sir, it was just the two. I encountered no one else last night."

"Are you quite sure?"

"Ah…yes." Kitch's voice was weak.

Rahaxeris stood up. He moved forward with a slow precision. Kitch had the urge to run as he approached him.

"Don't look so nervous, my boy. You're not in trouble." Rahaxeris gave him a reassuring pat on the shoulder.

Kitch exhaled so loudly his breath came out in a whoosh.

"How long have you been working for us?" Rahaxeris asked.

"Oh, umm, under a year, sir."

"Keep up the good work, and you'll have a bright future. I can tell. You have a curious nature—I value that. I bet you're just busting with questions, aren't you?"

Kitch smiled easily, thinking now that he'd been silly to worry he would be punished. Rahaxeris was taking a liking to him. He would have major bragging rights with his friends that night. Kitch envisioned himself sitting in one of those stone chairs before long. He was making friends in high places.

"Oh, yes sir! I have lots of questions."

"I bet one of your many questions is why I care about a random vampire and a Halfling? Am I right?"

"Yes, sir. I'd very much like to know that."

"Well…" Rahaxeris lowered his voice conspiratorially. "Can you keep a secret?"

"Most definitely, sir," Kitch said enthusiastically.

Rahaxeris leaned closer to Kitch and whispered. "The Halfling is my daughter."

Kitch's eyes widened in terror as Rahaxeris grabbed him around the throat. His long, razor-sharp finger nails stabbed deep into Kitch's neck, and he collapsed to the floor choking on his own blood.

Camber stood at attention as Rahaxeris came through the light door into the antechamber. "Ah, Camber, clean up the mess in there." Rahaxeris pointed to the small light beam on the wall.

"Yes, sir. Will I need to send a fabricated story of how he died to his family as well?"

"Yes. A simple story, Camber, for a simple man."

Camber nodded. "I did warn him against lying, Sir."

Rahaxeris clicked his tongue in response.

"Was his information useful? Shall we pursue the travelers he let go?"

Rahaxeris smoothed his hair and straightened his robe. "No. There were no travelers. He lied."

14

Forest choked as her heart stilled and refused to beat again. The werewolf behind her had her arms pinned in a grip she couldn't break. She'd been so distracted, arguing with Syrus, they'd walked right into an ambush. Where were all of her quick lies now?

One of the three wolves recognized her, and she had understood enough of their broken French to know that they planned to take her to Philippe, but they were going to kill Syrus.

The afternoon sunlight glistened on the amber pelt across the wolf's hulking shoulders as he knocked Syrus to the ground. He couldn't win. They had already injured him badly. She couldn't tell the extent of the damage to his right leg, but he couldn't put his weight on it. All three wolves were barking and laughing and taunting him. All their noise turned into a loud buzzing in Forest's ears. She couldn't watch Syrus die.

Forest tried to come up with a plan, even if it was nothing more than something to cause momentary distraction to the wolves, but nothing would come. *Come on, Syrus, think of something*! He rose from the ground, breathing heavily, totally disarmed. The two beasts circled around him; they'd been tag teaming him from the start. Forest recognized the gleam in their eyes. The moment had arrived. Both wolves lunged forward. Syrus knocked one of them back, but the other seized his arm in its shark-like teeth. He shouted in pain, the sound echoing inside her heart. The other wolf jumped back up and caught his other arm. They were going to tear him apart.

"FOREST!"

"SYRUS!"

" I'm right here."

Forest was panting and tears spilled from her eyes. It was dark, and she felt Syrus gently breathing to her left. She looked at the moon overhead and remembered where they were. They were camped at the edge of the

Wolf's Wood. She'd been dreaming. She looked over at Syrus. He lay next to her on his side, facing away from her. The moonlight fell along the planes of his back, and she couldn't think to stop herself. She scooted up to him, laying her cheek against his shoulder blade, gripping his arm tightly with her hand, and cried. Her chest quaked against him, her tears fell on his back.

Syrus went rigid under her touch. Given the experience he'd had with her dreaming last night, he thought it best to remain as still as possible until she was lucid, if not wiser to guard his sensitive areas in case she was about to attack. He waited for her to let go of him. It was only when her tears soaked through his shirt that he realized she was completely awake. He was perplexed as to what to do. Maybe he should just do nothing and wait until she had cried herself out and embarrassment set in and she'd turn back into the Forest he was familiar with.

"I thought I lost you," she whispered so quietly he almost didn't hear it.

She'd been dreaming about him, and now she was crying on his back. He slowly rolled over so he could ask her what she had dreamed, but he never got the chance. As soon as he faced her, she fused her mouth to his. He sucked his breath in, shocked. Her lips were throbbing and hungry and tasted of tears. The pain that always came with touching Forest was sharper than ever.

Syrus pulled back, wishing he could see her face. "What are you doing, Forest?"

"Uhh...Your dreaming, Syrus."

Syrus' face was set in irritation, and Forest began to come back to her senses, but she didn't quite make it. The next second Syrus was smiling the widest imp smile she'd ever seen.

"Oh, well, in that case."

He pulled her against his chest, his lips now intense and demanding. Within seconds, Forest drowned in sensations. He quickly and efficiently removed her from her sleeping bag and pulled her over him. The cold night was heating up around them and Forest was just going to let it happen, throwing caution to the wind. Her jacket went flying, and her shirt was about to join it when Syrus moved his lips to her neck, kissing the top of her scars. Pain sliced all the way down the length of her scars, and deep as the bone. She jumped as though she'd been startled and looked around guiltily as if Leith might step out from behind the nearest tree.

Syrus reached up to pull her back to him. She put both of her hands flat on his chest and pushed away.

"What?" he asked bewildered, his mind still in the bogs of desire, trying again to bring her back to him.

She pushed harder. "No!"

He exhaled in plain exasperation. "This is the worst dream I've ever had. You are the biggest tease I've ever met."

His words stung deep, and she moved off of him. "I…I'm sorry. It wasn't my intention to tease you. I just *can't.*"

"Why?"

She searched for an answer that was both true and stretched truth. Syrus rolled on his side and propped his head on his arm. "There's someone else, isn't there?" he asked quietly, hoping desperately that she would say no.

Forest shook her rumpled sleeping bag out and laid down on it again. "Yes," she said aggressively.

She immediately regretted saying it. Syrus sat up, all of his muscles tight and an expression like she'd dealt him a mortal wound.

Forest sighed. "No. It's not that there is someone else… It's not like that."

"There's no one else?"

"No. You…I can't…It's just that I'm not willing to mean nothing to you."

"Why would you ever think that you mean nothing to me? When have I ever given you the slightest impression that you weren't important to me?"

"I won't be your convenience!"

"There is not one single thing about you that's convenient, Forest. Why do you think I would use you? You mean a great deal to me."

Forest's heart flinched at his words, but she shut it down swiftly. "How can I trust that is anything other than pillow talk?"

Syrus' angry expression smoothed out into contemplation. He took a few slow breaths and lowered his head back down. "All right. Come here."

Forest looked sharply at him for a second, and then softened; he just wanted to hold her. She rolled her face away from him, and he moved against her back, spooning her. He smoothed the hair away from her face, tucking it behind her ear and kissed the back of her head.

"Trust is the underlying problem," he said quietly. "I can understand that. Trust runs thin on you, Forest."

They were both quiet for a while. Forest looked at the trees that marked the boundary of the Wolf's Wood repressing a shudder. It had been many years since she had gone in there. It really was the most wonderful and terrifying place in all of Regia. The trees here were three times wider and taller than any other trees in Regia, and they formed a tight line around the edge, like a fence around the Garden of Eden.

Wispy clouds began to slither across the sky, darkening the aqua light of the moon, and a chilly mist crept along the ground around them. Forest shivered. Syrus pulled her tighter against him. "Tell me your deepest secret," he whispered.

"No way."

"Please?"

"Tell me yours," she tossed back.

Syrus sighed deeply. "Not yet."

"Will you tell me something else?" she asked.

"Anything…well mostly anything," he chuckled.

"Why do you have so many scars?"

He took a deep breath. "Oh, well. After I lost my sight, I spent a year in total darkness. I don't mean visual darkness. It was internal, spiritual darkness. I wanted to die. Before the attack all I had to my credit was my title and my vanity; there was nothing else to me. Unable to maintain my arrogance with my disfigurement, I soon became completely insufferable. Redge was the only person I trusted, the only one I'd let near me. And when he wasn't around, I had to keep company with myself. I soon realized that I wasn't even a fit companion for myself. That sounds stupid."

"No, no, it doesn't. Go on," she urged.

"Redge had always been my servant and I considered him a friend, loosely. I used to commend myself on how generously I treated him. As time passed, however, I discovered my idea of generous was little better than bankrupt. When you are as lonely as I was, you come to appreciate company, and Redge was good company. He is better than a brother to me now."

"I'd like to get to know him," Forest said.

Syrus chuckled. "Oh, I think given the opportunity, you two would become fast friends."

Forest's heart gave a little pang as she realized she never would have the opportunity.

"So anyway, I had given up on everything, and it was Redge who encouraged me to take up the Blood Kata again. I wouldn't listen to him at first, thinking it impossible. But as he continued to nag at me, I began to wonder if I could do it again. I eventually caved, partly because I was curious and partly because I was terribly bored."

"Didn't your parents object; afraid you'd get hurt?" she asked.

"I'm sure they would have if they'd of known, but I had been so surly with them after the attack they had since left me alone entirely. Redge set up a place for us to spar in a forgotten area of the castle, where no one would bother or notice. As I'm sure you can imagine I got hurt a lot at first."

"I bet."

"My body remembered how to fight, but I was very disoriented. We trained in secret every day, until I was sure my skill had reached back to the level of master. I was ready to show my father and petition him to send for a lord master to come to the castle to continue my training. My father was pleased at what I had accomplished. He seemed…proud. He agreed to find someone to come. I begged to go to the mountain where all the lord masters train, but my mother wouldn't hear of it. There was a lot of fighting between my parents at that time. In the end I was allowed to continue my training in the confines of the castle and the lord master, Ithiel, was sent for."

"*Ithiel?* The Ithiel? The master that singlehandedly routed the northern wolf pack assassin squad?" Forest asked awed.

Syrus chuckled. "That's him, although that story, great as it is, has been greatly altered through the line of gossip."

"What's he like?"

"He's everything they say he is and more."

"Really?"

"Yeah, he's a major pain in the ass."

Forest laughed lightly. "So, he gave you all those scars?"

"Not all of them, but most, yes. He wouldn't let me stop. No matter how high I climbed, he knew I had the power to surpass him locked inside me. He said he felt it. For a long time I had nothing else in my life but training. Strangely enough, I mastered the knack of shadowing in my sleep. I went to sleep unable to do it and woke up perfectly at ease with it."

"I wish you would have done that when we were sparing," Forest said. "I've actually never seen anyone shadow."

"I'll try and remember that the next time I pick a fight with you." He grunted as she elbowed him in the ribs.

"So how did it actually happen? Becoming a mage?"

"Well, throughout all of the months that Ithiel had been training me, his greatest complaint was my temper. The Kata had given me direction and purpose, but I was still angry and bitter over the loss of my sight. He harped on and on how it would be my undoing, if I didn't harness it."

Forest chuckled. "I've been told similar things in the past as well."

"Yes, but you were probably told to choke it down. Ithiel took a different approach; one that blindsided me. The day my transformation happened began the same way of every other training day. It's really simple actually: focus, forms, then fighting. During my focus, Ithiel did something he never had before; he placed one of his hands on the top of my head. Such strong waves of energy came from his palm and it felt like my thoughts were torn from my brain and pulled into a deep abyss within me. When he removed his hand, it was like waking up from a long sleep. I had never felt so centered.

When I began my forms, again Ithiel did something unorthodox. Instead of doing forms alongside me, he stood opposite and mirrored me. I knew this because my senses were hungry and clawing at the world around me. It was the first time my mind's eye gave me an accurate and detailed picture of what was in front of me, and it was stronger than actual sight. I would have been elated, ecstatic even, but again Ithiel was doing something different that distracted me from my newfound 'sight.' He was stinging me."

"Stinging you? How was he stinging you?"

"With his aura. His aura began to fill the room around us. I began to feel frustrated and flustered. The stinging was not so painful; it was more confusing and irritating. But it wasn't until I finished my forms that he began the real abuse. Usually there was a short pause in our routine once forms were done before we began fighting, but not that day. The second forms were done, he launched at me and struck me in a…ah, a very sensitive area."

"What the hell?" Forest interjected.

Syrus laughed quietly. "That's what I was thinking at the time, only in more colorful language. As you can imagine, anger does not begin to cover it. As soon as I could stand upright again, we began the most aggressive and dirty fight I had ever been in. But not only was he using moves and tactics that were usually reserved only for real life and death combat, he was hurling abuse at me with his words. Ithiel told me exactly what he thought of me, without reservation."

"What did he say?" she asked.

"Ah, well. I'd rather not repeat most of it, but he did call me a coward and an angry baby."

"Why was he trying to provoke you?"

"Because it was what I needed. He worked me into a rage that was so overwhelming, I have never felt the likes of it before or since. Redge, who was watching, said he could actually see the moment the pressure exploded inside me. Ithiel stopped his attack and stood still in front of me. I was going to kill him. Logic was gone, focus was gone, and all that was left was murder in my heart. Even now, I don't know exactly what he did to me in that moment that would have been his death.

"I couldn't breathe. It felt like I had been plunged deep underwater, you know, sort of, compressed. And my hands were clasped around a hot solid surface, a burning, pulsating sphere.

'In your hands is your rage; objectified, weaponized. Use it.' Ithiel said.

"At first, I had no idea what to do. That was all he said. Every other master said to conquer your anger or it will conquer you, and all other sorts of little catch phrases that really are no help. So, after a moment of consideration I decided to act on whatever instinct came to me."

The energy emanating from Syrus as he recounted his memories dazzled Forest.

"I broke the sphere between my hands and the shards absorbed through my skin. I felt it running up through my arms and into my chest and that was where it stopped and collected. I was able to breathe again and there was Ithiel waiting to finish our fight. I had never been able to overtake him in a fight before, but now it was easy, pathetic even. I triumphed over him quickly. He asked for me to help him up from the ground and as I grasped his hands, that was when it happened."

"What? What happened?" Forest asked, totally absorbed.

"Again, I don't know what he did, but…I don't have the words, Forest. I can't describe it. What it felt like to transform, but there was this terrible roaring. It wasn't until later that Redge told me I was the one roaring. Every scar I had achieved in fighting broke open, and I turned red with my own blood. So, Ithiel named me The Sanguine Mage."

Forest was overwhelmed by his story. She was ashamed that she had ever treated him with disrespect. And in awe at the way he had treated her; in awe that *he* needed her. She felt a huge surge of pride; her mate was a powerful mage. And she almost told him right there that they were mates, almost. But she felt unworthy. Forest lay silent in the wake of his story, not trusting herself to speak.

"Are we going to make it in there?" he asked gesturing toward the trees of the Wood.

"Of course," she said quickly.

"I've never been there. The wolves had taken back possession of it long before I was born. As a kid, I was always sore about it. My history tutor taught me all about it though."

Forest snorted. "I bet I know the history better than anyone else in all of Regia."

"That's quite a boast. How could you make such a claim? My history tutor is seven centuries old. He has grandchildren older than you."

"I can make that claim confidently, because I was taught the history of the Wood by someone who has lived there for eons."

"What?"

"When I was a girl, I would often go into the Wood to escape my life. I could go on for hours about my childhood memories of the Wood. On one particular day, I was terribly upset, and I wandered deep into the interior, deeper than I had ever gone before. I found a tree there with an attractive sitting place in its roots. I nestled down there and cried and talked to myself about my troubles. Before long, I accidentally fell asleep with my head resting against the trunk."

"What were you so upset about?" Syrus asked.

"I don't remember."

"I don't believe you, but go on."

"I began to hear a whisper in my sleep. It was such a beautifully gentle voice, like the wind through the trees. When I woke up, Shi was sitting beside me, holding my hand."

"Shi?"

"It's more of a sound than a pronounced name, but I call her Shi for short when I'm not addressing her directly. It's more like, *ssshhh-hhiii* . Like a mother hushing her baby."

"Who is she?" he asked.

"Shi is the ghost of a Dryad. She's the keeper of the Wood. As soon as we set foot inside the boundary, she will know we are there. She may be a ghost, but you do not want to screw with her. I'm the first person she has shown herself to in thousands of years. Being able to call her my friend is the greatest honor of my life. I'm hoping she will be willing to direct us to Maxcarion. "

"That's amazing, Forest! I had no idea there were Dryad ghosts. I can't wait to meet her!"

"Ah…well…there might be a problem with that."

"What?" Syrus asked.

"She, ah, doesn't like vampires much."

Syrus was quiet a beat, his face twisted a little. "Oh how sweet. The two of you are joined forever as sisters in your mutual hatred of vampires. Terrific. I can just imagine it now: You going into the Wood as a girl and ranting for hours with a tree about how vampires suck…metaphorically."

"Don't be a twit. I hated vampires long before I met her; it was just some common ground we share. Maybe if you'd stop being so petulant I might say some nice things about you to Shi if she shows herself to me, and then you could have the chance to meet her."

Forest could tell that under his nasty expression was a strong childlike excitement to meet Shi. Forest could feel her face heating up as she thought about what Shi might think about Syrus. Shi would know everything there was to know about him as soon as he crossed into the

Wood. She would know that he was Forest's mate. How would Shi respond to that tidbit of information?

"What does Shi look like?" Syrus asked.

"A tree," Forest said shortly.

"So, you woke up and the tree-ghost was holding your hand?"

"No you moron, I was resting against her, but she appeared to me in a corporal form. She doesn't appear very solid though. She is so beautiful; I used to wish I could look like her. She doesn't resemble any other race I've ever seen. A woman-tree. She's very tall and skinny, twig-like arms and legs, and her hair is like the dropping branches of a weeping willow."

"What is a weeping willow?" Syrus asked.

"Oh, sorry, it's a tree on Earth."

"I'm glad you don't look like that."

"Why?"

"Because, that might be beautiful, but I don't want to make out with it."

Forest hesitated for a moment unsure how to respond to his remark.

"Umm, anyway Shi became my friend. I spent lots of time with her in my adolescence. She told me all about the Wood's history. I'm just hoping that she will talk to us. "

"Why does she hate vampires?" Syrus asked.

"If your history teacher was worth his salt, you wouldn't have to ask that. It's a long story and one filled with pain, so I'll give you the short version. Your great great great great great grandfather—there are probably more greats in there but you get the picture. Anyway, your grandfather King Leramiun is the one who brought the Dryads to their demise. He was the one who saw the potential lure the Wood could be for his enemies and began to work tirelessly on creating the perfect maze of death. Many Dryads were simply cut down like common trees. Those that were spared were only spared for a different death. Leramiun brought the shadow sand into the Wood. The effect on the unwary traveler was exactly what Leramiun hoped for, but the Dryads ended up being collateral damage. The introduction of shadow sand into their ecosystem made them instant addicts. The addiction was deadly. Shi was the last to die.

"Her prejudice against vampires is perhaps slightly ignorant. She has judged a whole race from the actions of few." Forest was quiet for a moment. "As have I," she added quietly. "Some of you are halfway decent."

"Praise indeed," Syrus said dryly, giving her a little squeeze. "It's going to be dangerous in there, isn't it?"

"Maybe…probably…yes. Yes, I'm afraid it's going to be very dangerous. Are you sure you want to go through with it?"

"Yes, I'm sure," he said. "I don't want to live the rest of my life without ever looking in your eyes."

"Oh, come on," she said annoyed.

"Are you really going to keep up this ruse? I wonder how long you can deny this…this…"

"All right! I admit it. There's something between us. It doesn't mean anything. You'll get over it once your home. I mean really, you're the *prince!* You can't make me your princess. It's ridiculous."

Syrus made a little grunt in the back of his throat. "Don't tell me what to do."

"Okay. I'm done talking. I'm going back to sleep for a little while. Are you all right?"

Syrus chuckled. "No, not at all."

"Are you able to keep watch?" she huffed. "Or are you too sleepy?"

"Go back to sleep. I'll wake you when I feel tired."

"You might want to move away from me now. I might start dreaming again and attack you without meaning to."

His arm tightened around her. "I'll risk it."

It took Forest a while to fall back asleep. Reason told her to pull away and finish her sleep in her own space, but her heart argued that she should relax against Syrus and enjoy this stolen time because it would be an anomaly in her life. Hell, they might die tomorrow. *Pull away! Pull away before this memory just becomes another brick on your wall of pain.*

Forest rested her cheek on his arm and sighed. The stupid sucker made her feel weak. She didn't need him. She just needed to get through the next day or two and get back to her crappy status quo. If Leith could see her in Syrus' arms, he'd kill them both. Well, he'd kill her. Leith wasn't even close to being strong enough or skilled enough to hurt Syrus. That thought alone caused her heart to win over her reason.

Once Forest was back asleep, Syrus relaxed and tried to work through his tangled thoughts. His chest ached against her back. She was so much smaller than he was; taught, formidable, and bitter but she was also soft and fragile; skittish like a small child who had been abused. She had admitted she felt there was something between them, and her actions had confirmed it. But he knew there was still a deeply rooted hatred she had for his kind. Syrus was fed up with not knowing why. How was he to change her bad opinion if he didn't know what direction it came from?

Well, he wasn't going to find out tonight. He sighed contentedly and lightly kissed her hair again.

Forest came awake slowly. The sunlight penetrated through her closed eyelids. How could the sun be up? She opened her eyes and gaped with shock. She was face to face with Syrus, lying in his arms, and he was fast asleep. She jerked out of his hold and smacked him hard on the shoulder.

"What? What is it?"

"Syrus! How could you fall asleep on your watch?" she demanded. "We could have been slaughtered! I can hardly believe we weren't."

"Oh," he said thickly, sitting up and rubbing his face. "Sorry. Holding you made me feel so peaceful."

Forest's mouth hung open. "I...you...peaceful...sleeping..." She spluttered. "How can you just sit there rubbing your eyes like nothing happened?"

"Something happened?" he gasped in mock horror.

Forest was so mad she couldn't speak or even look at Syrus while they packed up their stuff. He acted oblivious to her rage. At the very least, he could have the decency to act sheepish and shamefaced for falling asleep on his watch, but he didn't. He ate his breakfast with the casual nonchalance of a man on vacation. Forest had to keep unclenching her fists as they ached to pummel him.

"Get over it!" he ordered. "I can feel your hate gaze, Forest. I was wrong, I'm sorry. Now can we move on? We're about to enter the Wood and your attitude is far more likely to get us killed than anything I've done. Focus on getting us to the wizard, and you'll be rid of me in no time."

Forest's fists clenched again. She wanted to pummel him for being right. She looked at the tight line of massive trees and sobered. She took a few deep breaths, trying to let go of her anger. She watched Syrus pull his arms through his backpack straps and adjust his T-shirt, the trees at his back. They were here. This was the beginning of the end of their time together. And before she realized what she had done, Forest had gone to him and pulled him into a tight hug. He hugged her back just as fiercely. She knew as well as he did they were trying to reassure each other.

She let go reluctantly. "All right, once we're inside we need to make a beeline for the Heart. The outer rim is the most beguiling, and we'll need to get off the trail as soon as possible. It's good that you're a vampire and immune to shadow sand. It's also good that you're blind; the beauty won't stall you or lead you in the wrong direction. It is a shame, however, that you won't get to see the Heart or the Waterfall of Silverlight."

Syrus shrugged. "I'll see it on the way out. You'll show me, won't you?"

"Of course," Forest said lightly. It was the most awful and painful lie she had ever told.

Forest felt the surge of power through her veins as they crossed through the invisible curtain draped over the wood. She watched Syrus as they entered. He shivered, and she could see his senses pique and roll through him.

"Wow," he said under his breath.

"If you think that's something, wait till we get to the Heart. The power you'll feel there is, well, hard to describe...overwhelming. As we get deeper, you'll understand why the Heart repels instead of drawing. I'm sure Maxcarion will have made his home near the Heart."

Forest's heart expanded as she threw her head back, looking up through the trees, and taking deep breaths. It had been so long, so very long, since she had beheld the beauty of the Wood. She had traveled to some of Earth's most beautiful places, but nothing she had seen there could compare to the transcendent heartache caused by beholding the glory of the Wood.

Syrus reached for Forest's hand. She took it easily. For a few moments, Forest allowed herself to daydream they were doing nothing more than taking a morning stroll. If she wasn't careful, she would fall victim of the hallucinatory power of the outer rim and lead them in circles and probably into the hands of a few wolves. The amount of time that had passed since she had been in the Wood made her more sensitive to its seductive power. The dust particles floating on the air were tainted with shadow sand. It entered her lungs as she breathed, reaching in with soft skilled fingers that tickled and stroked the hidden desires buried deep in her mind.

Forest shook herself, she had almost walked right passed the fallen tree with the branch that looked like a man's arm, where they needed to turn and pass under, off the trail.

"How do you withstand against the sand?" Syrus asked.

"I know where it's concentrated on the ground, so the only problem for me is what's floating around in the air. I have to remind myself to stay focused when my mind starts to wander, but that's about as bad as it gets for me. I think the amount of time I spent here in my formative years gave me some level of immunity." Forest laughed darkly. "Either that or it made me toxic and my system hardly takes notice of it now."

"Did you use it when you were a youth in revolt?" Syrus asked with a little smirk around his mouth.

Forest chuckled. "I'm still a youth in revolt, but no. I've felt its effects transdermally a handful of times. But I only tried snorting it once. One nostril of that stuff was enough for me. Becoming lucid after that was just too depressing. I see why so many become addicted. And I almost fell into it; it would have been so easy. But I had ambitions and being a sand junkie wasn't one of them."

"Before I became a mage, I welcomed any addiction that could grab me. It used to irritate me something fierce that I was immune to sand. I tried it once too, just to see if it would have any effect at all on me."

"Did it?" Forest asked.

"Oh, sure, it had an effect, but it was far from the desired one. Mostly just a lot of sneezing and blowing gritty snot from my nose for the better part of an afternoon."

Forest laughed and had to cover her mouth with her hand. "Don't make me laugh, Syrus! We have to be quiet."

"Sorry."

"The first time I ventured into the Wood alone, I was a child. I got stuck on the outer rim and did nothing but walk in circles for hours. When my mom found me, she said I was totally glazed. I have this fantastic memory of those hours. It's too bad it was only a cluster of hallucinations. I was rather disappointed when I learned that nothing I experienced that day actually happened. Watch your head, Syrus. There are some low branches here."

"So, Leramiun created a toxic, living labyrinth."

"Yes," Forest said. "That is very much what it is."

Shi drifted silently overhead, watching them as they traveled the hidden path she had taught to Forest many years ago. She was bemused by the situation. How could it be that her little Forest was the life mate of the vampire prince? Even though Shi had a fierce desire to talk to Forest, she held back, not feeling she could trust herself to behave the way she considered an ancient should.

Shi examined Syrus thoroughly, grudgingly pleased with his internal makeup. She did not object to him being paired with Forest, except for the fact that he was a vampire. Why did Forest always get tangled up with suckers? She examined the newness of their relationship and their incomplete connection. It wouldn't be incomplete if Syrus knew they were mates, but he was still holding his tongue and keeping his secret. Shi might grow to have some affection for him, but for now, she would remain silent. She would watch over them and keep them as safe as she could.

15

Netriet's cheek pressed against the cold stone floor. Her breathing was shallow and labored. Sweat beads glistened on her forehead and cheeks as she trembled with a fever. Horror assaulted her as the memories of the last round of Philippe's experimentations on her surfaced. In his attempt to master the workings of the collar, she lost her left arm.

She knew the second the collar began to spread its needles and poison through her hand, and she remained silent. Through sheer force of will, she had not cried out when the pain washed through her arm like water running down a pipe. Another few moments, and it would have reached her heart. But no such luck was hers. Philippe noticed just in time and chopped her arm off in one swift slice from the dagger he carried in his belt.

The flesh pulled together quickly over her short stump, her quick healing capabilities preventing her yet again from dying. The last thing she'd seen before losing consciousness had been Philippe removing the collar from the hand of her severed arm. She had thought that at least if that happened again she would have no more fingers and the torturous experiments would be over.

The warm nectar of blood filling Netriet's mouth brought her awake. Through the haze of wounded, feverish exhaustion, she fought to reclaim her wits. Philippe wanted her to regain her strength so he could continue to torture her. Her eyes dragged themselves open slowly and shock roused her further. It was Philippe who fed her from a small cut on his wrist, no low ranking foot soldier or serving wench, but Philippe himself. How could he be so foolish?

Their eyes met, and he smiled knowingly. "Go ahead. Bite me. I can see what you're thinking. It won't work. I won't fall victim of your brainwashing persuasion," he said confidently.

Netriet hesitated, wondering if she should try it anyway. She sank her teeth into his flesh, took one strong pull from his veins, and spat the mouthful into his face. For a long moment, she hoped. His eyes sparkled with rage. Then he blinked and smiled at her, getting to his feet and wiping the blood from his face.

"Still clever, Nettie, even in your physical state. I'm impressed. I'm not going to kill you in a rage, though. And I'm not going to let you die of starvation while I still need you to help me master the trick of that damn little thing."

"A girl can dream," she said feebly.

Philippe laughed, shaking his head. "If only you were a she-wolf. I'd have made you my queen."

Netriet smiled weakly. "Yeah. If only."

Philippe laughed again and picked her up off the floor. To her amazement, he laid her down on his bed and covered her up with a wolf pelt. She was too weak to kick the disgusting thing off so she tried to ignore that she was lying under a corpse. The pelt was warm and soft and she was soon asleep again. She had strange wolfish dreams and the traces of Philippe's blood, still in her mouth, went down her throat, giving her back a small measure of strength.

****

Forest was fighting down the panic creeping up her body. She was unsure if they were lost or not. Had she taken a wrong turn? Syrus waited silently behind her. They stood on the edge of a large clearing that Forest had never seen. The trees appeared to have been cut down recently. This must have caused Shi great heartbreak. They had obviously stumbled upon an area where werewolves frequently gathered. The smell of them was everywhere.

It looked like a place used for relaxation and revelry. The silver river snaked through the clearing, and she could tell where they used it as a swimming hole. The ground was flattened with footprints, paw prints, and a wolf's partially transformed beast prints. Cold fire pits and forgotten or discarded articles of clothing littered the ground. Forest's eyes carefully scanned the entire area. Off to their left was clearly the path the wolves used to travel to and from this spot. They would have to skirt that path at all costs.

Syrus stiffened next to her. She had heard it too—voices approached down the wolf's path. Forest momentarily froze as she considered fight or flight. Running would put the wolves on the hunt and that was the last thing they wanted to happen. Fighting was a good option if they weren't too outnumbered. Hiding was impractical in such close range; the wolves would easily catch their scent. She listened closer, trying, to determine how many might be coming when a familiar voice whispered in her ear.

"Wolves are coming. You must hide, Forest."

"Ssshhhiiiii?" Forest hissed through her teeth.

"You must hide," Shi's disembodied voice said again. "This way."

A light breeze sailed past Forest, lifting her hair. She watched the direction of its wake. Forty feet away, the leaves of a very large tree swayed in the ghostly breeze. It was the only tree the breeze caressed. Shi was directing them to safety.

"Over here!" Forest whispered urgently to Syrus.

They ran silently to the tree. Forest couldn't see how standing behind a tree was all that great of a hiding place. Did Shi want them to climb it? Forest placed her hand on the trunk and walked around it until she saw the concealed opening. The trunk was partially hollow. She grabbed Syrus' hand, and they both squeezed into the tiny crevice hidden in the base of the massive tree.

Forest's heart thundered in her ears. The wolves hadn't spotted them but could this hiding place cover their scent?

"Don't worry," Shi whispered in her ear. Syrus apparently couldn't hear her. "They will smell nothing."

Forest exhaled in relief as she heard the wind pick up and blow their scent away. The dark confined space sandwiched her and Syrus together face-to-face. The pain that lay sleeping in both of their chests awoke and began winding searing ropes around their hearts. Worse than that was the knifing sting within the eyes. Forest winced in pain, and Syrus hissed through his teeth. After a long moment of agony, the pain eased and mutated into a pulling sensation that drew them tighter together.

The two wolves tromping through the area were both in man form and grumbling to each other in broken French. They clearly weren't there doing anything official or stealthy given the amount of noise they were making. Forest strained her ears to catch some of what they were saying.

"Pour quoi suivons-nous Philippe du tout? Il est fou."

"We follow him *because* he's crazy. Do you want to stand up to him? Oh…uh… *parce qu'il est fou. Voulez-vous se tenir jusqu'à lui ?* Did I say that right?"

"Yes. I mean *Oui. Je pense ainsi.*"

Forest was afraid that if she kept listening she might laugh when Syrus captured her mouth in a slow and devastatingly sweet kiss. She barely had enough room to pull her head back from his.

"Are you crazy?" she whispered. "What do you think you are doing?"

He smiled broadly. "Taking advantage of the situation. Duh."

"If those wolves discover us, we may both be dead."

"Exactly my point," he said under his breath and captured her mouth again.

Forest could have protested further, but her heart wouldn't have been in it. So she merely sighed and sank into him. Mortal danger all around, and she couldn't remember ever enjoying herself more than making out with him while squished into the trunk of that tree.

A long time after the wolves had passed them they still had not resurfaced to the world, even though it was perfectly safe for them to do so. Syrus' lips were so tender and intense; Forest could almost feel the folds of her brain unraveling.

"We need to go, Syrus," she said against his lips.

He shook his head back and forth. "I don't think it's quite safe yet," he murmured crushing her mouth again.

"Don't you want to find the wizard? Get your sight back? Kick lots of wolf ass and become the king?"

"All in good time."

"We've been here for over an hour," she protested feebly.

He smiled against her mouth before kissing her deeply again. "And I'm not even close to being finished with you."

"This is ridiculous, Syrus. Let me go."

Her tone had returned to its usual lilt. He sighed in defeat and they both grunted and pushed themselves out into the open again. Forest squinted in the afternoon sunlight. Syrus rolled his shoulders and cracked his neck. Likewise, Forest stretched and took a few deep breaths of fresh air.

Forest looked around, trying to locate the hidden path that the wolves play area had disrupted. They skirted the clearing before getting back on track. The scent of wolves was everywhere, but it all smelled old. Syrus followed her without a sound, and she could feel the outreaching of his senses, scanning for danger in a vast circumference around them.

The day was wearing thin, and they needed to make it to the Heart before they stopped for the night. Forest's body was set in motion like the gears of a clock. She pushed on steadily, though her feet ached and her stomach was empty. Comforted in the knowledge Shi watched over them, and with Syrus so focused on their surroundings, she could move them along quickly, their destination her only care.

As the afternoon moved into evening, Forest's comfort began to slip. The massive trees grew very close together, and their intertwining branches gave off the feel of being under a basket. They had covered a good amount of ground, and she was anxious to keep going, but her stomach was tugging petulantly on her esophagus. Syrus had not made a sound or spoken a word, but she was sure he must need a break as well. She was disquieted that they had met no one and nothing. She told herself not to buy trouble, but her instincts were growing jumpy.

"Let's stop for a minute," Forest said quietly.

"Fine by me," Syrus replied emphatically, shrugging off his pack and sitting down against a tree trunk.

Forest rummaged in her backpack until she found a granola bar. She practically shoved the thing down her throat whole. She washed it down with some Mountain Dew and fished out a bag of gummy bears from the side pocket of her pack. Syrus had finished off one of his bottles and was drinking deeply from another.

"I found some gummy bears. Want some?"

"Oh! Yes please!" Syrus said enthusiastically.

Forest shook her head in amusement as she watched him over-chew the candy before feeling a pang of sorrow that they would be parting soon. She would miss him and the silly little ways he made her laugh. She fought down the urge to hurry them along and decided to take another few minutes.

"Are you excited?" she asked.

Syrus' face went strangely blank. "I can't let myself get excited."

"You're just holding it at bay. You're excited underneath."

"Yes. You're right, Forest. But I'm trying to not be excited. I'm trying not to think about getting my sight back." Syrus leaned his head back against the tree and sighed. "I smell water."

"Yes. We're very close to the waterfalls."

"There's more than one waterfall?" he asked.

"Oh yes. There's the main falls, but if you know where to go, as I do, you'll find a whole network of smaller falls with the most beautiful pools and caves. I like the smaller falls better because they are fairly hidden and provide privacy if you want to take a little dip."

"Hmmm. Taking a little dip sounds really good about now," Syrus said with a little smile.

"Yeah it does. You ready to go? Night will be here soon, and I want to get to the Heart. Maybe we'll find Ol' Maxi tonight."

Syrus got wearily to his feet. "I dare you to call him that to his face when we find him."

"Ha! I've done some stupid things in my life, but I think I'll refrain from adding that to my list."

They began walking again. Again, Syrus stretched his senses out around them; Forest could feel it. It was like walking inside a bubble. She looked back at him and could see the strain around his eyes and in the tightness along his jaw. She continued to glance back at him to see when he would begin to feel the beating of the Heart. She was sure he would feel it before she did. Forest decided to circumvent the falls as they drew near them. If she detoured there, they would not keep going tonight.

The trees pulled closer together. The ground cover became so thick that it slowed them down considerably. They had to walk over many layers of exposed tree roots and twisting vines. It was so compact and jumbled that for the first time since Forest had met him, Syrus truly looked and acted blind. His feet tested every surface before putting his weight down, his hands outstretched around him, groping through the space.

"Why is it like this all of a sudden?" he asked.

"It's the ribcage protecting the Heart. We're very close."

Syrus took another ten paces and stopped short. The protective bubble popped. Forest looked at him. He was feeling it now. His skin covered in goose bumps and his hair stood on end.

"Forest," he whispered, "there's a …I feel…wow…it's like a buzzing through my whole body. The force of it is astounding."

"Just wait till we get closer."

Syrus moved faster, drawn to the Heart like a magnet. As they approached, Forest began to feel it as well, only she didn't feel buzzy. She felt the pulsations like a cold burn that shot right through her with every throb. The trees and foliage were so thick around the Heart that it hid the marvel from sight, until you were right upon it. She was sure Maxcarion would be close.

Forest spotted the Heart and paused, watching the black flames dance. She had feared it would be so. The last time she had seen the Heart, the flames had been green. Regia's heart was manifesting sorrow. Syrus stood next to her and took her hand.

"Describe it to me, Forest."

"Oh, well…" She said rather breathlessly. "There are twenty trees of the Heart and they stand in a perfect circle around the manifestation. The trees are all identical, and they are all as clear as crystal so they look like they are made of the fire they protect. Their leaves chime the music the manifestation bids them. Do you hear it?"

"Yes," Syrus whispered reverently. "It's heartbreaking."

They stood there hand in hand, silently experiencing the personal affects the Heart had on them. Forest began to feel drained as the Heart pulled energy from her, while Syrus had never felt more alive or powerful. He began to pull her forward, but Forest dug in her heels.

"It's too painful for me, Syrus. I don't want to get much closer."

"It's painful for you?"

"Yes, very."

"It's not painful for me," Syrus said.

"I can see that. You're practically radiating."

"You stay here. I want to go to it. I have to."

Syrus' hand slipped from hers, and she watched him as he moved slowly towards the flames. The only thing she could think of was that it was affecting him like this because he was a mage and his powers were somehow tied to the world's spirit.

Syrus reached the Heart, walked between the crystal trees, and stood in the fire. Forest didn't move, mesmerized by the sight of him standing in the manifestation. It seemed like he was there only a few moments, but when he returned to her, the night had fully fallen.

Syrus was wrapped in what felt like strong static electricity, but apart from that, he looked unchanged.

"What happened?" Forest asked.

"Other than the fact that I feel terrific, I can't really say anything *happened.* I didn't know if it would kill me, speak to me, or bless me in some way, but there is no deity in the fire. No singular personality."

"So what is in the fire?" Forest asked.

"Emotion. It told me nothing, but I certainly *felt.* I don't understand why it exists, but it seems to be the accumulation and outpouring of the world's emotions."

Forest smiled at him. "That's why it is called the Heart."

"So what do we do now?" he asked.

"We backtrack a little to the hidden area of the smaller falls and we make our camp there."

They walked hand in hand again. The throbbing in their touching palms was painful, but Forest didn't pull her hand away because his excess of energy began to feed her lack. She held tightly to his hand as she reminded herself again that their time was almost over, and the knowledge began to choke her. How could he not know they were mates? Would she have known by now? If she had not seen her true form reflected on his eyes, would she have guessed?

Forest found a small sheltered area amid some towering boulders to make their camp in for the night. Would this be their last night together? She wondered sadly, as she laid her sleeping bag out on the ground next to Syrus'. She looked at the two separate sleeping bags side by side and was seized with the urge to zip them both together. If he touched her tonight, if he kissed her, if he acted at all amorous, could she refuse him? Could she refuse herself and the desire of her hard and battered heart?

Maybe the real question was not *if*, but did she have the guts to take something for herself? Just a few hours, that's all, a few hours to feel worthy, a few hours to feel loved.

Forest's breath shuddered, and everything inside her pulled to the center like a fist. It was nothing more than a fantasy, she told herself. To indulge would carry too high a price. She took a deep breath to relax the clenching inside her. The fist slowly eased open and then hung limp. She was simply exhausted.

"Forest?" Syrus was standing high above her on one of the boulders protecting their campsite.

"Yeah?" there was hardly any strength behind her voice.

"Could we go to the falls before you go to sleep?" he asked.

Her arms hung like dead weight at her sides, and her head felt thick. "I don't think I can right now, Syrus. I'm just too tired. Let's go in the morning, okay?"

"Okay," he said easily.

Syrus jumped down next to her as she crawled into her sleeping bag. She could still feel the energy he'd gleaned from the Heart pulsing off of him. He probably wouldn't need to sleep for a week. He sat down next to her and stroked the hair off her forehead. She was three-fourths asleep already.

"Don't worry. I'll protect you."

"Yes, and Shi will protect us."

"Really?" Syrus asked.

"She saved us from the wolves today. She'll keep us safe." Forest's words were slow and slurred.

Syrus said something in reply, but Forest didn't comprehend the words; she was tumbling through the darkness and the mist.

Syrus waited until he was sure that Forest was sleeping deeply. So, Shi was protecting them? Well, if the dryad ghost/goddess of the wood was watching out for them, he couldn't see any reason why he shouldn't take a little stroll down to the falls alone. It wasn't that far away, and if there was a problem, he could be back in a moment's time.

He got up and walked out of the protective circle of boulders before using the same incantations to open his eyes as he had back at Forest's house so he could look at her while she was sleeping. Forest didn't stir an inch as he whispered the words over and over, nor was she disturbed by his quiet moan of pain as his pupils released and opened.

The darkness was a blessing; it eased him into processing what he was looking at. At first, there were only shadows and shapes, and then gradually his sight grew stronger until it was like looking through very dirty glasses. Excited and energized, Syrus loped off towards the sound of the waterfalls.

The night sky was clear overhead, the moon buoyed up by the surrounding stars. The whole wood around him felt empty. The vacant feeling was alarming, but he reminded himself that they were secure in Shi's protection. The light from the falls ahead undulated through the trees, making everything around it appear to be underwater.

Syrus' breath caught in his throat as the falls came into sight and involuntary tears instantly welled up and ran down his cheeks. It was the most astounding natural beauty he had ever seen. Silverlight was an apt name, the proper name, the only name for this place. He had never seen water with these properties before. It had the same opalescence that other Regian water did, but it moved slower, as though thicker, and the violet/silver light was not a reflection on the water. The light came from the water itself.

He breathed deeply, enjoying the fresh fragrant air, heavy with mist. If only he could gaze upon all this clearly. He would come back here once his sight was restored and spend a good amount of time. He stepped into the water not minding that it soaked the bottoms of his pant legs. The temperature was perfect to refresh without giving a chill. It felt like his skin gulped the water up, and the pain in his feet from walking barefoot all day, was gone. The stones around the water's edge all glittered and sparkled, imbued with the water's light. He understood why this place was constantly fought for over the eons. And his mind snapped into, 'I will be king someday' mode. Wouldn't it be fantastic if the Wood could be made neutral like Paradigm? Open for the enjoyment of all? Could such a plan be executed successfully? Surely with Forest's help and her connection to Shi, it could be done.

Syrus wished he could stay there all night, but his sight was fleeting, and he wanted to look at Forest again before it was gone completely. He sighed sadly, taking in the beauty, but now that the idea of looking at Forest was back in his head, he found that more enticing than the falls. He hurried back to their camp; his sight growing dimmer every second. He landed on his knees next to her, she was still sleeping deeply. He had expected her face to have changed since he'd first seen it, but it was the same.

Even though he had a mental image of her that he looked at constantly in his mind, the blurry reality in front of him affected him as strongly as it had before. His lungs constricted, and again he felt it was entirely unfair. A force so strong he couldn't even give a thought to holding against pulled him to her. Just one kiss was all he needed to ease this terrible ache. As the last glimmers of sight faded into blackness, Syrus pressed his lips against hers.

Forest did not wake.

16

Annoying noises poked at Netriet's unconscious state. She was deeply submerged in a dark and quiet place, but the distant noise hooked through her flesh, pulling her toward the surface. The closer she came to waking, the more her subconscious fought against it. As the surface loomed, the pain began screaming. She imprisoned a cry in her throat. All that escaped her mouth was a shuddering hiss. The sounds and the smells slapped her with the awful truth of where she still was before she opened her eyes. Keeping her eyelids clamped shut she reached around herself, groping for the arm that was no longer there. Her hand passed through the space where her arm should have been, and she found the strength to weep.

The resonance of two voices drew her attention. One was the familiar gruff, commanding tone of Philippe. The other was new to Netriet's ears. Flat like some strange type of automation, it gave Netriet a deep sense of dread. When she finally opened her eyes, everything looked hazy. Philippe sat at the far end of the chamber in his high backed chair, rolling the collar between his thumb and index finger. The figure belonging to the flat voice stood in front of him with his back to her.

"Oh look, my little pet is awake!" Philippe said jovially.

The figure turned and locked his eyes on Netriet. She instantly pulled back a little farther under the pelt she was covered with. He was the smallest werewolf she had ever seen, with weak shoulders, and eyes as flat as his voice. He didn't look as wolfish in his man form as most did; he looked like part rat.

"Nettie, this is Ambassador Marius. He's just returned from Paradigm, and he's got the answer we've been looking for."

Netriet said nothing and curled up tighter. Ambassador Marius stared at her with his dead eyes. She hoped Philippe would send him away. Her gaze shifted pleadingly onto Philippe for a split second, something Ambassador Marius noticed.

"I find the fact that you thought to keep her most fascinating," Marius said.

Philippe merely grunted.

"And you've been using her to try and figure out how to master the collar, experimenting on her?" His voice gave its first inflection when he'd said the word 'experimenting', like a slithering caress.

"Yes. I'm glad I didn't kill her, she's been very useful, and she's often quite witty too."

"How nice," Marius said flatly. "Can I see the collar?" He held his hand out to Philippe, who dropped the ring into his hand.

Marius held it up close to his face and twisted it all the way around. "Yes, yes. I can see why you've had trouble with this given that you had no instruction. Damn wizards think they're so clever. See here, around the stone, the engravings in the wizard's language? I don't understand all of the words, but there is one I have no doubt about. This one." He indicated which character he was talking about to Philippe with his pinky finger. "It means 'teeth.'"

"Teeth?"

"Yes. This collar will not recognize you as its master until you have allowed it to bite you."

"Bite me?" Philippe sounded alarmed. "What do you mean, bite me?"

"You must put it on one of your own fingers and press down on the stone. The spikes inside the band will pierce your skin and absorb a small amount of your blood. You see how the stone is clear? Once it has accepted you as its master, the stone will change colors. There's no knowing what color it will become. I assume the stone was colored when this messenger arrived?"

"Uh, yeah. It was a yellowish color," Philippe said.

Ambassador Marius handed the collar back to Philippe who looked at the object dubiously for the first time.

"So, once I'm its new master, how do I give it a task?" Philippe asked.

"When you have someone you want to perform a task, all you have to do is slip it on. It won't bite you a second time. Tell the collar, inside your mind—there is no need to speak aloud—what the person is to do, and the collar will change colors again. It will remain the color it changes until the task is completed or the collared person dies."

"And what will happen if the person dies far away from me and I cannot get the collar back?" Philippe asked.

Ambassador Marius shrugged. "There is no way to claim the collar forever unless you never use it. It will eventually pass on to someone else, but if the people you use it on are able to stay alive, then you may have control of it for a long time."

Philippe grunted as he considered Ambassador Marius' words. "Thank you, Marius. You may leave now."

Netriet watched as Marius bowed and turned to leave. He hesitated for a second, looking down at her lying on Philippe's bed. She shivered again under his gaze. Why didn't he just leave? His eyes were like zombies, dead things mindlessly trying to devour anything living.

Philippe noticed Marius' staring at her. "You are bound to silence, Marius. You may tell no one about her."

"What are you going to do with her now that you know how to work the collar?" he asked, not taking his eyes off her.

"That is none of your concern," Philippe said icily.

"I only asked because I was wondering if I could have her?"

"Why?"

"The same reason you've kept her. I have a few *experiments* of my own I'd like to try."

Netriet looked pleadingly and panic stricken at Philippe. No matter how he had tortured her or how much she hated him, she would rather spend the last little bit of her miserable life with him than the likes of Ambassador Marius.

Philippe noticed her panic and understood it. "I'm not yet finished with her, Marius," he said dismissively. "Be sure to have the cook provide you with dinner on your way out."

Marius lingered a second longer before he slunk out the chamber door.

Philippe came over to her and sat down on the edge of the bed. He pulled the wolf pelt down so he could examine the stump just below her shoulder. Then he looked sharply in her eyes with the examining gaze of a doctor. "You're still very weak, but you are better." He smiled wickedly. "I see you took quite a liking to Ambassador Marius."

Netriet gave him a droll stare, and he laughed. She wasn't sure how she felt about this weird codependency they seemed to have formed. The thing she feared most was that his affection for her had mutated into something so unnatural that he would try to keep her alive indefinitely and keep her with him like a real pet.

"So let's see if Marius was right about this thing," he said holding the collar up close to his face.

He slid the large ring onto his smallest finger, his others being entirely too big to fit, and pushed down on the clear stone. She heard the spikes engage, and Philippe grimaced but took the pain like a man. The stone swirled with red that she was sure was his blood then it turned a solid black. The faint sound of metal on metal told her that the spikes receded, and Philippe pulled the collar off his finger. He held his pinky up for her to see the little puncture wounds encircling his finger before putting it in his mouth and giving it a little suck.

"Nasty little thing isn't it?" he asked.

She gave him a dirty look. "No, not at all," she said sarcastically. "It only cost me my arm."

He laughed again. "Okay, you're right, you win." He looked at her seriously then. "Are you ready?" he asked.

She sighed and reached up with her remaining hand. He took it and pulled her into a sitting position. The room tilted sickeningly for a moment.

"I'm going to give you a task that I know you could never do without being collared. Well, at least not convincingly." He put the ring back on his finger and closed his eyes, telling the collar he wanted her to do inside his head. Then he put it on her middle finger. The collar's teeth bit down into her flesh.

"This is going to be hard for you, but if you don't succeed, I'll just have to chop off your arm again. Failure is not your ticket out of here, Nettie. I won't let it kill you. Now, tell me you love me. " Philippe ordered.

"That is my task?"

"Yes. Convince me."

Hate and bile rose in the back of Netriet's throat. And she wondered, just how badly did she want to keep her arm?

****

With the exception of the occasional werewolf party, Shi's existence had been mostly peaceful for the last few years. Now she seemed to have her hands full all of a sudden. Philippe was preparing for war, Maxcarion had been attempting to conceal himself from her, Forest had come back to the Wood with a blind vampire mage who just happened to be the prince and her life mate, and now a whole troop of vampires from the Onyx Castle had just crept through her southwestern border. Shi quickly perused through each of them in turn, reading their hearts and their minds. They were following Forest and Syrus on Royal orders. Their leader, Redge, was a good man. Well, good for a vampire. But the presence of the vampires could cause Forest serious problems and possibly ruin her whole mission. Shi decided to contain them.

Until she chose to release them, the troop would wander in circles, confused and directionless in an area where they would not be discovered by the wolves. Setting up the parameter around the vampires was not difficult for Shi but it required her attention and time, leaving Forest unguarded.

17

Syrus was in deep meditation, trying to figure out how he could keep Forest with him once his sight was restored. He could give her a title, but he knew she would hate him for it. She wouldn't accept anything she didn't earn. Why couldn't he shut off the relentless mantra inside him that forever chanted she was his? Was it merely a strong physical attraction? Sexual chemistry and nothing more? Thinking that was painful. It wasn't true. She was his friend. But did she really consider him her friend in return?

A distant growling brought Syrus to the here and now with a sharp jolt. He had been lulled into a false sense of security, thinking that the dryad ghost was protecting them. He immediately stretched out his mage senses. From the sound of their movement and their breathing, there were three of them and they were in beast form. Damn it. Wolves were at their best in combat when in their half man, half wolf, beast form. Syrus listened intently. They were doing more than taking a stroll; they were skulking this way for a reason. They knew Forest and Syrus were there and they wanted blood.

Syrus covered Forest's mouth with his hand before roughly shaking her awake. As he anticipated, she struggled against him and screamed into his hand.

"Three wolves are headed this way in beast form," Syrus hissed in her ear.

Syrus pulled his hand away from her mouth. She asked nothing but instantly got to her feet and reached for her sword. The wolves would be right on top of them in seconds.

"We fight together," Forest said under her breath. "Back to back, as long as we can. I'll become invisible and you shadow."

"Agreed." Syrus turned and pressed his back to hers, pulling his short swords from their sheaths.

The wolves climbed the boulders, their claws scratching and skidding on the rock. The moon fell on their disfigured backs, outlining them. Three silhouettes like black paper cutouts with glistening eyes, claws, and teeth.

Forest had never been in this kind of fight. She had never fought against a wolf. She was always on their side. One of these wolf monsters might be someone she knew, maybe even a friend. But there was no reluctance in her. They wanted to kill her mate. She would show no mercy.

The wolves looked down at Forest and Syrus though they could not see her and he blended into the darkness, their weapons however were plainly visible, hovering in midair at the ready. They all growled and salivated revoltingly. The one on the right moved prematurely and jumped down before the other two. He died the second his feet hit the ground in front of Forest. She swiftly hacked a large x on the front of him, from his shoulders to his hips, and he went down without causing any more trouble.

The other two barked angrily but made no move to join their comrade. They exchanged a glance, and then backed down out of sight. Forest's heart pumped harder. These two would not die as easily as the first. Syrus' back pressed against hers though his flesh felt insubstantial now that he was shadowing. The two beasts stood between the boulders, motionless except for their breathing.

The moment hovered before them. Forest knew when it happened it would happen fast and they could be dealt victory or great loss; a possible bump in the road or the moment when everything would change. She had never felt this kind of fear before. Cutting your way through enemies for the sake of your job or your own life was one thing. Protecting what you held most precious was something else entirely. It was the first time she had ever doubted her ability to win. She and Syrus had stealth and weapons and mad skills, but the beasts had abnormal size and strength and animal instincts.

The two beasts charged at the same time. Forest slashed at the neck of the one in front of her, but he dropped and skidded into her, knocking her off her feet. She slashed again at him but from her poor position only grazed his shoulder, a mere scratch. Syrus had thrown one of his swords at his opponent, stabbing the beast deep in the torso, but not piercing any vital organs. Forest scrambled desperately to get to her feet while the beast she fought swung and grabbed at the air, trying to catch his invisible adversary. Forest had to duck and roll to avoid his claws. She came up behind him and thrust her sword at his back, in what would have been a killing strike, had she not been knocked in the back of the head by the flailing arm of the other beast. The blow sent her skidding sideways and turned her strike into a long, deep gash along the beast's back.

The monster howled in rage and pain. Whirling around, it finally caught Forest by the hair. She was pulled down, the wind knocked out of her as she hit the ground. The beast wrenched her sword from her hand.

"Syrus!" She gasped.

The beast was now aware of where she was. It landed on its knees, hovering over her, about to tear her throat out with its teeth. Syrus had heard her breathless cry for help, and he moved so fast the dust twisted in his wake. The beast he'd been fighting, like the one now over Forest swung wildly through the air at Syrus. He ducked and ran behind it. He launched himself up with one step on the nearest boulder, twisted in midair, and the beast's head hit the ground with one precise cut.

Syrus turned to the beast that had Forest pinned and placed his hand on the back of the wolf's head as though he might be giving him a genial pat. The beast's body went rigid. Its eyes widened in surprise. Syrus' face contorted with rage, and red waves of light pulsed down his arm like lightning made of fire. Forest remembered his story about becoming a mage and gaining the ability to weaponize his rage. What looked like a softball-sized red and black marble sphere appeared on his chest. It moved to his shoulder, down his arm to his hand, and absorbed into the head of the werewolf. The wolf got to his feet and staggered to the center of their little arena. Then a sound like breaking glass erupted from inside him. He gave one lurch and fell in a heap at Syrus' feet.

Syrus picked Forest up off the ground and held her in a tight embrace. "Are you all right? Are you hurt at all?"

"I'm fine," she said and then giggled with relief and hugged him tightly. "Are *you* hurt?"

"Just this." He held his hand up for her to see. A ragged gash on the fleshy area under his pinky ran to his wrist. "Caught me with one of his claws." Syrus kicked the nearest dead body spitefully. "Rabid puppy!" He spat at the corpse. "It stings something awful."

"Maybe he infected you with something and you'll start to turn half wolf," she teased.

"Shut up! That's not funny!"

"Maybe not," she laughed. "But you are."

She realized then just how scared she had been, and now that it was over, she couldn't remember a time when she felt so light and happy.

"Yuck," she surveyed their camp. They needed to move the bodies and cover them with something. "We need to move our camp."

"Naw, *we* don't. I'll handle it. You might want to step back though."

Forest backed up out of the little protected area that was now disheveled and blood spattered, watching Syrus bemusedly. He stood with his back pressed against one of the boulders and stretched his arms out. His body began to crack and snap with the same red lightning that had danced along his arm. A cyclone began to twist in front of him, throwing everything in the small space into the air. Their backpacks and sleeping bags flew around the top while the bodies circled the bottom. A hole began to open on the ground like an ant lion's, and the dirt swallowed up the dead. Forest's mouth was hanging open in amazement, and she caught a handful of dirt in her teeth.

The little tornado spun itself into nothing as quickly as it had appeared. Their packs and sleeping bags sat neatly on the ground again, and Syrus emerged, shaking dirt from his hair.

"Syrus, you're awesome!" she sounded like a fourteen-year-old fangirl .

"Thanks." He shook his head at her, sprinkling her with dirt, and she shoved him away, laughing.

"The dust scrubbed the whole area and our stuff clean of blood," he explained.

"I can't say it did anything for your level of cleanliness, or mine." She spit some dirt out of her mouth. They both were filthy, caked in sweat and blood.

Syrus grimaced as he rubbed his hands on his grimy jeans. Then his face lit up a little, and he smiled at her. "How about we take that little dip we talked about earlier, right now?"

"Oh yeah! Race you!" She took off toward the smaller, secluded falls.

Syrus laughed and followed at a leisurely pace. He was in no danger of losing her; the trail she left behind smelled too bad.

As soon as Forest hit the small beach, she kicked her shoes off, threw her shirt in the air, and peeled off her nasty jeans, leaving it all in a pile. She plunged under the water, wearing only her bra and panties, and her brain did an immediate *AAAhhhh!* She stroked to the falls ahead. Nine total fell over the crescent shaped cliff. Most of the falls hit the water in a deep place, but Forest knew where to go. She put her feet down on the wide rock shelf, waist deep, the shimmery water splashing over her head and torso. The sheet of water concealed a cave behind it, and Forest fully intended to loll in the pool inside the cave once she felt totally clean.

The water splashed down on her, washing away the grime. She turned to look for Syrus and spotted him moving through the trees. He came running, barefoot and bare-chested. As his foot hit the shore, he launched into the air, soaring like an eagle in a wide arch before plunging into the water in a perfect dive, fifty feet from where Forest stood. She watched him sliding under the water toward her and an intimate emotion punched her right in the gut. Forest felt her cheeks stain with heat. She turned away from him and lifted her face to the water as he came up for air behind her.

Syrus had been enjoying the cool cleaning refreshment the same way Forest had when she hit the water, but the second he broke through the surface and inhaled, he snapped to his feet behind her. He inhaled again greedily. The smell of her skin and the water sluicing over it was intoxicating, but there was something else. The energy pulsing from her hit his skin and absorbed deep into his core. Everything about her was screaming for him.

She could feel his heightened senses reaching out from his body, upping her already throbbing adrenaline left over from their victory. He said nothing, but stood a foot behind her. Even through the splashing water, she could hear his breathing. Or maybe she could just feel it. He moved closer slowly. Awareness rolled down through Forest from the top of her scalp. She held still as he closed the empty space, moving slowly, slowly closer until his bare chest pressed against her back. She leaned back against him, feeling him breathe in and out. The moment drew out into a tantric aching.

Please. Please. He thought. *Please, Forest, don't fight what you feel for me.*

Just once, she thought. *Now, here. Just once let yourself be loved. Know your mate once, and then you can let him go.*

Forest turned to Syrus and wrapped her arms around his shoulders. Wariness came into his expression. She pulled his wounded hand up close to her face; it was already mending.

"Does it still hurt?" she asked quietly.

"Not much."

She raised it to her mouth and kissed it gently. Goosebumps covered his skin at the touch of her mouth. He pulled his hand from hers and dragged his fingers through her hair. She stretched up on her toes and pulled his face down to hers.

"Forest…Please," he whispered.

She placed her hand gently over his mouth. "Yes, Syrus. Yes to everything."

Syrus' touch, Syrus' lips, drowned out her reason and her thoughts until all she could hear was her own pulse and the falling of the water. He held her tightly against him and pulled her into the dark cavern behind the waterfall. This would be her one true memory of him, of them. However short the night might be, every second would be forever burned into her soul. The cavern was small, and the water pooled around their waists. Light danced on the wet stone walls in a ceaseless echo of silver shimmer, and the falling water made an undulating diamond curtain over the mouth of the cave. Their breathing, like the light, echoed around the confined space.

The moments flashed by, and Forest's mind had completely turned off. The water they stood in would surely begin to boil soon, just as steam was literally rising off their skin. Emotion built pressure inside her, and she began talking breathlessly without any thought as to what she was saying. "I need to tell you something," she said against his lips.

He moved his mouth to her ear. "You're not going to tell me to stop, are you?" he whispered.

She chuckled. "No…I…" She bit down into his shoulder. Why was she talking? She didn't have anything to say. Her mouth stayed happily employed on his skin for a few minutes when the words began to bubble up again. Her brain was a thicker fog than the one they were creating. So lost in her senses, she hadn't noticed that his touch had changed from sexual to curious.

"I need to tell you something," she said again not sure at all what was going to come spilling out of her mouth.

His arm wrapped around the back of her waist, pinning her left arm to her side and her whole torso against his. "Oh? Is it about this?" The venom in his voice sucked all the heat out of the cave and flipped the switch, turning Forest's brain back on.

His hand moved up and down along the length of her scars. Forest cursed herself for stupidly believing she could make love to him without him noticing. She couldn't breathe when she saw the look on his face— disgust, pure and undeniable. Her eyes broke like full glasses of water, and her heart collapsed in on itself. She tried to pull away but he held her fast.

"They're just battle scars," she muttered through her tears.

"Don't lie to me!" he shouted, insane with rage. "Do you think I don't know what this is?" he demanded. "Do you?!"

"Please..." she whimpered.

"Why didn't you tell me?! Why, Forest?"

"I couldn't, Syrus," she sobbed.

"Who did this to you?"

"Please let me go, Syrus."

"*Who did this to you? TELL ME!* I'm gonna kill him. I'm gonna tear his arms off and cut out his tongue and gouge out his eyes. No, he'll watch me pull his heart from his chest and drink the blood from it before I show a single shred of mercy."

Forest couldn't stand this. The repulsed look on his face and his irate ranting was too much, and she began thrashing against him. "Let me go! Let me go!"

Syrus held her tighter and felt slowly and meticulously down the length of her scars. This was so much worse than anything she had ever imagined.

His expression began to morph from disgust to utter shock as he touched every last ridge of her skin.

"What the hell?" he muttered under his breath.

Forest stumbled backwards as he abruptly let go of her. She bolted through the water before he could change his mind and pin her again or ask her any more questions.

Syrus stood still, his body weighed down with immeasurable heaviness. How could it be possible? Who could be capable of doing such a thing? The vampire that had marked Forest had broken ancient law and placed two different kinds of marks on her. The lovers mark was only used by vampires in committed relationships in a ceremony setting. The lovers mark on Forest entwined with a slave mark. She was the property of the sucker who had marked her. He had total control over her, forced obedience. Against his will, Syrus' mind blurred with images of things he wished he'd never imagined. He had to know the truth.

Forest ran through the darkness back to their camp. How could she ever face him again? What could she say? Her mind got stuck on one thought that repeated over and over, *Damn you, Leith! Damn you!* She had wanted one night, just one night to love Syrus, and Leith had ruined that. Now it would never happen. Now Syrus found her gross, and he wouldn't want to touch her ever again.

She quickly rummaged through her bag and found some clean jeans and a shirt. She put them on as fast as she could, in case Syrus came back to camp. She didn't think she could face him now. She needed to regroup and come up with a convincing lie that would explain her scars. Maybe she could convince Syrus that they weren't what he thought they were.

But she wasn't fast enough. Syrus came charging out of the darkness and hit her with a spell that lifted her three inches off the ground. The spell held her immobile in the air. She could talk and look around, but nothing else.

"What are you doing?" she demanded.

"I need the truth, and you won't give it to me, or you can't."

Forest had thought her horror had reached its pitch for the evening but she'd been wrong.

Syrus held his hands next to the sides of her head. His jaw clenched so tightly she could hear his teeth grinding together.

"No, Please! Please, Syrus don't do this! All I have is my pride. Really, that's all. I'm begging you, don't make me debase myself."

His look of determination faltered, and he turned away from her, pacing back and forth. His fists clenched and unclenched over and over. He muttered and argued with himself.

"No! I have to know, Forest." He put his hands back next to her head.

"*Please!*" she sobbed.

"I'll only take the memories directly connected to your scars."

"NO!" But her protest was cut off as she was forced to look at the memories that were now transferring into Syrus' mind. She had never wanted to die so badly.

Syrus was disoriented as he began to experience Forest's memories. It wasn't like watching a movie or being a bystander. He saw through her eyes, from her perspective. Forest watched as Syrus lived what she had. He shut his eyes as if that could make him more blind and continuously shook his head back and forth. It didn't take long for him to see all he needed to.

Syrus turned his back on her. The spell broke and dropped Forest in a heap on the ground. She watched him walk away until the shadows swallowed him. Forest turned her face into the ground and wept. A second later, Syrus raised his voice in a roar of rage and agony that split the sky and rippled through the entire wood. Forest got to her feet and ran in the opposite direction, to the Heart.

Syrus returned to the camp as soon as he had regained some level of self-control and found Forest gone. He didn't know if he was relieved that she was gone or not. He needed more time to digest the truth. The last thing he wanted was to injure her further by saying something stupid. He sat down and placed his head in his hands. She'd been so young, so very young to be the victim of such a terrible crime. Seeing it through her eyes had been traumatizing to Syrus and it helped him understand to a level he certainly didn't desire. Experiencing the memory of the first time Leith had raped her had caused something inside Syrus to break.

Rage boiled the blood in his head again as he thought about how the bastard had stalked her, and laid in wait with a handful of shadow sand that he threw into her eyes the second she walked around that corner. She had been covered with his bite marks that time, giving him a strong, persuasive power over her. He made her come to him over and over, and she'd had no choice. But she fought, and he was in danger of her killing him or reporting him, but that was before he'd truly marked her.

Syrus had to remind himself that they weren't his memories. He felt what she felt, and he wished he could wipe it from his mind. But he needed to examine closely what Leith had done to create the mark he left on Forest. Reluctantly he brought her memory back to the forefront of his mind from where his subconscious was already trying to bury it.

Leith had brutalized her that night, worse than any other time before. Forest focused her eyes on the pile of her ripped clothes by her head and concentrated her mind on how best to repair the spilt seams while Leith satiated himself on her. He'd abruptly gotten up and left the room when he was done, leaving her exposed and broken on the floor. She was about to get up and try to leave when he came back with a rope. Syrus shuddered and forced himself to continue watching.

Leith had an old book open on the floor next to where Forest was tied up.

"What are you doing?"

"I'm going to make you mine forever. I love you that much."

Leith studied the book for a few minutes. Forest knew it was futile to scream, no one would hear. If they did, they wouldn't care. It was futile to beg—he would only get off on that. She had no weapons, nothing to bargain with. She couldn't even move. So she lay quietly, watching the person she hated most in the world as he poured over a book in the last minutes of her freedom.

Leith lay the book aside and began her slave mark first. Slave marks were supposed to be small straight lines on the upper part of the arm. Leith started just under Forest's ear, and using his sharpest incisor sliced an unbroken line to her elbow. Then he bit into one of his fingers and bled a line of his blood into her wound. It was the first time Forest wished for death. Her flesh pulled together and began healing. She was property now. Her inferiority was complete, the knowledge imbued inside her.

Syrus didn't know if that was worse than what came next. His rage had grown into an inferno and was salivating for Leith's blood. There was only one tiny shred of sanity inside him, and it demanded that he finish watching her memory.

Lover's marks were simple. Two vampires in a loving, committed relationship often marked each other as a symbol of monogamy. It's simply a deep bite with transference of blood. Before biting, each vampire will pool a small amount of their own blood in their mouth, usually by cutting a small place on the tongue by running it along a sharp tooth. The bite mark heals into a crescent scar. Lover's marks strengthen the love between the two, but it is by no means unbreakable. Ending a relationship and taking a new lover will erase the previous mark.

Leith began again just under her ear and bit her seven times, entwining the crescents with the straight slave mark. The lover's marks confused Forest's heart. At times, she believed he loved her, and occasionally she questioned if she might love him in return. Leith had created something new with Forest, and Syrus didn't know if it could be removed.

Syrus took a few deep breaths and let his mind release the memory back into the dark recesses where he wanted to wall it in. He hated himself for taking her memories. He had raped her as well, just in a different way, and he'd give anything to undo it. He feared she'd never let him close to her again.

He thought back to right before, when they were together under the waterfall. Her willingness to be with him, wanting to be with him, and he knew now how all those scars must have hurt every time he touched her. That alone was a testament to how much she really must feel for him. His heart pulled as he realized the extent.

Syrus stood abruptly and calling on the strength of his senses, he ran after her.

Forest reached the ribcage with the thought of finding Shi, but now she was so distraught she didn't even know which direction she had come from. She fell at the base of a tree and tried to will herself to die. She pressed her hands over her heart and closed her eyes.

"Stop," she whispered to her heart, her voice growing faint. "Stop, stop, stop, stop... just let me die."

Her heart didn't listen. "Don't you get it?" she said to the stupid organ. "He doesn't want you. He'll never want you."

"That's not true."

Forest startled at the sound of Syrus' voice behind her. He strode up to her, bent over, and scooped her off the ground. Forest went limp in his arms. She had no more fight left. He turned around and began carrying her back towards their camp.

"You love me, don't you?"

She sighed heavily. "I did."

"You will again."

She collapsed into sleep on his shoulder and knew no more until morning.

****

Forest's head throbbed when she awoke, her eyes reluctant to open. Awkward didn't even begin to describe the way she felt about facing Syrus. Now that she had rested, she was determined to regain some level of respect. She had to rebuild the walls he had toppled. She had to push him away again. *Damn it*, she'd even told him that she loved him. At least she'd used the word in the past tense.

She could hear him moving around next to her and kept her eyes clamped shut before she reminded herself stupidly that she couldn't fake him out by keeping her eyes closed. He probably knew she was awake before she did.

He sat cross-legged on the ground, his face smooth and contemplative. He'd put on a clean T-shirt, but he still wore the same jeans as yesterday. There was a tear over his right knee, and the hems were dirty and beginning to fray.

Forest felt overwhelmed with sorrow as she looked at him. Stealing her memories was unforgivable; just like a vampire to take whatever they wanted no matter what it cost others. She nestled down into the familiar feeling of hate. But hate in regards to Syrus was shallow. She stared at him. His short hair was a mess in a way humans thought fashionable; she wanted to comb it. She remembered when she'd cut it and he'd touched her face. If only he could really look at her without it bonding them together forever. When the wizard healed him, she wanted him to see her just once. But that was a desire that must always remain unfulfilled.

Forest groaned as she sat up, rubbing her thumping temples. He said nothing. She waited, but he kept silent. Why did he have to be so composed when she felt like she'd just woken up with a hangover in a strange bed, hardly knowing what she'd done? Forest opened her mouth in a silent scream, which she directed at him.

"What are you doing?" he asked.

"Nothing."

"Your breathing was strange just now."

"So?"

Syrus shrugged. There was a long uncomfortable silence. Forest began to busy herself with rolling up her sleeping bag and straightening up her stuff. Her stomach rumbled, but she didn't think she could eat anything. She wanted to get searching again for Maxcarion, and she was thankful that it was still necessary for them to keep their talking to a minimum.

"All right, I want to move our camp to the Heart for tonight if we are unsuccessful locating the wizard today."

"Whatever you think is best," he said vaguely.

"Have you eaten? Are you ready to go?" Forest hated the nasty tone of her voice, but she didn't think she could do anything about it.

"I'm ready."

Forest strapped on her backpack and adjusted her shirt. She gave a quick second look around to make sure they were leaving nothing behind. Syrus put his pack on, and before she could give him orders, he walked slowly into her space and reached for her forearm. Forest's eyes went wide, and she contemplated jerking out of his grip, but she waited to see what he was doing. His face was pained and it broke down her new defenses. She frantically grabbed at them to put them back up.

"We need to get moving, Syrus," she tried to keep her voice firm.

"I want you to forgive me for what I did last night."

"What you want is irrelevant."

"Tell me what you want me to do, and I'll do it."

Forest's heart trembled. *Be cold*, she told herself. She lifted his hand off her arm and took a step back. "Give me some space, Syrus. That's what I want from you."

He sighed dejectedly and nodded. "All right."

Hours passed as they searched for Maxcarion. The day grew unseasonably hot, and Forest found it harder and harder to concentrate. Syrus followed her as she led them nowhere, to the middle of it, and back around the edges, over and over. With every new line of sweat that slid down her back she grew more and more frustrated.

Syrus kept his distance as she had asked him to, but the space brought her no peace. He was a walking volcano of emotion, churning and brewing, and impossible for her to ignore.

Her frustration level was at its breaking point but it was nothing next to Syrus'. He imagined that his mouth was a walled-over gate that could not be opened. There was a raging beast behind the composed exterior of his body that he must keep jailed. He had an idea he was sure would work but the words he desperately wanted to let loose had to wait for the proper time, if there was one. Waiting to speak to Forest, to present her with his proposition, was taking all of the force of his mage power. And so, they went in circles through the trees and inside themselves, searching and reaching for things just beyond grasping.

When they stopped for lunch, Forest could tell Syrus was on the edge of losing it, though she was unsure as to what 'it' was, exactly. Forest felt like the taut string of an instrument, constantly being picked by a ragged fingernail. Fraying had begun, and she too would snap eventually.

She kept her distance as they sat down to eat. He unscrewed one of his bottles, but he didn't drink. His jaw clenched so tight, she could see his facial muscles tremble with the strain. How long had he been like that? What could he be fighting that hard not to say?

"Syrus, what is wrong with you?" she demanded.

Syrus' teeth stayed locked together. He really had no idea how she would respond to what he had to say. He wondered if he could just swallow it. It was the worst timing imaginable. He needed to focus his mind on finding the wizard. He'd been telling himself that over and over since the idea popped into his head, but he couldn't focus on anything other than Forest. Now that he knew the truth about her life and what she was forced to go through on a regular basis, and now that he was sure he could make things better for her, it made looking for the wizard seem like an annoying fly in the background.

Indecision and pain twisted all over Syrus' face. It was obvious to Forest that he was going through some internal battle, and the moment dragged.

"Oh, for goodness sake! Just say it, Syrus, and get it over with!"

Even in the face of her irritation and the pressure she'd just put on him, he mulled it over. He put his bottle back inside his backpack and stood up, moving closer to her.

She watched him warily as he sat down again, cross-legged in front of her so that their knees touched. Whatever he was about to say, it was heavy and Forest held her breath waiting for the weight to fall on her.

Syrus held both of his hands up in surrender before he uttered a word. When finally he did speak, his voice was quiet and collected, though obviously nervous underneath. "I have no idea the right way to say this. Please realize that I would never intentionally hurt you, and I speak out of genuine friendship."

Oh, crap. Forest took a deep breath. "All right."

"I can remove one of Leith's marks from you. If you'd let me. I cannot, unfortunately, remove the slave mark. At least not yet. But I promise to find a way."

"How could you remove the lovers mark?" Forest asked.

"I could replace it."

Forest let his words sink in, and she fought down the knee jerk reaction to knock his head clean off his shoulders. She took a slow calming breath, remembering that he said that he was speaking out of genuine friendship, and that she hadn't acted as though she had any aversion to him as a lover last night under the waterfall. However, a one night fling was something worlds apart from the commitment of a mark. Everything was just backwards and wrong. There was no way she could or would take a lovers mark from Syrus, especially when it came out of pity.

"Thank you, but no."

"But Forest, don't you understand that…"

"No!" she said forcefully. "Look, I appreciate your concern for me, and yes being tied to Leith is a terrible way to live, but I'm used to it. I'll find my own way out, eventually."

He looked not only shocked but also hurt and disappointed. Why at this moment did she feel guilty for hurting his ego? She wanted to kick him.

His cheeks looked a little red. "It wouldn't have to be anything other than an arrangement if you found being with me like that… objectionable."

"Oh? And what about you? Why would you give up the chance to be with someone else in a real relationship? You might find being with me objectionable. It wouldn't work anyway. No one would allow it. You're the prince, and I'm a disgusting Halfling, unworthy of the air I breathe. I don't think you realize all that you would be giving up just to help me out. And for me, I'd just be trading one kind of slavery for another."

Syrus' mouth fell open, but before he could protest, she pushed on. "I know that you are nothing like Leith, and that you would be good to me, but even though it's trading up, it's still trading one kind of prison for another. Like I said, I appreciate it and all but…hey!"

Syrus had heard enough. He stood up abruptly and grabbed Forest by the shoulders, lifting her to her feet. Before she could ask him what he was doing, he crushed her mouth with his. The fiery snake inside her uncoiled and snapped painfully. Her head spun, and she clung tightly around Syrus' neck. His kiss didn't push or demand, it just gave warmth and sweetness and sorrow.

"Forget friendship. I only said that to soften you up. My offer is real, and it stands until you accept it. It's not charity. *I want you.* I want your heart."

Forest buried her face in his chest and cried. "What good is my heart? It's angry. It hates."

TENAYA JAYNE

Syrus took a deep breath, holding her tightly against him. "All hearts are capable of hate, Forest. That doesn't make them worthless. I understand your hate, now. Hell, I even condone it. But you don't hate me."

Forest wailed. "Oh, I do! I most certainly do! I hate you more than anyone or anything else."

Syrus let go of her and stepped back, his face shocked.

"Yes," she said tears running down her cheeks. "I hate you more than Leith."

"How could you say that?" he asked in a deadly whisper.

"Because, look at what you've done to me! You've weakened me! My hate for Leith made me stronger, but you make me weak. You don't have to ask for my heart, black as it is, it's yours already. My love is not a blessing to you, Syrus! It's a damn curse! You are the necromancer of all that was dead in me. I hate you for that! I feel pain and fear…fear above all else. I had killed my fear. Buried it. And now it's back, choking me! *Damn you!*"

She reared up and struck him in the chest over and over and hard as she could. He grabbed her arms, restraining her. She pushed against him with everything she could as though she could crash through him. A feral growl broke out of her. "I want to hurt you, Syrus! I want you to feel the agony you've created inside me. But you never will. You'll never understand." She let herself go limp, and she slid back to the ground sobbing. "How could I not hate you? You've robbed me of my spirit. I can't trust you. Can't trust what you are. You think you mean well, but I'm nothing but a toy to you." She wept bitterly.

He knelt with his heart ripping in pain and reached for her. She didn't pull away. As soon as he touched her, she curled up in his arms.

"It's not true," he whispered.

She raised her tear-streaked face, and again he kissed her. He meant to show her, if only he could, if only she would let him. Love seemed to flow from her mouth into his, staggering him. His fangs began to throb, not from a desire to drink from her, but a scorching rage to tear Leith's throat out.

"You don't belong to him. You belong to me," Syrus said through his clenched teeth.

Forest stiffened in his arms, and he knew that in his rage he had said the wrong thing. She pulled away slowly, stood, picked up her backpack, and strapped it on. Syrus didn't move.

"I can't belong to you, Syrus. I don't even belong to myself."

The next second, she darted through the trees and was gone, leaving him all alone.

18

Forest ran, the world around her blurred by tears. She ran like a small child to its mother for comfort. But the mother she was seeking was her surrogate, Shi. Everything she'd felt since the first moment she'd laid eyes on Syrus seemed to meld and roll up into a ball. The combination equated only to sorrow.

Forest tripped and fell on her face three miles from where she left Syrus. She pulled herself into a sitting position, her tears momentarily stymied as she looked at her surroundings. She was in the Dryad graveyard. The monuments of stone trees were broken and toppled. The whole graveyard was a ruin. The destruction had happened long before she had been born, and it was the one story Shi would never tell her. She said it was too painful for her to discuss.

Forest sat against a large broken trunk and pulled her knees into her chest. "Shi?" she said quietly. "Shi, please answer me."

She felt the breeze first then she heard the faint, whispering voice. "I'm here child."

Forest looked around. Shi materialized in a sitting position next to her. She looked the same as she always did, green and long, twiggy arms and legs with large wise eyes that were reflective and insect like. Forest immediately placed her head on Shi's lap, and Shi stroked her insubstantial fingers over Forest's forehead.

"Oh, Shi, tell me what to do."

"About what?"

"Me…and Syrus."

"In the past I would have, but not now. Not with this problem. You alone must answer it so you have no one to thank or curse but yourself when you finally land on your feet."

"You don't hate me for having a vampire as a mate?" Forest asked.

Shi chuckled lightly. "You didn't choose him. I don't know why you are always mixed up with their kind. But I am a little amazed at what is inside you for him and also what is inside him for you, especially since he doesn't even know that you are mates."

"What is inside him, Shi?"

"Hmm. . .It feels like cheating to tell you anything else."

"Is he sincere, or just confused by our partial connection?" Forest asked.

"Are *you* confused by your partial connection?"

Forest was quiet, biting on her lower lip. Shi continued to stroke her hair back from her face. It felt more like a light breeze than tangible fingers.

"My strong adopted daughter, how I long to see you free from that which binds you."

They both were quiet for a few moments.

"You are so tangled up inside, Forest. Just answer one simple question. Are you really willing to turn your back and never see him again?"

"No. That's the simple truth, Shi. No."

"There you are then. I've always told you to simplify things, haven't I?"

Forest chuckled. "Yes, you have, countless times."

Shi continued to stroke Forest's hair. After a moment she laughed. "Silly girl, you haven't even asked me where the wizard is."

Forest gasped and sat up. "Yes! The wizard! Where is the wizard?"

Shi smiled and pointed straight ahead of her. "How many times have you sat in this graveyard, Forest?"

Forest shrugged. "Too many to count."

"And since you know this place so well, tell me, do you recognize that stone tree over there?"

Forest looked where Shi was pointing. Sure enough, there was a stone tree more intact than any of the others. It was an anomaly among them. She had never seen it before.

"Look there at the base, the fracture line running down the length of it. Do you see?" Shi asked.

Forest nodded, and standing up, she took a step toward it. "It's an illusion! That's his front door!"

"Yes indeed. Now you know where he is, and how I wish we could sit here and have a nice long talk, but right now you must run."

Forest felt it a millisecond before Shi said anything about running; her heart seized in a terrible panic. It was unlike any distress she had ever experienced. She started her hand over her heart, unable to breathe.

Shi's form was still there next to her, but Forest could tell that her eyes were elsewhere in the wood.

"What has happened?" Forest gasped.

"They've taken him. Eight wolves in man form. He surrendered; too outnumbered. He's injured, but alive. What you're feeling is your connection to Syrus, alerting you that he is in mortal danger. They are taking him to the Lair."

Forest hesitated only long enough to shift into a form she had not used since she was a youth, a she- wolf. Shi watched her fly, contemplating how best she could help. She had no powers past the boundary of the Wood. She traveled to the other side of the Wood in the blink of an eye and looked down on the troop of vampires she had confused. She appeared before Redge.

Shi had to admire the way the vampire covered his alarm at the sight of her. The rest of his troop was more obvious. One even made to run in the opposite direction.

"Listen well, Redge of Halussis. Your prince had been captured by werewolves and is being taken to the Lair as we speak. Forest will do all she can to save him, but I fear she may need your assistance in the end. I have kept you here wandering in a loop, but I now release you. Follow me swiftly. I will cut a path for you straight through the wood to the Lair. I will keep any wolves away from you. Come now!"

Redge didn't need telling twice. He waved for his men to follow, and they all fell in behind him, single file. With Shi flying ahead, they moved like a bullet train, the sun glinting off their clinking armor.

Forest ran on all fours, faster than she had ever moved before. Her sword, clinging awkwardly around her animal body, was the only catch in her fluid speed. Panic made her crazed, and the fear of loss drove her focus to unnatural heights. The trees and foliage and uneven terrain was nothing to her—she exploded through it all, gaining in speed and momentum. She knew she couldn't just charge in, kill them all, and take Syrus back to Maxcarion. She needed a watertight plan.

As she drew near, she could smell Syrus' burning flesh. They had chained him with silver. Since they were all in man form and she was in wolf, she had to wait for them to emerge from the wood before she could charge through the boundaries of the Lair. She quickly decided how she would handle the situation and hoped with everything she had that it would work.

Forest hunkered down, hidden from view in some bushes at the edge of the Wood. *Remember the plan! Remember the plan!* She screamed to herself as she saw Syrus pulled behind four of the wolves, the other four bringing up the rear. Silver chains wrapped around his wrists, one tangled around his neck. Smoke rose off his skin. They had obviously beaten him—he was bloody and bruised. The desire to kill had never pulsed through her so strongly. *If you fight, both you and Syrus will die.*

She stayed still as they emerged from the wood and approached the wolf community's low-lying, solider training camp. Luckily for her, soldiers were whom she preferred to deal with in this circumstance.

"Hey! Hey! Hey!" one in front shouted to someone in the camp. "Look what we caught in the Wood!"

A wolf Forest recognized stepped out to meet them—Gahu. She had met him back when she was making regular tips to the Lair, bringing Philippe smuggled French wine. Gahu had purchased some grape soda and a package of Twinkies from her once and had been friendly to her every time she visited. It looked as if he had gained some rank. She hoped it was enough and that he remembered her fondly.

Gahu approached Syrus, his lips twisted back from his teeth. The wolves that had brought him in backed away.

"He was alone?" Gahu asked.

"Yes, sir."

"Maybe you didn't see anyone else, but I doubt he was alone. Look at him. Look at his hair. He's someone's servant." Gahu turned his attention wholly on Syrus. "Who are you with?"

Syrus said nothing, keeping his face tilted toward the ground.

"How many of you are there? Where is your master?"

Still, Syrus said nothing. Gahu growled at him from deep in his throat. "It seems you have a high pain tolerance." Gahu gestured at the silver chains. "I don't mind a little challenge. Let's see what it takes to open that sharp mouth of yours."

More wolves had come out from tents and stopped their sparring exercises to see what was going on. As soon as they laid eyes on Syrus, they all had the same malevolent light in their eyes. Gahu drove his fist deep into Syrus' stomach, sending him to his knees. Howling and barking erupted around them. It was time for Forest to make her appearance before Syrus was torn apart.

The crowd had their backs to her as she came charging towards them on all fours. She broke through, knocking aside those in her way. Shouts of surprise and alarm went up as she crashed into the center, using her body as a barrier between Gahu and Syrus. Gahu's mouth fell open as this unknown she-wolf snarled at him, protecting a vampire.

"What the hell is this?"

The crowd fell silent in confusion. Forest saw Gahu's nostrils flare as he caught her scent. She needed him to recognize her before he gave the word and they were both killed. Forest shifted back into a woman, pulling from her mind one of the sexiest forms she had ever assumed; long curly black hair, playboy bunny curves, and full pouty crimson lips. The response to her new shape from the surrounding soldiers was expected and exactly what she was wanting. They howled, whistled and made lewd comments.

Gahu looked closely at her pointy ears and her forever-unchanging eyes, and the light of comprehension dawned on his face.

Knowing she had bought them only a few moments she continued with her performance. Forest turned to face the group with a deadly stare. "Idiots!" She spat, reaching down to remove the silver chains from Syrus. "You'll jeopardize my whole mission!"

She quickly felt his pulse. He was even weaker than he looked. The silver had burned its way deep into his skin. She pulled on it gently so she didn't cause any more damage. Pretending to examine the wounds on his neck she leaned very close to his ear and whispered, "Don't believe anything I'm about to say."

She turned back to Gahu and threw the silver aggressively on the ground.

"Forest, what in all of Regia do you think you're doing? Have you lost your mind?"

"Under different circumstances, I'd say it's good to see you, Gahu."

She heard murmuring through the onlookers. "It's Forest. The Shape shifter. The smuggler. She's friends with Philippe. She kills vampires for fun, why is she with one?"

"I've got strict orders, Forest. I must kill any vampire I encounter. New orders recommend the same treatment of Elves now that they have lumped in with the suckers. Shape shifters are welcome on a case by case basis," Gahu said severely. "Seeing as you are a Halfling, you are regrettably half my enemy. The fact that you have always had a good standing relationship with Philippe has bought you a few seconds to explain yourself."

"I, unquestionably, know how bad it looks for me to be in the company of a vampire. Believe me, enduring his company has been the foulest trial of my life. You know how I hate suckers. Unfortunately, his life is tied to the success of my mission; a mission for the Lair and for the victory of the wolves in this war." She gave a meaningful look around at the bystanders. "But that is all I can tell you here. I must see Philippe at once!"

Forest watched Gahu as he considered her words. She knew she had said all the right things. He was an officer of the army and acted predictably. If in doubt, escalate the problem up the chain of command.

Gahu looked at the men standing around. "Back to work!" he barked loudly. Within seconds, they were alone.

"All right, Forest. Let's go see Philippe."

"Thank you, Gahu," she said, bending down and pulling Syrus' arm across her shoulders, helping him to his feet.

The three of them began walking towards the ground entrance of the mountain. Many wolves hissed and growled at Syrus, but none did any more than that because of the warning look they got from Gahu. Forest maintained her solid exterior, but inside she felt like a scared little girl. At any moment, Syrus' presence would push one of them a little too far, and in the blink of an eye, Syrus could be dead. She was relived once they stepped through the entrance of the mountain out of the open.

The air inside the mountain was cool and slightly moist with a smell of minerals. She had been in this place many times before as a guest. It was a huge entrance hall with many doorways leading off to various locations within the mountain. Gahu seemed as relieved as she was that there was no one in the large room except a few guards.

Two massive and menacing wolves guarded the entrance to the long ascending hallway that led to Philippe's chambers. Chosen, no doubt, for this post because of their natural ability to invoke fear. Gahu stepped up to them and began talking quietly. One of the guards bristled at Syrus, but the other eyed Forest closely. She could see the light of male appreciation in his eyes. She winked at him, causing his cheeks to color red.

Gahu came back to her. "Okay. You can go up, but the sucker has to stay here."

"No," Forest said forcefully.

Gahu raised his hands in surrender to her vehemence. "Sorry. If you want to see Philippe then you have to leave the sucker here. I doubt he could make the climb anyway by the look of him."

"That's just the problem. He can't take much more abuse, and as much as I'd like to see him dead, as I told you before, my success hinges on his life. I need him alive and able to travel. I can't just leave him here where anyone can see him and have access to him."

Gahu nodded. "You're right. Okay, let's take him somewhere more private."

He turned, and Forest followed, pulling Syrus along. He led them into a side hallway and through a low door into a small weapons room.

"You can leave him here with me. I promise that nothing will happen to him. I'll guard him myself until you return. Okay?" Gahu said.

Forest eased Syrus down to a sitting position on the floor, propped against the stone wall. She felt his pulse again and squeezed his hand reassuringly. He didn't respond at all and kept his face to the ground. She wanted to hold him and tell him she was sorry for leaving him alone. She wanted to weep over the pain he had suffered because of her weakness. He would most surely scar around his neck and wrists. The silver had burned deep. And she wished she could offer him the remedy of her blood to help heal him, but she could do nothing but leave and hope that it was not the last time she would ever see him.

The guards at the entrance to Philippe's hallway stood aside as she approached and let her pass. Her feet moved swiftly as she built lies inside her mind to convince Philippe to let them go. All she had to do was get them out. If they could get out, they could go directly to Maxcarion and then escape all surrounding danger completely.

She wound through the heart of the mountain in the dark passage and met no one on the way. Philippe's ornate wooden door loomed before her, and she crossed her fingers, praying that his affection for her had not waned since she had last seen him. If only she had a bottle of French wine on her.

She knocked. There was no answer. She knocked louder. Nothing. She pushed the door open. The antechamber was empty. She strode through it to the double doors of the bedchamber and knocked; again, there was no answer. She pushed the doors open and walked in. Philippe was not in his chambers. Forest's hands were shaking, and she had to concentrate on breathing slowly. Why hadn't they told her that he was out?

A gust of warm afternoon breeze blew through the open balcony doors, but it didn't feel good to Forest. She shivered. This was bad. The longer she had to be away from Syrus, the more likely everything would fall to pieces and they both would end up dead. She moved toward the balcony to look out. She could see the army bellow, amazed at their number. Her old loyalties would have delighted in this sight. How could the wolves fail now? They looked more than ready to overthrow the vampires. However, she didn't delight in the sight at all. Syrus had caused everything inside her to shift, and she found herself on the other side of the fence now.

"Who are you?"

The voice that came from behind Forest made her jump. She whirled around but saw no one. She drew her sword, her eyes darting over every inch of the room. She spotted the eyes buried under fur on Philippe's massive bed.

"Show yourself," Forest said, moving forward slowly.

Netriet moved out from the pelt into a slumped sitting position. *I've seen it all now*, Forest thought. A sickly, one-armed, female vampire on Philippe's bed; she scarcely believed her own eyes.

Netriet smiled at the look on Forest's face. "Shocking, I know. But don't worry, you're not hallucinating. What is your name?"

"Forest," she said weakly. "Are you sure I'm not hallucinating?"

"I wish I was only a figment of your imagination."

Forest sheathed her sword and came closer to the bed. "Who are you, and how did you get here?"

"My name is Netriet, but I'm no one, obviously. I was sent here as a sacrificial messenger. Most regrettably, for me, after I delivered my message, Philippe decided to keep me instead of kill me. He's been experimenting on me." She took a deep shuddering breath, her emaciated frame shaking with the effort of talking so much. "So, what brings you here?"

"I have to convince Philippe to let me and the vampire I travel with, go."

Netriet raised one eyebrow. "How are you going to do that?"

"Philippe is very fond of me. I have a chance."

"You're an Elf, right?" Netriet asked a confused look on her face.

"Half. I'm also a shifter."

"And you travel with a vampire?"

"Yeah. He's down in the base of the mountain under guard. I have to get him out before they kill him."

"Who is he?" she asked.

Forest hesitated. "I can't tell you that. We're on a mission for Fortress."

"*Fortress!*" Netriet said through her teeth like it was a dirty word. "I was sent here by a traitor inside Fortress. A mole who feeds Philippe secrets."

Forest's eyes widened. "Who? Who is it?"

"I don't know, an elf. A woman with lots of power."

Forest's mind crashed through the possibilities of who the mole might be. "Is she a member of the *Rune-dy*?" Forest asked.

Netriet shrugged. "Could be...yeah...possibly."

"Does Philippe know the identity of the mole?"

"No. He's asked me many times."

Forest's thin hope grew a small layer of fat. "Will you help me?" Forest asked. "I promise once I get out, I won't leave you here like this. I swear on my life, I'll send someone back for you."

Netriet hesitated, seeming to mull it over. "You know if you would have showed up yesterday, I would have begged you to kill me. But last night I came up with a plan. Don't bother sending anyone after me. I'm going to end Philippe. I'll help you any way I can, not that it will be much."

"Thank you."

An hour dragged along like a snake with a wounded belly. Forest paced the floor restlessly, waiting and constantly beating back the emotion that screamed and clawed at the bars she put around them.

"Forest!" Philippe bellowed jovially when he finally came back to his chambers. "How are you?"

Forest couldn't answer because Philippe swooped down on her, picking her up off the ground and planting a hard kiss on her mouth. She stumbled to the side when he dropped her back on the ground. "It's fantastic to see you. I love your new shape." His eyes raked her hungrily. "Very appealing," he half growled. "So what is all this nonsense I hear from my guards that you've brought a vampire into my mountain?"

"He's not the first," she said smiling, gesturing to Netriet.

"Ah yes." He blushed. "Has she told you why she's here?"

"She didn't need to. I'm the one who sent her."

Philippe narrowed his eyes at her. "So you're the mole?"

She smiled confidently. "Didn't you guess? I thought for sure you would have."

Philippe twisted a strand of his beard around a finger. "You did come to mind from time to time." He raised his eyebrows at Netriet who nodded in agreement.

"So, you're here yourself now. What is going on? Why did you tell me to wait in the message you sent with Nettie?"

"I hadn't intended to be here until tomorrow. However, a little pack of yours captured my slave and brought him here, so here I am. I told you to wait because I have, or will have if you let me leave tonight, a weapon for you that will take away all doubt of victory."

Philippe's eyes widened in excitement. "What is it?"

"There is a wizard residing in your Wood. I have been in contact with him, and he will join your army against the suckers, but he insisted that I come personally and complete the transaction."

"Well, what are we waiting for? Let us go now together, you and I."

"No. I must follow his instructions. That is why I brought the sucker downstairs. The wizard wants him for some kind of ritual sacrifice. But it is private, evil magic. The wizard demanded that I come alone with a vampire no one would miss. He said he would only deal with me."

Philippe sat down and eyed her closely. "You can't expect me to just take your word for it."

"I don't," she said plainly.

"You play marvelous games, Forest. I know you. But I cannot fathom why you would lie to me about such a thing. Or why you of all people would be in the company of a sucker if it weren't for the reason you said." He chuckled darkly. "I believe you hate them more than I do."

Forest smiled as though this were a great compliment.

"Still…I sense there is something …something wrong with this picture…perhaps something you're not telling me?"

"Philippe," she drew his name out seductively. "There are many things I've not told you…" She gave him a hot look that did not fall short on him. " I'm a woman."

Netriet, who watched silently from the bed, had to commend Forest on her wiles.

He stroked his beard a few more times before getting to his feet again. "All right, I'll let you go, but since I'm not sure how far to trust you, you shall go collared."

"Of course," she said shrugging, but her insides were filled with dread. Netriet had told her enough about that thing.

Philippe rolled the ring in his fingers. "Let me see…" he said to himself. "How best to command you? Hmmm…"

Forest saw the fearful look in Netriet's eyes; it did nothing to calm her.

"Aha. I have it," Philippe said putting the ring on his own finger. Forest watched unsure what was happening. He closed his eyes for a moment before pulling the ring off, smiling at her. "Which hand would you prefer?"

Forest held out her left hand.

"You know it caused me quite the problem when you sent me this without instructions how to use it. That's why I kept Nettie. Why she doesn't still have both of her arms."

"I'm sorry about that. I was in a hurry to get the message to you, and I was remiss."

Philippe took her hand and slid the heavy ring onto her index finger. The stone was a deep iridescent grey just like Syrus' eyes. It was beautiful, she thought, before it bit down into her finger. The spikes on the inside of the ring pierced all the way through the bone. She swore loudly.

"You have nothing to fear if you told me the truth. The collar will pose no threat to your life so long as you reach the wizard before the sun rises and complete the transaction."

"That's all?"

Philippe chuckled at her. "The collar is tied to the life of the vampire you brought with you. It will kill you at sunrise if he still lives."

All the blood drained from Forest's face.

"What's wrong?" Philippe asked.

"This damn thing really hurts," she said holding up her hand. "Well, I'd better get my sucker and get going if I'm to make your time limit."

Philippe walked down with her to the little room where Gahu was still guarding Syrus. Syrus looked a little better, able to stand on his own. Forest thanked Gahu and pulled Syrus behind her by the wrist. Philippe sent Gahu ahead to clear the way for them so random wolves didn't spot them, and to send the order that any and all wolves in the Wood were to return to the Lair immediately.

Everything around the Lair was quiet, devoid of prying eyes when Philippe and Gahu walked Forest and Syrus down to the edge of the Wood.

Philippe smiled broadly at her in parting. "I'll see you soon."

Forest only nodded and turned her back on them, the two of them disappearing into the trees.

Philippe waited for a few moments. "Get a team and follow them, Gahu."

The sun was setting as Forest and Syrus reentered the wood. The pain around the collar throbbed and made her whole arm feel heavy. The words had not yet formed inside her head before then. *I'm going to die in the morning*. Syrus followed her as he had at the Lair, silently and with his head down. When she felt they were sufficiently away from where Philippe had sent them off, she turned to him and wrapped her arms around him.

"I'm sorry, Syrus. I'm so, so sorry! I should have never left you."

He made no reply and was like a dead weight in her arms.

"Please, Syrus. Please forgive me."

"What difference does it make?" he said in a low flat voice. "It's all over now anyway."

"It's not! I found Maxcarion when I ran away from you. I know where he is. It's not far at all!"

She stepped back from him, and he raised his head a little. "How did you get us out of there?"

"I told him half-truths, and he believed letting us go was in his best interest." Forest turned and began walking again. She couldn't tell him about the collar. She just had to get them to the wizard so he could have his sight back. When she had thought about this time before and how she would say good-bye to him, she didn't realize how final it would be.

"So that's it? You're really not going to tell me the whole of it?" he asked incredulously.

"I'm tired, and we have to move quickly."

Syrus didn't push the issue further; he seemed too weak and dejected to argue. The shadows stretched along the ground as the sun sank below the treetops and the sky slowly undulated with its dusk colors. Forest looked up at the sunset, realizing with a sharp pang that it would be her last and she couldn't even sit and enjoy it. She pushed ahead; she had to complete her mission. It was the only gift she could give Syrus. She wouldn't die whining and crying. She would die with the stiff upper lip of a warrior.

Forest slowed her pace. They would be there soon enough. She reached for Syrus' hand. He moved away from her. A sob rose in her throat. She couldn't let it end like this. She reached for him again. "Please," she whispered. "Please, hold my hand."

He raised one eyebrow, but his face softened, and he held out his hand to her. She made sure to grasp it with her right hand. Her left felt so heavy now. She would have to hold it up with the other one before much longer.

The Dryad graveyard loomed in the distance ahead, and she couldn't stop the tears in spite of her determination not to cry.

"What's wrong?" Syrus asked. "I can smell your tears."

"Oh, I'm just so happy," she lied. "We're here."

The stone trees gave off a faint green glow in the darkness. They stood in the center of the graveyard. There was no noise here. The silence of the dead was absolute.

"I can feel his presence," Syrus said quietly. "My magic recognizes his."

"It's time to say good bye," she said facing him.

"What do you mean?"

"I'm not going in there with you. You don't need me anymore."

A number of different emotions flashed across his face. "Fine, don't go in with me, but don't leave yet. Please don't leave before I get a chance to see you with my own eyes. It's not over yet, Forest."

"All right. I'll stay right here and wait. You go. Do you need me to show you the door?"

"No. I can feel where it is."

He framed her face gently with his hands. "Forest," he whispered leaning his forehead against hers. "I *do* need you. Don't run away."

She could say nothing as he left her, knowing her voice would betray her; her words would confess the truths she'd hidden from him. She watched his retreating back disappear through the optical illusion into the tree. Her heart sobbed for him to come back.

Forest sank down on the ground, cradling her screaming arm in her lap and listened to the tortured cries of her heart as the darkness of her last night closed in around her.

19

Syrus walked slowly into Maxcarion's home. He didn't want to come off threatening, especially since he was unarmed. The wizard calmly allowed him to approach, pausing his Wii bowling. Maxcarion's home overflowed with various kinds of magic and magical objects from many different worlds. If Syrus could have seen it, he would have found it beautiful, fascinating, terrifying and occasionally disgusting.

The wizard himself, ancient and wizened, had lost some of his edge over the last century, mostly out of boredom.

"Well, well, well." Maxcarion's voice was dusty from lack of use, and he had to cough and clear his throat before he could say more. "Prince Syrus. It's about time you showed up."

"You were expecting me?" Syrus asked.

"Oh yes. I have the power to see the future. I know all about you and Forest. A more bumbling pair of lovers I've never seen." He chuckled.

"Forest and I are not lovers."

"Ha! We'll come back to that. You've changed so much since the last time I saw you, all of it for the better, I might add. Even your hairstyle is better. I don't know why vampires insist on wearing their hair so long. But anyway, as you have guessed, I *am* the wizard who attacked you five years ago."

The excitement of this confirmation bubbled up inside Syrus. "Then you can restore me! You know what it will take to fix my eyes!"

"Not so fast, my boy. I'm sorry to tell you this, but I cannot restore your sight."

"But…but…you're the one who did this to me. Surely you must know a way."

"I'm sorry. The damage is permanent."

All of Syrus' hopes crashed like glass falling on marble.

Maxcarion sighed. "Look, I'm a mercenary through and through. I was hired to kill you. Something I could have done easily. I took the job and intended to see it through, but when I came in contact with you, mere seconds before I blinded you, I saw what great potential you had. So I spared you, and I did you and everyone else a huge favor. By taking your sight, I took from you that which truly blinded you: your arrogance. I gave you a chance to become who you were meant to be, and you have."

Syrus was numb. "I came all this way for nothing."

"Now, now. Don't make me take that compliment back. What about Forest?"

"What about her?" Syrus spat angrily.

"She's sitting in that graveyard crying tears for you as she prepares to die."

"Die? Why would she die?"

"Philippe collared her before he let the two of you go. The collar will kill her unless you die tonight."

"I don't understand," Syrus said.

"Your mate has traded her life for yours."

"Mate?" the word fell stupidly off his tongue as if he did not understand it. "Forest is my mate? My *destined life mate?*"

Once he said it aloud, Syrus didn't need confirmation. He knew it was true. Now it all made sense. The desire and the pain, the fiery lightning that snaked inside him, their first kiss. Syrus threw his head back and laughed before smacking his forehead.

"I'm so stupid! She knows, doesn't she?"

"Yes."

"How long has she known?"

"Since the time you first touched her face. She saw her true form reflected in your eyes."

Syrus considered the amount of unfinished business between them but that would have to come later. Her life hung in the balance.

"You can stop the collar can't you?" Panic seized him at the thought of Forest dying.

"Certainly I can, but I told you, I'm a mercenary. What do you offer me as payment?"

Syrus swore angrily. "I've paid you already! You took my sight. You owe me!"

The wizard scratched his nose unconcernedly. "I suppose I could do you a favor. Or would letting her die be better? She's not really suitable if you're going to be king, you know. I mean that's really why she's hidden it from you all along."

"You disgusting little…" Syrus proceeded to call Maxcarion names that even he had never heard before. The wizard listened amusedly to his rant, unaffected.

"All right, all right," Maxcarion said in lazy retreat from Syrus' anger. "Since you love her so much."

"I do!" he said defiantly. The omission made in the midst of vehement anger gave it concrete validity. He did love her.

"The collar will be disabled by the time you go out to her, but I require that you give it to me once it is off."

"Deal."

The wizard smiled to himself, "Now go do what you've gotta do."

20

The pain in Forest's hand generated all the way up her arm so terribly, she was on the verge of dementia. Her vision blurred around the edges. Cold sweat ran down her face and back. It would be many hours yet before the sunrise when she would actually die, but these were her last moments of lucidity. She wished she'd had the chance to see Syrus' eyes healed, to tell him all that was in her heart, and say good bye. She closed her eyes as a shadow slithered up behind her, wrapping its black hands around her, pulling her down. She sighed, leaning back, letting it take her.

"Forest? Forest! Wake up!" his voice alarmed her, loosening the shadow's hold.

Then the shadow ripped away along with all the pain, waking her completely with a burst of adrenaline. Forest opened her eyes and looked down at her hand. The collar was gone.

"Are you all right?" he asked.

"Oh!" she said breathlessly. "Yes." A laugh burst out of her. She was alive! This was not the end of her life. "Where is the collar?"

"The wizard took it. Stand up, Forest." Syrus ordered rather rudely. He took both her hands and pulled her up.

With a nasty jolt, she saw his eyes were the same. "Your eyes?" she asked desperately.

"Yes. My eyes, let's talk about my eyes, Forest." He took a few steps back from her and squared his shoulder, his face taut and somber. "I need to tell you a little story, and I need you to not interrupt me."

"Okay," she said slowly.

He gave a deep sigh, pulled out the little flask he always carried, and began turning it in his hands. "Back when I was a terrible person, before I lost my sight, I was addicted to human blood. I never went to Earth, but I made Redge get it for me. I never asked him how he acquired it. I didn't care. I was the worst blood junkie ever, or so many told me. For an entire year, I gave myself to it without the slightest restraint. My parents finally intervened. I mean, really, what kind of a king would I be if I didn't kick the habit? Getting clean was…difficult."

He drew a deep breath. "But I got clean, and I stayed clean. Then I lost my sight, and I told you how broken I was at that time, before I took the Kata back up. In a moment of weakness, when I felt I had nothing left to loose and longing to anesthetize my pain, I drank human blood again. It had a strange and different effect on me…It opened my eyes."

"What?"

"Shh!"

Syrus took another deep breath continuing to twist the flask in his hands. "One drink of human blood restores my vision perfectly for a short period of time; only a matter of minutes. And naturally you're wondering why I don't drink it all the time. Because having my eyes opened by human blood is painful. It's painful in a way there are no words strong enough to describe the excruciating tearing of it, and it leaves me physically weakened."

He paused for a long, thoughtful moment. "So that's what's in this flask. I always keep some human blood with me in case the need arises that I must have my sight. I don't have to worry about falling back into addiction because the pain is too great to tempt me in the slightest. And I'm sure you're wondering why I didn't use it before we had that battle with those werewolves who came to our camp."

She was indeed wondering just that.

"Because I needed my strength more than my sight right then. But more importantly, I never wanted to confess to you that I had ever been an addict. It's something I'm ashamed of, and I didn't want it to taint your opinion of me. But now here we are, and it's time for confessions. Mine and yours."

Forest gulped hard.

"Aside from human blood, I have developed my own way of seeing for a short burst of time. I use my mage powers and an incantation I designed, but the vision I get from that is weak and blurry. I have used it twice since you and I have been together. I went to the falls alone and looked at them and…and once when we were back at your house. I came into your room at night while you were sleeping to look at you."

"Really? You snuck into my room?" She chuckled. "Perv."

"I *just* wanted a mental picture of you, even if that picture was not your true form. And what I saw, well, it knocked me to my knees, literally. I couldn't breathe. I kissed your hair, and then I ran away, fearing I'd lost my heart completely. It has tortured me, thinking that all I saw was some random shift you had created. But now I know, weak and blurry as it might have been, I saw your true face."

Forest's chest tightened. He knew.

"I think I understand why you didn't tell me we were life mates when you discovered it. Your own prejudice against me, the difference in our stations, the racial bigotry you've suffered your whole life, and Leith. Am I right?"

"Yes, but there is more."

"What?"

"I was afraid you wouldn't want me."

"Oh, Forest," he said sadly shaking his head.

"I have endured all these years being tied to Leith and having my emotions scrambled by the lovers mark he forced on me. The last thing I wanted was to end up finding my life mate and always questioning my feelings for them and their feelings for me. Was it real love or just the unbreakable connection? And would I end up torn in two? How could I be mated to one and forever tied to Leith? I thought it would be better to leave our connection incomplete."

Syrus nodded gravely. "I, stupidly, just discovered that you are my destined life mate. I didn't know before now. What I did know was that I wanted you more than I have ever wanted any woman. I knew your friendship had become more important to me than even Redge's. I knew I respected your skills as a warrior. You are a badass with that sword, baby."

Forest giggled like a little girl.

"And now," he continued. "I know that I need you. I don't have to think about needing you. Just like I don't have to think about my need for the air. The knowledge is innate and primal. The need just is, and it's too vast for me to question. I asked you earlier today for your heart. I meant it then. I mean it now."

"You know I want my freedom."

"I know. I want my freedom as well. I only want you if you come freely, just as I come to you. That's why I've told you all this." He unscrewed the cap on his flask. "I'm going to drink this. It's your last chance to turn away from me."

Syrus put the flask to his lips. Forest had only a second to decide. Instinct stomped reason into the ground. He asked for it, she thought. She would be his Cinderella, and his Juliet, but she would be much more than that. She would be a raging forest fire, an all-consuming crisis, too big to be ignored, too powerful to stop, and too hot to put out. She would be herself, and she would be his. It might be surrendering one desire for another, but life was far from perfect. You can't have everything.

Forest held herself still as she heard him swallow. Then she gasped and made to go to him, but he held out a hand to stop her. He'd said the pain was excruciating, it certainly looked like it. He doubled over, his eyes shut tight. His whole face clenched, and a cry of pain escaped his lips. It was torture for her to watch him going through such pain while she was unable to stop or soothe it.

Then all of his muscles relaxed while all of hers seemed to tense. His straightened up, his eyes still closed. "I love you, Forest," he whispered.

He opened his eyes.

All the breath was pulled from her lungs as their first eye contact was made. The fiery whip of pain that she had lived with ever since their first kiss, uncoiled and exploded through her whole body. They came together without seeming to have moved their feet. Looking into each other's eyes, their foreheads pressed together. There would be no more questions of turning away or choosing. A spiritual bridge formed between her irises and his; a bond that only death could break. But this bridge was only the first of many. His eyes, her eyes. His lungs, her lungs. His heart, her heart. His hands, her hands. It was done. The power that tied the knots between them and had taken control of their bodies now relinquished control back to them.

Forest and Syrus stumbled backward gasping. There was no more pain, and they looked openly at each other. Finally looking into Syrus' eyes and him looking back into hers was one of the most amazing moments of Forest's whole life. All of the attraction she felt for him before now seemed weak in comparison. As if those small black dots in his eyes magnified his beauty one hundred times.

Syrus could feel the seconds ticking before his sight would be lost again. His eyes devoured Forest. Never, never had he seen or imagined anyone as beautiful as her. And he felt the rush of this virgin moment. No one could see her the way he could! This beauty was his private possession, his alone. He would never treat *her* as though he owned her, but the vision of her true form *was* his to own.

When he had looked at her sleeping, he had only gotten part of the whole picture, and he hadn't seen her eyes at all which were devastating in the extreme. He didn't know how he held himself still as he looked at her full mouth, realizing that he had kissed it many times without knowing how exquisite it was and how it begged for his . Her curly chestnut hair hung long in a riot down her back. And her body, oh how he was blessed! His hands throbbed as he looked at her body.

Forest smiled at his obvious pleasure. "Like it, do you?"

Syrus couldn't even articulate an answer. His mouth opened to reply, but nothing came out. Forest's smile turned wicked, and she turned in a slow seductive circle.

Syrus moaned and then turned demanding, "Come here! Now!"

She rushed into his arms, but as she did, the hateful sound of approaching wolves registered in her brain. Syrus swore loudly.

"I'm really beginning to think we're cursed here," he said.

"I've always been cursed, and now you've inherited it, being mated with me."

They both listened. They were more than a little outnumbered. Wolves in wolf form, man form, and beast form were closing in on them.

"What do we do?" she asked. "They'll chase if we run."

"Yes, and I'm too weak to run very fast. I'm too weak to fight, and I don't have my swords anyway."

"Maybe Maxcarion will hide us," Forest suggested.

They approached the tree, but before Forest could touch it, she knew it was no good. The optical illusion had changed, and she could feel new defensive magic blocking them.

"Well, I guess this is my last night after all." She looked tearfully into Syrus' eyes. Tears surfaced in his as well.

He folded her into his arms and rested his cheek on top of her head. "I couldn't have chosen a better end than with you," he said.

"I love you." Her voice trembled. "I've never said that before. Not to anyone."

The wolves were closing in, bringing death with them. And in this moment of would-be terror, Syrus held her face gently in his hands and gazed into her eyes. Everything around them faded away. A lifetime of tenderness, and passion, and I love yous, were concentrated into that moment. The world was nothing but the two of them, and it was full of peace.

A crash of metal made both of them jump. Redge in the lead, the troop of royal vampires charged into the graveyard and formed a protective circle around them.

"Protect the prince!" Redge ordered.

The approaching wolves roared and charged faster through the trees. They were still outnumbered. The vampire's swords flashed through the air, hacking the wolves in front to death. Syrus' arms tightened around Forest. In the noise and movement, Redge came to the center to Forest and Syrus.

"I've got the end of the bridge!" he shouted. "I'm going to open it!"

Redge pulled the ball from the chain around his neck and smashed it between his hands. A glowing portal opened, and a fierce wind kicked up, pulling all of them into it. Forest closed her eyes and held onto Syrus as tightly as she could. The wind rushing around them was deafening. Something crashed into the back of Forest's head. Everything went black as the portal dumped them, and the entire vampire troop, unceremoniously in the throne room of the Onyx castle.

All Forest knew was gleaned from the blurry snatches of things going on around her. She didn't care about anything except that she could still feel Syrus' arms around her. Heated arguing filled her ears like water, thick and muffled. She was trying to come back when Syrus tensed around her.

"NO!" he shouted.

Something was wrong. She was trying so hard to come back. Then she was covered with hands. Harsh strong hands pulled her from Syrus. She tried to hold on, but her arms were useless. His voice resounded in her ears, moving further and further away from her, and she couldn't answer.

"Forest! Forest!"

She could feel the stone floor beneath her, about to regain consciousness, when someone lifted her shoulders and brought her head back down on the floor with a crack. Blackness enveloped.

****

Unfamiliar voices talked in hushed tones above her. She was no longer on the floor but in a bed. She could feel the smallness of the room around her. Pain spiked in the back of her skull, bringing back the memory of being smashed on the floor. Oh, if she ever found out who did that to her!

"Is she dead?" a soft female voice asked.

"No, my queen."

"Then kill her."

"I cannot. The king gave orders that she was not to be harmed."

"So? Pretend that you did not hear the orders. I'll get you out of any trouble."

Forest decided this was a good moment to open her eyes. Her would-be killers both gasped at her sudden awakening. One was an ogre the other was Queen Christiana. She'd heard of bad mother-in-laws, but this seemed a little extreme. Forest considered for a second before she thought, *To hell with it.*

"SYRUS!" she screamed. "SYRU—"

Christiana clamped a hand over her mouth. "I've heard the whole story, you grasping little Halfling! I won't rest until you're dead. You will never see my son again. And you will never sit on the throne!"

Damn the consequences, Forest was going to kick her royal ass, with all due respect, of course. Unfortunately, she was tied down.

"You really won't kill her?" she asked the ogre.

He shook his head severely.

Christiana huffed in exasperation. "Fine!" she spat. "Open a portal!"

"To where, my queen?"

"Earth."

"To the place where she lives there?" the ogre asked.

"Whatever! I don't care."

The ogre struck the air, and a swirling black portal opened next to him.

"I, Queen Christiana, speak into law, that Forest, the Halfling, is banished from Regia, forbidden to ever return."

She kept her hand over Forest's mouth as the ogre untied her. Then Christiana stepped back and the ogre scooped her off the bed and threw her into the portal. Forest screamed for Syrus as she fell through the black hole that pulled her back to Austin. It dumped her on her bed, back in her condo, and closed behind her.

Forest drowned in sorrow marbled with rage. This wasn't the end. Her stomach twisted with nausea at being separated from Syrus. It was as though her heart had been cut from her chest and she was kept alive on bypass. She could almost hear him calling for her. Almost feel him reaching for her across the universe. She knew he would never stop reaching until he held her in his arms again.

The End

Turn the page for a preview of

FOREST FIRE

The spellbinding sequel in Tenaya Jayne's all-new fantasy

Series, The Legends of Regia.

Coming soon from Cold Fire Books!

Prologue

"Protect the prince!"

Redge's yelling voice was the best sound Syrus had ever heard. Fighting erupted around them but rather than join in, Syrus pulled Forest tighter into his chest. He was whole now. He was hers and she would always possess him. Chaos, danger and death all around yet there was nothing but silence and peace inside him.

Redge opened the end of the bridge.

The harsh wind pulled them into the portal, but with Forest in his arms, he felt shielded from it. They were encapsulated in the heart of the raging noise. Regrettably, his vision would fade soon. He wanted to use the time to get lost in Forest's eyes but she had her face buried in his chest so he contented himself watching her hair dance in the wind around them.

The soldiers in the portal tumbled in disarray. Mesmerized by Forest, Syrus didn't react fast enough to stop the foot of one of the soldiers from slamming into the back of her head. He felt the force of the blow in his own head, coupled with an insane fury that she had been hurt. She had been clinging tightly to him but now her arms were limp.

He didn't fear for her life. Since they had forged their connections, he would know if her life was in danger and the extent of any injury she might suffer without ever having to see it; the knowledge was innate. His heart could feel the beating of hers. The blow to her head had only knocked her unconscious.

In the next second, the portal dumped them and the whole troop of soldiers in a heap in the throne room of the Onyx castle. Syrus' sight blurred around the edges. The soldiers untangled themselves and got to their feet, leaving Syrus in the middle of the floor, cradling Forest against him. He tipped her head back and gazed at her face for the last remaining moments of his vision. He was only dimly aware of the movement and talk around him. The unmistakable lilt of his mother's voice was trying to break its way into his attention. He paid no mind. The world was nothing, there was only Forest. He stroked her cheek with the pads of his fingers and kissed her lips.

"I demand to know what is going on!" Christiana yelled. "Syrus! Syrus, stop it! You debase yourself in public! Get off the floor! Let go of that disgusting aberration! Syrus!"

The only thing his mother said that registered in his brain was the insult to Forest.

"She's my destined life mate, mother," he said calmly, without taking his eyes from Forest.

"No!" She seemed to scream in a whisper. "No! It can't be!"

She turned her wide furious eyes on Redge. Redge merely shrugged.

"Syrus, it's not the truth," she said in forced composure. "You've been bewitched. You're sick and you need medical attention."

Christiana clapped her hands and five ogres came rushing into the room. Redge fled down the hallway. He had to find the king as quickly as he could or something terrible that could not be rectified would happen. Zeren jumped as Redge came bursting into his study, wild eyed and out of breath.

"What?! Is it Syrus?" Zeren demanded.

"Yes! In the throne room. You must come now!" Redge wheezed.

Christiana sent the soldiers away before giving the ogres any orders. The less witnesses the better.

"Alright. Three of you take the prince to his chambers and keep him there. Subdue him if necessary but do not let him out."

Syrus' vision was almost totally gone now and the sum of his whole day left him too weak to have a prayer of fighting off three ogres. Six huge hands grabbed him.

"NO! NO! Mother, don't do this!"

His heart cried out as loud as his lungs as Forest was wrenched from his arms.

"FOREST! FOREST!"

The last thing Syrus saw was Forest lying unconscious on the floor with his mother standing triumphantly over her. Then his eyes slid into darkness. His cries reverberated through the whole castle until he was shut in and locked down.

Forest's eyelids fluttered and she moaned. Christiana grabbed her roughly by the shoulders, lifting her, then slamming her head back down on the floor, knocking her unconscious again.

"Now, one of you, get this piece of filth out of my throne room," Christiana ordered.

"What shall we do with her?"

"Christiana!" Zeren came barging into the room. " What is going on here?" Zeren looked down at Forest and then over to the ogres waiting to do the queen's bidding. "Put her in a clean room and get her a doctor. No harm is to come to her. "

The ogres looked over at the queen.

"Now!" the king yelled.

Forest was picked up and taken from the room.

"Now," Zeren turned his attention on his wife. "Tell me what is going on. Where's Syrus?"

"He was injured. He is resting in his chambers," she said innocently.

Redge was dying to yell, "liar!"

"Remember your place, Christiana," Zeren said sternly. "I'm going to see my son."

Zeren turned to leave the room when a messenger came rushing in.

"Your highness! Fighting has broken out in the shifter colonies. Philippe's armies are moving out. They march on Kyhael!"

Zeren looked over at Redge. "Come with me."

The two men left the room without a backward glance at the queen.

"Give me orders, my king," Redge said.

"I want you to stay close to Syrus. Pay attention to what the queen does. I don't want her interfering in anything."

"Yes, my king."

Redge watched Zeren's back as he rushed from the castle to confer with his generals. He didn't have the power to control the queen. The only thing he could do was protect Syrus the way he always had. Christiana had no authority to relieve him from that duty. Nevertheless, it wasn't Syrus that needed protecting, it was Forest, and Redge was powerless to help her.

Chapter 1

The aquamarine moonlight reached down, caressing Netriet as she lay on the stone floor. She ached to open the closed balcony doors and let the moonlight fill the room but the chain around her wrist would not permit it. She was beyond the pain. The cold of the stone under her clawed deep into the tissue of her flesh for hours and hours, finally releasing her to the pleasure of numbness. Perhaps this would be her last night. She turned aside her feelings of failure and let her eyes slide out of focus in the beautifully dim light.

Netriet was positive she had missed her window to kill Philippe. He had left two days ago in a towering rage after he learned that Forest had lied, escaped his grasp, and he'd lost the collar in the process. She'd heard the movement of the army far below her at the base of the mountain and now all was quiet. Death moved around the edges of the room, whispering peaceful seductions. Her eyelids became heavier and heavier with every blink. Sleep descended as gently as the moonlight.

"Nettie," his voice sounded strained. "Nettie, wake up."

The smell of blood woke her more efficiently than his shaking her. Philippe's face was close to hers when she opened her eyes, his beard tickling her neck. He had come back. Either that or she was dreaming. He looked as though he had been in a fight. There was a cut on his forehead and scratches on his cheek.

"So," she said weakly as he picked her up off the floor. "You didn't forget me after all."

"No, I was..." he looked at her sharply, his eyebrows drawn down as her hand gently cupped his cheek. His eyes searched her face for a moment before a small smile pulled into one side of his mouth.

"I have wondered," he said before hoisting her up and crushing her mouth in a harsh kiss.

Netriet felt smothered under his ardor as he dumped her on the bed.

"Wait," she said desperately as he pulled his cloak from his shoulders and dropped it to the floor.

"What?"

She held up her wrist. "Please take it off."

He narrowed his eyes at her for a second then shrugged and went to get the key across the room. Her arm was freed and he again smothered her. She let her muscles go lax and she lay there like a corpse. He noticed soon enough.

"What's wrong with you?" he demanded.

"I'm just so weak. I haven't eaten in days and days. I'm sorry. I *really* want to participate."

He smiled broadly and pulled his shirt over his head. His torso was covered in deep purple bruises.

"What happened to you?" she asked.

"Here," he said offering her his forearm.

She sat up a little and sank her teeth deep into his flesh. This was the opportunity she had been waiting for. She pulled as hard as she could on his veins.

"My position was challenged," he explained. "I had to fight two contenders. They're both dead now. The army is marching to Kyhael. I will join them tomorrow, but I had to come back to tie up a few loose ends. I've got to get the...the...uh..."

It was starting to work. Netriet pulled harder and harder. She had never taken this much blood at one time from anyone. She looked up at his face. His eyes were getting glassy. She continued to drain him.

"Those idiots keep using the wrong words. I swear it didn't take me half this time to become…become fluent in French. I don't think they…um…understand why I made them…I mean…aren't you done yet?"

He was on the brink. She felt flooded but with two more deep pulls, he would be right where she wanted him. He stroked the back of her head and then staggered to the side, pulling his arm from her mouth. She sat upright, her strength returned, but she felt nauseated. He looked at her confusedly, his eyes dilated.

"Come here. Lie down. You need to rest," she said.

He obeyed her instantly. "Yes. I'm so tired."

Philippe lay down next to her, all his carnal intentions had vanished, and he closed his eyes. She smiled to herself. He'd been so arrogant before that if she bit him, she'd have no persuasion over him. What a crock. She sat still for a moment. There were numbers of things she could do to kill him, but she wanted to make sure that when he was found, his death would be one of humiliating circumstances. A new werewolf leader would emerge but with Philippe dead, there would be discord. The new leader would need time to establish his authority and make changes to the whole community. The future of Regia lay in her hands, well, her hand.

She watched his chest rise and fall and considered the matter carefully. The vampires would write songs in her honor. Oh, that would just burn the queen's ass. No one even knew she was still alive and she was about to hand her race the war.

Over the next hour, Netriet monitored Philippe's vital signs. She continued to take blood from him to keep him right on that dangerous edge. Everything still seemed quiet and empty in the mountain, but she locked the heavy doors and slid a long sword through the handles just in case. She kept the set up simple. She unhooked the chain that had held her captive all this time from the wall and dragged it out onto the balcony. It would be an adequate trip line.

Netriet gazed into the night sky and out over the land. She could see Halussis like a speck in the distance. *Home*, she thought. *Goodbye*. Positioning herself at the very edge of the balcony, the wind and gravity attempted to pull her over the side. Netriet braced her arm on the railing. Her muscles shook with the strain every time the wind gusted. She began to whisper to him.

"Philippe," her voice came drifting into his dreams. "Wake up, Philippe."

He sat up and looked around for her in the darkness.

"Come to me, Philippe. Come…"

Philippe stood up, his body propelled haphazardly towards Netriet.

"Hurry!" she ordered.

Netriet braced herself as his bulk moved towards her. Would the chain hold? She held her breath. His foot caught the chain. He tripped, his arms flailing. He crashed into her, grabbing her, taking her with him over the edge. Philippe held her tightly against his chest as they fell to their deaths.

Made in the USA
San Bernardino, CA
26 January 2014